Tears
of a
Statue

BY WALTER BRUNT

The Alchemist Series

Gold into Lead

Transmuted Heart

Tears of a Statue

Tears

of a

Statue

Book three in the
Alchemist
Series

Walter Brunt

ISBN 978-1-9994668-4-8
eBook ISBN 978-1-9994668-5-5

To my loving wife,

who helped me with my story.

Most of the good ideas in this book

were mine. No truly they were,

just don't tell her I said so.

Tears

of a

Statue

Chapter

1

Kole ran. The legs of his Power Armor pumped through the thick mud of the battlefield. Thinking back, this was entirely his fault. The Human engineers did well. They had modified the Dwarven Armor he'd traded them during his first visit to Winter Haven, but at first he didn't like the look of the massive suit of Power Armor. Once the engineers saw his disapproving gaze they told him that the suit could be modified for a variety of environments including underwater and the vacuum of space. It sounded great but didn't wow him. It was bulky and weird looking. He didn't need the suit for aquatic farming or asteroid-mining. He needed it for combat and they made the suit look like a giant bullet magnet. It was too big. He could almost fit a full set of Dwarven Armor into it.

He examined his soon to be Power Armor standing in its station, looking like a smooth brick with rounded edges. It had equally proportioned appendages, minus the head, and though the exterior appeared smooth, shifting plates that protected its joints. Over all, it appeared weak and Kole worried about the pilot's protection, but the cockpit, they called the pill, sat encased in armor inside its movable torso. The pill, mounted to the suit's spine was located in the armor's center of gravity. The pilot would enter from the top and climb down to sit on a long curved chair.

In training, it took time for Kole to get acquainted with the suit, but it was the view screen that impressed him the most. Fixed to the internal wall, the screen wrapped around and down the front half of the pill, exceeding Dwarven design. It was fancy and the most advanced tech Kole had ever touched, but he didn't like being strapped into the pilot's seat wearing the tight interactive sensor suit, he called jammies. Once the pilot's arms, legs and torso were secured, the seat tilted forward suspending the pilot, allowing the pilot to move their arms and legs to control the suit, making it a physical machine where a small action translated into a larger reaction.

The suit's many eyes were equally scattered over its body and overlapping sensor suites feed data to the view screen, giving the pilot whatever view they wanted, depending on the task at hand. The Power Armor could be made to run on all fours, flipped around and used backward or upside down, the appendages would adjust accordantly. A light flickered in Kole's eyes encouraging the engineers to keep selling. They told him that the computer takes the information from the overlapping sensors and renders a clear picture of the pilot's environment even if half the optics were obscured. They finished their pitch telling him that the suit was his and all he had to do was choose the paint.

It was Sarah's idea to put him in charge of the project, allowing him to choose the Power Armor design that'd change the face of the world. For a guy who had spent most of his life alone, being crowded by people who wanted his attention, unnerved him. He thought of himself as a free spirit whose only major decision was what he was going to manifest for dinner that night. It was difficult for him to deal with the technical aspects of the suit when he'd normally manifest what he needed. Half the time he didn't know the details of what he made. He only knew what he wanted it to do. His subconscious did the heavy lifting and he took all the credit for the results. When it came to transmuting, the more he stepped out of his subconscious' way, the cleaner his manifestation would be. And by working with other people, it bettered him, forcing him to learn to communicate his ideas in a different way. In the end, he agreed to the project knowing that Sarah wanted to amalgamate Kole, Eric and Enora into Winter Haven, giving them some authority as Agents. At first it was tough pretending to be normal, but they soon connected with the world around them and came to enjoy their new role in life.

Back on the Battlefield, Kole splashed through puddles, sinking into the mud. The wind howled through the trees and pelted his Power Armor with sheets of rain. Even through the thick layers of armor, Kole heard the rain spray against his suit, striking it like small pebbles, but Kole barely felt the wind's nudges. It was sunny when they had landed. The storm came out of nowhere in waves of rain that could be seen bouncing off the ground, forming a thin layer of water that turned the ground into mud.

A week before, they had searched for a suitable target and found a Troll stronghold on the other side of the continent. It was very inviting, sitting atop a small hill in a forested valley with multiple Human life signs, a giant cube building surrounded by a tall fortified wall with little defenses. Kole and Enora's first impulse was to strategically bomb the Troll targets, but they couldn't separate the Troll's signal from the Human prisoners and assumed that the Troll tech blocked their scan.

Some of Sarah's people didn't want to go in and waste life to save life while Kole wasn't comfortable with their new tech. In the end, Sarah cut the arguments and ordered them to go in and rescue their people anyway. She pushed it as an exercise to test their Power Armor and trainees on what was thought to be a soft target. With James leaving with his Cruiser to rescue other settlements, those that disagreed with Sarah, refuse to go, creating a small division within her ranks. It was all bad.

But with the new Power Armor came advanced Drop Ships capable of providing air support. The engineers offered a small pro-filed ship capable of carrying an armored cargo container that could be dropped onto the battlefield and used as cover by those inside. Again it was about versatility. They chose a long craft with the al-mond shape cockpit and gunnery remote station located near its front and at its back. At each of its four corners, the landing gear extended out of a large ball that held an antigravity engine and re-mote controlled gunnery turret. Two spines that ran the length of the ship allowing a cargo container to be locked into place between them. The Drop Ship could be outfitted to fill whatever roll was needed, sacrificing armor for speed and agility. The engineers wanted to load up the ships with advanced weapons that fired energy bolts, but Ripper Rounds and flamethrowers were the best for han-dling Trolls.

Their plan to take the stronghold was simple. Split their forces and attack from slightly opposite sides, meeting in the middle. Upon hearing that there would be two teams, Eric insisted to be on his own team away from Kole. Concerned, Kole took Eric aside, re-minding him that it'd be safer if they stayed together, that they could-n't use Alchemy and that even though they had authority, they weren't part of the command structure. Eric's eyes glazed over and his jaw went slack making Kole want to slap him, but Kole had to let him go. Eric hadn't been the same since his fight with the Lollypop King and no matter what Kole advised, Eric did the opposite.

Enora didn't want to play soldier and encouraged Kole to do the same, not wanting him to get entangled in Sarah's agenda. Instead, she tucked herself away in her small lab in Winter Haven designing her satellite network. She promised that it was the only way to get rid of the Trolls and that it wouldn't damage too much of the planet. But Kole didn't believe her. Her eyes went a bit crazy when she de-scribed how she'd make the Trolls burn, making him think that her personal grievance with the Trolls dominated her thinking. All he wanted was to maintain a little balance in his wobbly world, so he went along with Sarah's plan to help save as many Humans as he could. It was sad, but her plan was the only one that sounded sane.

Kole pulled on his jammies, climbed into his suit then walked over one of the open sides of an armored cargo container. The cargo container fit two rows of Power Armor that secured themselves into place using hand holds on the floor and ceiling. At first when he'd practice moving upside down, he kept forgetting the quick procedure to interchange his hands and feet which would fill his foot hands with debris, making his hands hard to use once he became right side up again. Eric refused to use the hand option, boasting that he'd be able to kick punch any Troll to death. Kole argued that he should get used to the versatility of the Power Amor and gave scenarios where Eric would need to use both sets of hands, but Eric said he'd never be in those situations anyway. His flippant disregard for his own personal safety irritated Kole until from afar, he watched Eric practicing. It wasn't hard for Kole to spot him on the obstacle course. Everyone had the standard camouflage paintjob while Eric went with hot pink. It was just another thing Eric did to annoy him.

After securing himself into his suit, Kole tuned into the cargo container's com channel that was quiet and rather peaceful compared to when he was with the Dwarves. It was nice to be in a room with a bunch of people, relaxing while waiting for pickup, but a part of him missed his team's banter. When it was time to go, the long sides of the container folded like a box then locked into place. A minute later they shook and after a series clicks and bangs, the Drop Ship lifted off.

The screens on the ceiling and the upper part of the doors of the cargo container flickered on, displaying the outside. They lifted off the huge landing platform that had been built near Winter Haven's exterior wall, over a section of smaller buildings with elevators that went down to the new underground base. Winter Haven had grown too fast. The city couldn't afford to waste building materials on a new outward expansion wall and they weren't prepared to build upward because they didn't have a proper support structure in place. They had only one choice, building down, pouring their resources into their military. Kole turned his head and watched the side screen. The Drop Ships formed up, flying in formation around Winter Haven to meet up with one of the new Battle Cruisers. The Cruiser's job was to sit back and if needed, provide support for the new Power Armor, if they get into trouble. The plan sounded good on paper and no one expected it to go so wrong.

The Drop Ships gained altitude, flying high over the clouds. Kole relaxed his mind and released his expectations, imagining that the clouds were the first layer of snowfall on the waste. Transforming the landscape in his mind gave him some serenity, telling him what he truly felt. It was all outside his control, the direction of the war, Enora's rekindled hatred for the Trolls and Eric's foolishness. It was a luxury, perhaps his delusion to think that he had control over anything. It was all about being in the right time and place to encourage a small change, the little bump that sends the stuff in your hands crashing to the floor. He wanted the best, or what he thought was the best for Eric and the world without thinking about what Eric or the world wanted. He had to let it all go, so he could be there, waiting to become the pebble underfoot.

The Drop Ship continued on and the cloud cover dispersed revealing the long rock walls of a forested valley. Kole couldn't see where they were going, but felt their decent. They all knew they'd be landing soon and in anticipation of confronting the unknown, a nervous and excited energy filled their group com, but Kole stayed calm, refusing to partake of their energy, believing that a calm hand would be stronger and move faster.

Kole's Drop Ship set down in a small clearing with three others while the rest split up, landing where they could. He released his hand grips and readied the Gatling Gun Pods in his suit's arms. The Drop Ship released its crate then lifted off, hovering above the tree line to provide cover. In the cargo container, the Troops lined up using the screens to search the forest for Trolls. Not seeing any they opened the top half of the container. Though it was daytime, a spooky oppressed feeling forced Kole to pay attention to quiet forest.

There was nothing. No birds happily chirping or wind rustling the branches.

The lower part of the door opened onto the carpet of pine needles that stretched across the forest's floor. They left their cargo container, running to the tree line. Kole tried to hide behind a tree, but the tree wasn't fat enough to hide his bulk. He shrunk down, doing his best to lessen his profile then peeked the camera eye of his shoulder around the tree, looking into the forest. He expected a hoard of Trolls to rush them, stomping, a rumbling wave of flesh aimed to devour them, but nothing happened.

"They know we're here right?" asked a trooper.

"I'm bored," another said.

Kole ignored them then heard their leader bark the order to move out. He didn't budge. Instead he took a moment to stretch out his awareness. The Trolls were there. His awareness brushed against their dark and putrid presence then recoiled. He never liked mentally touching them, fearing that their presence would contaminate his mind and corrupt the very way he thought, never allowing him to get clean. His eyes scanned the forest looking through the trees while he moved his view screen between the suit's sensors, but nothing in the forest moved. He reached out again and felt for the closest group of Trolls, finding that they weren't in front of him.

His eyes shot open. He spun with his arm stretched out and in the clearing behind him the ground erupted, sending pine needles, small rocks and dirt into the air. The cargo containers rocked then through the dust, a gigantic grey Troll emerged, grabbing a container with one hand. The Troll spun on his heel then launched the container into the air, hitting Kole's Drop Ship. The container crashed through one of the Drop Ship's spines almost flipping the ship. The pilots cried out in surprise and fought to regain control while the ship's powerful anti-gravity engines compensated, twisting its frame. The Drop Shop spun out of control and followed the container, crashing through the trees. Over the com, the pilots' screams were cut off when the Drop Ship exploded. A burst of static crackled over the com as the shockwave carrying debris through the trees struck Kole, pelting his suit with shards of wood.

The rolling cloud of dust and needles washed over him. Kole focused, tuning out the trooper's yells and death cries and through the dust he saw the Troll's fat, round head. It was the ugliest thing he'd ever seen. A half dead deformed monster with strange growths over its skin. Its puffy face looked like an angry baby's that had droopy ears and nose. Kole braced himself, his arm swayed and pointed at the Troll. He wanted to look into the Troll's cloudy dull red eyes before he pulled the trigger and felt a smile spread across his face, but before he could fire, he saw movement behind the massive Troll and came to the grim realization that many of the troopers were about to die. The dust thinned revealing two more gigantic Tolls. They lumbered out of their underground hiding place, pushing trees out of their way and at the bottom of one of their pits was the mouth of a tunnel.

Normal sized Trolls flooded out of the tunnel and stormed out of the pit. Kole targeted the swarm and fired his arm's Gatling Pods. There were so many Trolls, Kole didn't have to aim. The Trolls charged, slamming their bloody chewed up torsos into him, covering the cameras of his Power Armor with blood and chunks of flesh. Inside, Kole's screen took on a reddish hue. He spun around and swept the smaller Trolls out of his way then reversed his armor to see out his back. The Trolls climbed over the dead to grapple him, but the thick blood coating his back made it too slick for them to hold on.

Kole didn't need his eyes to see, through Alchemy, he could feel them scurrying around him. Screams and shouting filled the com spurring Kole on. He tried to step pushing against the mound of bodies piling up at his feet. He then opened fire, chewing through the bodies until he could climb through the gore to free himself.

His screen was a mess of red and black smears. He couldn't see anything. He assumed that the horde of Trolls had swarmed past him, charging into the forest, following the three gigantic Trolls and now he stood on the lip of pit. He paused, stretching his senses and felt more Trolls about to come out of the tunnel and also felt Troll weaponry. The second wave was armed and through the smeared blood, he saw movement, a flicker on his screen and opened up, firing into the Tunnel's entrance. A bright light flashed on his screen as the force of an explosion penetrated the spine of his suit knocking him forward. His mind hiccupped, forgetting he had spun his suit around and was now facing the wrong direction. He ignored the error messages flashing in the top corner and tried to run for cover, but his suit's legs failed to move. He kicked wildly, trying to make his suit run while he returned fire. He was blind, but his senses told him that he was still killing Trolls then two more explosions rocked his suit. The explosions drummed against him, rupturing his suit's left arm, setting off his ammunition in a massive explosion that shredded his side, spraying shrapnel and tarring up the ground beside him.

His screen flashed then died with his com. Darkness and silence swallowed him and he fell, sliding over the bloody sludge and bone fragments into the pit. Kole erected his shield expecting the Trolls to pry their way into his suit to get at its tender center, but all he heard was thumping of Trolls climbing over him. Kole wanted to scream a string of profanity in frustration to anyone or anything that'd listen, but he clamped his mouth shut. His frustration built and his body trembled. Things like this constantly happened to him and he knew that he'd never hear the end of it from Eric and Enora. They were right, all his stuff was jinxed.

His screen flickered, turning on and he could see the sky. He felt grateful to the Trolls who cleaned off some of his lenses when they used him to climb out of the pit. It was a positive in thing his growing negative day. Then his suit's damage report told him that the left side of his armor was trashed, but the self repair unit was working on restoring him to full power. He lay there deciding his next move watching the sky darkened and the wind forced its way through the forest bending the tree tops. Then with a flash of light-

ning the sky opened up releasing a deluge of rainfall washing the
gore off his armor. He lay there listening to the rain pelt his armor,
waiting for his suit to reroute its systems, watching the rain flow
around him and into the tunnel. The ground softened, turning into
mud under him. He sank a bit before slowly sliding further into the
pit.

He could see that he was alone and couldn't feel anyone nearby
and was tempted to use Alchemy. He is the Alchemist Kole, limited
only by his imagination. He didn't need armor. He could get up, lay
waste to the Trolls and rescue everyone, but then what? He thought
about Sarah and what she had accomplished and felt saddened by
his past. It took him this long to realize that he should've kept to
himself. It had never been about balance. Like everyone else, he
tried to find his place in the world thinking that he could fix everything, what balls he had. In the name of balance, he imposed his
will on everyone else, but what else was he supposed to do. Life
doesn't come with an instruction manual.

Kole thought back to his suit's training and remembered that on
the battlefield he could eject the suit's damaged limbs and replace
them. All he needed was to find another set of armor with a dead
pilot. With all the Trolls running around, he was confident he'd be
successful. He rolled onto his stomach then struggled, fighting his
suit's damaged limbs to drag himself along as he clawed his way
through the mud to the lip of the pit. The mud made it suck and he
wanted to cut his suit's damaged limbs loose, but needed to keep the
suit's sockets clean. He thought about calling for help, but his com
and some of his sub systems were still down. He had thought he
was having a bad day, but when he crawled out of the pit and looked
into the tree line, he realized that he was the one who got off lucky.

The forest around Kole was a mess of dead suits, Troll gore and
bullet riddled trees. The troops who landed with him did their best
to cut down the Troll swarm, but were overrun making Kole feel
terrible for lying around doing nothing while people died. He pulled
himself on to a log and adjusted his sensors to follow the trail of

destruction. He could see that the three gigantic Trolls spared nothing leaving a trail of toppled and trees. The Troll had moved on
leaving their dead who were in the middle of regeneration. Even
now in the rain, Kole could see parts of the Troll's gore bubbling.
Soon those parts would grow into those hateful little monkey Trolls.

Things looked bad and were going to get worse for any survivors.
Kole had to hurry. He asked his computer to scan the forest to find
suitable parts then dragged himself along the gigantic Troll's path to
a set of armor face down in a heap under a pile of broken branches.
The upper half of its body had been twisted and crushed, leaving
no room for the pilot to survive. Kole went to work replacing his
suit's limbs and once done his com reconnected. There were
survivors.

Chapter

2

It was going to be a great day. Eric could feel it. He felt charged, super pumped and remembering the look on Kole's face when he saw his hot pink Power Armor, made him giggle for days. He thought the color would ruffle feathers from the rest of the troops, but it didn't. At first, they were mad, glaring until they found out who he was. He was one of the Agents who were sent into the Dwarven Lands to acquire one of their suits, an Agent who had fought the Trolls in their swamp and won. His brand of crazy inspired the younger troops to express themselves with paint and attitude. Multicolored artwork decorated their armor, begging the Trolls to come and see. The pilots even reflected the look of their armor, changing their uniforms, adding colors then wore makeup to become the first Human Berserkers. He was so proud.

The pilots' superiors had a meltdown over their disregard of the uniform and Eric, being the one who inspired the change, was called in to stand before a group of old military people to explain. He didn't see what the problem was because most of troops were going to die anyway and should be free to live the way they wanted. The old guys didn't like his attitude, or answer and it wasn't hard to get into an argument with them, forcing Sarah to step in and smooth things over, but by the time Sarah showed up, Eric had forgotten what they were arguing about. She walked in all graceful, looking like she took lessons from the Elves, wearing her simple robe, but when she spoke, her words sounded oily. He watched her weave her magic soothing the old guys, making Eric want to take a shower to wash her stink off. Her smooth talk made it sound like Eric intentionally brought this new attitude out to inspire the troops and help them combat their fear, giving them power over what they couldn't control. The youth were now part of a unique family who'd band together to face the coming darkness. At the end of her long winded explanations, Eric felt heroic.

Despite all the warnings Kole said about her and how Sarah made him feel at first, after hearing all the good things she had said about him made her suddenly looked sexy. The old guys slopped it up and when she looked over then smiled, he was sure that she'd invite him over for tea. Of course he'd accept and see where things went, but after she was finished with the old guys she didn't offer, disappointing him. But before she left, she did tell him after how happy she was that he was fitting in, which confused him. He wasn't sure what meeting she had walked in on because those old guys may have looked calm to her, but their words were still heated. He was an expert at pushing Kole's buttons and he could tell that they were angry without showing when she was around. It was lies from people who'd forgotten how to live and be truthful about their feelings.

When he returned to his Berserkers, they thought he was a hero for facing down the brass to defend them. He liked the attention, but told the truth, giving full credit to Sarah. They were awed by the fact that Sarah personally came to help him, adding to his growing image which he felt good embracing. The girls were also noticing him, confirming that he was right all along, chicks dig tattoos and piercings.

In his Drop Ship, the clouds parted. They flew in their cargo container over the forest and even though Kole drilled the fact into his head that he wasn't part of their chain of command, his Berserkers were on a separate com channel chanting the chants he'd made up. Eric liked the Dwarves way of doing things, but their songs suck. Instead he developed chants based on breathing to inspire a feeling of connection between his troops and to elevate their energy level. Eric joined in their chant, feeling a pumping pressure in his chest, breathing with them as one.

Eric watched the screen that ran down the side of the cargo container as the first Drop Ships landed in their targeted clearing. Through the breathing and chanting, Eric couldn't tell what he felt. A strange calm blanketed him and all he knew was that he wanted to hit the ground running. His Drop Ship circled above the trees while to ones on the ground dropped their containers then took off.

His Drop Ship banked and was coming in for a landing when the ground opened up between the containers, spraying dirt into the air. Through the dust, Eric could see Trolls. Insisting on being in the first position, Eric lunged forward stabbing the open door controls with his armor's fist. The side of the cargo container opened and Eric leapt out, falling toward the hole. He extended his arms then opened fire at the Trolls pouring out of the hole, diving into the mess of exploding body parts. His Ripper Rounds forged the way, making a slick path of gore, quickly submerging him in a black mess of innards. His barrels plugged, triggering the safety mechanism in his Gun Pods. He squeezed his triggers, but his guns refused to fire. He wanted to push his way through the mess into the tunnel turning, but he had to find solid ground and clear his barrels. His people followed, ramming into him, pushing him through the disgusting mess of Troll chunks. Like a plug, the gore pushed its way through the advancing Trolls and flowed into the tunnel behind them. Feeling ground, Eric hunkered down with his arms outstretched, thrashing side to side in the waste deep mess, tagging the Trolls he could touch.

"I got you, Eric," a Berserker said from behind him, then pushed him out of the way.

He hit the tunnel wall, feeling useless. He couldn't see and his weapons were all gooey. His men passed him, fighting their way down the tunnel then one stopped to wipe his gore down and pick the chunks of flesh out of mouth of his Gun Pod. But before Eric could thank the person an explosion shook the tunnel. Rocks and dirt fell from the ceiling, slowly pouring at first then picked up the pace, signaling the time to retreat. Eric ran back with a pack of his men up the slop to the surface and was surprised at how far his mad dash down the tunnel had taken him. The only thing he was grateful for was that the first wave of Trolls was a swarm of unarmed thrashers.

The rumbling tunnel collapsed blasting a cloud of dust behind him, trapping some of his men underground. The loose dirt coated Eric's armor sticking the gore blinding most of his sensors. He pushed his way through his men looking through his smeared lenses for the Trolls that got past them. He swung his arms around, pointing at the tree line ready to open up, but a gruff sounding trooper told him to calm down. The surface was secured by the troopers from the other Drop Ships and the Trolls that had made it out of their tunnel before Eric dove in were dead, torched. The troops were regrouping, getting ready to push forward and once Eric realized that he had time, he ran back to the tunnel and thrust his arms into the loose dirt to dig his men out.

Through his com, the trapped troopers told him that it wasn't time for them to be rescued and told him to stop. He didn't want to let them go, but was reminded that they'll be freed because people will have to dig them out to burn Troll guts. It was their weak transmission that made him stop. They sounded hurt and far away, but they assured Eric that they would see him again. It became a race for Eric to get the job done then return to help free them before their air runs out.

After being bathed in fire and having his lenses cleaned, Eric was forced to stop and listen. They were to advance in waves in case the Trolls had more underground pockets that planned to attack them from behind and after Eric's suicidal rampage into the tunnel, he and his men were ordered to be last. Eric thought about arguing then remembered that he didn't have to listen to them. He wasn't part of their chain of command and decided he was going to do his own thing anyway.

The sky darkened and a weird storm came out of nowhere, bringing strong winds and heavy rain. Eric waited for the troops to advance then entered the forest in a different direction. He quickened his pace, bumping into trees and squeezing between others. Kole was right. He needed more practice to get used to the armor's size. He lumbered through the forest, scratching his armor against the trees and without the noise from the wind and rain he'd be the loudest target there. He circled wide with the plan to be the first one to charge the stronghold when screams and yells erupted over the com. For a second, he was glad their yelling took his mind off his troops trapped in the tunnel.

Eric stopped moving, listening, trying to hear through the howling wind and the rain bouncing off his armor. He had no idea where he was and asked his armor's computer to bring up a map to find everyone. A small topographical map appeared below his line of sight displaying the information. He realized that bumping into the trees had knocked him off course and that he should've been using the map from the start. He remembered his instructor going over all the armor's features, but the guy's voice was so drab it almost put him to sleep.

He read the map. The green dots were his people and they were surrounded by red dots. Eric watched the dots movement and discerned that the Trolls were now using weapons instead of charging in. He looked around making sure he was alone then ran, stomping through the muddy ground, trying desperately not to bash into the trees. He didn't have a plan. He found a concentration of red dots and was going to hit it. The Dwarven songs echoed through his mind and all he wanted to do was make a hole, cause some chaos and have a little fun. His mind was full of static and he felt great.

He was going to be the hero for Sarah.

Lightning flashed, shadows moved and the wind brought the forest to life. Eric charged through the bushes and stumbled upon his target, a large group of armed Trolls wearing thermo protected gear. He caught them building gun nest with their large caliber weapons. All he could think was that his map had lied to him. There was a second where he and the Trolls stared at each other then chaos came. Eric sprang sideways into the air, pointing all four of his limbs at the group. He remembered to open the Gun Pods in his legs then fired. He did his best to control his limbs and sync them up to aim true, but it didn't happen the way he saw it in his head. He envisioned hang time, where he'd hover for a couple of seconds while his limbs fired, mowing the surprised Trolls down. In reality he popped into the air, flailed his legs, shifting his body which forced him to compensate, aiming low. His rounds shot into the ground, splattering the mud and hit the odd Troll while they dove for cover. Eric landed hard in the mud, coating half his body muddy pine needles. He looked into the darkness then his eyes went big in surprised.

Lightning flashed above and out of the darkness the Trolls with their hateful eyes, clenched teeth and sharp features, opened up on him. The noise from their rounds punching into his armor was worse than the rain. Eric screamed, forcing himself to sit while firing three of his limbs. It worked better this time, but he was only able to aim two of his limbs while one of his legs shot high into the trees. He couldn't go anywhere and took their punishment while he delivered his. Alarms sounded in his ears and a damage report flashed to his left as their rounds passed through the outer layer of armor into the sensitive machinery beneath. His sensors winked out, the forest darkened and the only light was from the muzzle flashes. He invoked his Alchemy and put his shield up, tight around his body and kept firing.

His stupid plan angered him, but what made it worse was the Troll's refusal to die, showing him how stupid his plan really was. He tried to convince himself that it was a good idea to attack them

head on and not to find cover. And it was another really good idea
to attack the Lollypop King with everything he had, destroying a city
filled with innocent people.

His feeling of helplessness returned his mind back to the terrible
day in the Ork city, trapped in a vortex with the Lollypop King. He
went into that fight angry, summoning everything he had to pit his
power against The King's, but the King was stronger, slapping away
his efforts. He felt like a child who refused to lose. He opened himself, giving everything he had to delve deeper into his power, finding
more power than he knew he could possibly have until a crushing
pressure dropped on him. Something cracked then popped within
him releasing everything he had, ripping him open. The world went
silent and he felt cut open, hemorrhaging energy from his core. He
felt death, but couldn't stop. He wanted to pull away and run, but
he couldn't move. He could barely breathe. The pressure had him,
pulling at his very soul. His rage melted away showing him his truth.
All he ever had was fear and in that moment, he knew it would end
badly, but he refused to lose to the monster before him. His body
ached and a terrible cold filled his core. The world around him
dimmed all that he could clearly see was the frightened little boy
within, but now he had a choice. To allow his fear to consume then
kill him, or take The King with him, he was dead either way. Choosing to make his death mean something, he gave himself completely
to the vortex and it hungrily gorged itself on him then sweet darkness came.

He snapped back to fighting the Trolls with a renewed determination pumping through him. His hands clamped tight around
his triggers till his muscles shook. He no longer needed the sensors
to tell him where the Trolls were, he could feel them. He shot
through trees and stumps to kill those hiding. He didn't care. They
could destroy his armor, chop up his body and consume his flesh.
He will kill them all. He no longer used his eyes to see. He felt nothing, empty, pure void. His body felt light, his limbs floating. He
moved without mental command and when he had finished, the

Trolls had shot through his armor destroying half of his suit's mechanics and left him with a quarter of power.

Then the pain came. His jaw clamped shut, his body convulsed against his restraints and rather than face his trauma, he suddenly found himself outside his body standing next to his suit in the middle of the shot up group of Trolls who were in the middle of regenerating. Even with the flashing light above and the rain, the forest felt peaceful. Calm washed away his anxiety. He thought he was dead and turned around. His armor lay on the ground shaking, shooting his Gun Pods wilding into the air until they emptied. He waited for his armor's tantrum to end and watched the Trolls gore bubble, wondering what was going to happen to him next. His life was slipping between his fingers. His dreams, desires, hopes and fears. He didn't want to go. He had Trolls to burn, but standing outside his body waiting for something to come get him made him accept how powerless in life he truly was.

But nothing came to collect him and whisk him away into the afterlife making him wonder what was actually going on. His life continued to fizz away, his expectations and all the things he wanted to do, felt empty and unimportant. He thought of Kole and wanted to see him once more to thank him for being there for him. Believing he was dead, he took a step to find Kole, but found himself back in his sore and drooling body. Confused, he rolled his suit onto its feet then switched from front to back. He thought about his experience. He had let go of the world and found a level of peace he had never felt before, but now he was back. He didn't know what to think, or feel. He'd let everything go and now he had to care about the regenerating Trolls at his feet. He didn't even hate the Trolls anymore.

He waved the arm of his suit, gesturing to the middle of the Troll mess, manifesting a bomb that'd torch their bodies and burn in the rain. It was easy. He didn't even have to try. He extended his shield and filled the gaps of his suit's ruined mechanics then forced his suit to move. His suit came to life and the topographical map appeared on his screen telling him where everyone was.

A moment ago, he was sure he was dead and had been set free, but realized that under the stress of his memory of the Lollypop King, he'd only fallen out of his body. Rage filled him. He was robbed of the deepest peace he'd felt, having it replaced with a powerful will to survive. He didn't need bullets. He was still in the fight. He had his limbs and the Trolls had skulls that needed crushing. He wanted to punish whatever pulled him from his body only to slap him back in. He didn't know what it meant, or why it happened, but his angry demanded revenge, something had to pay.

He charged through the forest, running like a burly skater, shouldering the trees, busting their bark and when he was a safe distance away, he set his bomb off. He didn't look back or cared if the rain spread its burning chemicals. He was there to kill. He ran up a small hill and circled around a dense section of brush to see three gigantic Trolls swinging their fists, crashing through the trees to strike at the troopers. He skidded to a stop, sliding in the mud and was transfixed. He watched them stomp and slug their way through the forest. He admired their horrific beauty then felt a chill of energy run across his skin, filling him to the point of bursting. Rage, anger, he didn't know what the feeling was that filled him, but he had to act to keep the feeling fed. He charged the closest behemoth. In the dark, its haunting shadow used a full tree as a club, swinging its muddy roots in a wide arc, batting away two suits that were firing into its abdomen.

The Troll's club followed through, shattering trees in a noise that rivaled the thunder above. At the end of its swing, Eric stretched his senses out. He couldn't see with all the mud and needles stuck to his armor, but he could feel the Toll's wounds. It was a powerful creature with advanced regeneration and though the Troll was sucking up all the Ripper Rounds, it was regenerating faster than was thought possible. Eric ran up its club then when the Troll reversed his swing, he jumped, diving into one of the Troll's open wounds. Multiple Ripper Rounds had torn into its flesh, punching a big hole in its side that was in the process of closing. Eric wiggled, thrashing his way through the Troll's hardened flesh to hook the broken hands of his armor under a rib and pull himself deeper into the Troll's guts while listening to the rhythmic beating of its heart.

The thought of his men buried in the tunnel flashed through his mind, reminding him to hurry. He kicked off the Troll's ribs and thrashed through his soft and regenerating innards. It became clear to Eric that he wasn't doing as much damage as he'd hoped. At most the Troll felt that he suffered from a bad case of gas. Eric's suit slowed, his thrashing had wrapped the Troll's intestines tight around his armor binding him. If he died now, he and his suit would become like a surgeon's lost tool after a botched surgery. He doubted the dumb Troll even knew he was there and stretched his shield beyond his suit creating blades whipped around him, cutting himself free. Being inside the Troll, he finally understood Enora, when she had refused to use her Alchemy to empty his bowels. He didn't want to think about it, but knew he was now covered in waste. He didn't mind the blood and guts so much, but knowing what the Troll had eaten, hit him sideways.

There was only one way to stop this monster and keep him down. Eric thrashed again, climbing onto the Troll's heart then used its beating to push his way further up its body. He stopped, hearing a new loud meaty thumping only to realize that the Troll knew he was there and wanted to remove him the only way it could. He had to hurry, or the Troll would rip his own body open to get at Eric. The whole idea tickled him. He laughed and thrashed his way up the Troll's neck while the monster ripped out his own throat.

He quickened, squirming his way into the back of the Troll's mouth, but its tongue bucked, pushing him forward, allowing the Troll to grab him, squeezing, crushing the lower half of his suit. The Troll pulled, but Eric was too slick. Eric slipped out of his grasp, but the Troll leaned back, opening his neck then managed to get a hold on his legs. Eric laughed again then ejecting his suit's caught limbs. He maneuvered himself into the Trolls nasal cavity then used his shield to slice his way into the Troll's skull scrambling its brains.

The Troll wobbled and Eric laughed as it fell.

The Troll's head bounce off the ground, shaking Eric against his suit's restraints. When he stopped to think about it, it was an atrocious experience, but he couldn't stop laughing. He wanted out, not to free himself, or to get clean, but to find the next Troll and teach him the reverse way of eating a Human. He wedged himself against the Troll's skull and punched his way out, cracking its skull open. He dramatically emerged to inspire terror in any Troll watching because he was the monster that'd haunt their dreams. Covered in guts and brain matter, he gave up on using his suit to see. The Power Armor had failed miserably.

Eric stretched his awareness feeling the battle raging around him. The two other gigantic Trolls had spread out, thumping the fleeing troopers while the smaller Trolls regrouped outside the forest, close to their stronghold. Eric ignored the smaller Trolls, he had bigger aspirations. He flipped himself upside down and ran on his hands screaming, ignoring his throbbing head. He hungered for the kill. He was going to find the next Troll and enter him from behind and do what he did to the last one.

Chapter

3

Earlier, Sarah stood on the enclosed observation deck of a Battle Cruiser looking out the window at the passing Drop Ships. The room wasn't big. A grey steel deck more white walls and a couple of seats with two benches that were fixed in place. Why always white walls? She didn't know. Perhaps it was habit, or the cheapest paint. Bright plain white without any tint wasn't a color that calmed her mind, or made her think of space. She took a breath then released her annoyance and focused her attention outside.

She thought the warm sunny day was a good omen, one that would bring another victory to her people. They planned to try out their new Power Armor and rescue more Human captives to add to their numbers and she felt lucky. They were on a roll and have won every engagement against the Trolls, removing the fear in her people's hearts. Their emotions were shifting. They had hope, but mostly anger and resentment. What they felt was understandable. The Trolls were now seen as ravenous brutes, dying by the thousands to eat those too weak to defend themselves, a picture in a person's mind that didn't inspire mercy or compassion. But Sarah didn't want hate, anger or pity to replace their fear. She needed to provide an emotional balance to keep her people out of the extremes.

Depending on the type of anger, it's not hard to push a person to violence and in her mind there's only one answer. She needed to guide her people out of fear and into contentment. All other emotions would place her people into a position of imbalance. The ocean of emotion has many waves and a powerful positive emotion can be just as destructive as a negative one. But people must feel. It wasn't feeling that was the problem. It's the overindulgence in what they felt that causes them harm, an emotional high that they'd want to revisit. Her people needed to be taught to catch and release their emotions, becoming content.

She watched the Drop Ships become dots on the horizon then felt the Battle Cruiser move. She silently wished the troops luck then closed her eyes, centering herself. In her heart she didn't like the idea of sending them in alone to test the armor against the Trolls, a lot could go wrong. They should be doing a proper smash and grab, hitting the Trolls hard with everything they could spare. Why mess around? They'd still be able to find the suit's flaws without jeopardizing everyone, but her people demanded it. There were too many factors involved with creating an army and she had to sit back, allowing them to gamble with time, materials and bodies.

Thinking about the coming fight spiked her anxiety, swirling unease around her tummy. She needed to dump her nervousness before she left the room, so it wouldn't be seen on her face, or heard in her voice. The door slid open behind her and when she turned, she expected to see one of her servants, but was pleased to see Adrian standing in the doorway wearing his tan uniform.

When she sat in the quiet of her home, she had called up the Mayor and told him that she wanted to observe the battle from the bridge of the Battle Cruiser. The Mayor looked shocked and didn't like the idea of her seeking out danger. At the end of their talk, the Mayor insisting that she'd take protection. She laughed thinking that he was joking, but the worry in his eyes told her otherwise.

She was going to weave her power into her words and soothe

his spirit, but remembered her officer from the war room. The way Adrian had looked at her put all kinds of ideas into her head. She wanted to brush those ideas away, reminding herself that saving humanity was more important than matters of the heart, but what is life without love? She didn't need a partner to make her feel complete, but was willing to see if he'd be her equal. Giving in to her desires and feeling wicked, she asked the Mayor for him. She still didn't know his name and asking would've created questions, so she had to describe him to the Major, in a manly way. Sticking to the basics, she described him as having short brown hair, brown eyes and with speaks an accent. She skipped that he was handsome, smelling clean and masculine with strong broad shoulders and deep brown eyes. Lost in the memory of him, the Mayor told her his name three times before she clued in. He explained that a lot of women clamored for his attention and that he didn't blame her for asking for him. But before she could lie and tell him that she didn't choose him for those reasons, the Mayor agreed, saying that he was a good officer. Her face burned with embarrassment. She could see the rumors floating behind the Mayor's eyes and thought that she had thrown everything away to hear Adrian say her name.

"Mother Sarah," Adrian said with his accent that tickled her.

She met his gaze and stood tall, pitting her presence against his to impress him with her strength. She'd heard some women say that a woman should yield to the man and show him that he's needed, but she couldn't play the swooning damsel, she needed an equal and if he couldn't take her strength, she'd walk away. She looked into his eyes, building the powerful silence between them and got lost in him, forgetting what she was doing.

Her heart quickened and her face flushed. "Please, call me Sarah," she said trying to sound firm, but to her ears, she sounded strained and washed out.

He smiled then stepped into the room allowing the door to close behind him. "I apologize for the intrusion. I wanted to take this time and formally introduce myself before things got hectic."

"Oh, the Mayor told me who you are," she blurted.

"And everyone knows who you are," he said, almost making her giggle. "I am Adrian and I've been assigned to protect you for the duration of this operation. I'm looking forward to working with you."

Drawn to him, she took a couple of steps, surprising herself. She stopped and pretended she meant to do that then tidied her robe. She then collected her wits before saying, "I'm looking forward to working with you as well."

"Call me when you're ready and I'll escort you to the bridge."

She nodded with a slight smile then convinced herself that their conversation had gone the way she had planned it and watched him leave. The door slid shut and she waited a second to make sure no one else would come in then threw her head back and groaned. She slapped her shaking fists to her sides, ruffling her robe and threw a micro-tantrum. She had spoken to him twice and in both times she had behaved like an idiot. She stopped thrashing. Part of her re-fused to straighten her robe, but she did it anyway. Asking for him to be her protector was a mistake. Somehow, when he was around her brain took off and abandoned her. She was Mother Sarah and her people looked to her for guidance, but would they still listen to her if they knew that some boy turned her into a blubbering idiot. This wasn't her. She wanted to show him who she really was, but he made her feel so many things she couldn't control her mouth, or even her feet.

She pushed away her negative thoughts and calmed down, re-membering how she was going to bring contentment to her people. How she was going to teach them to experience emotion then release it before it became an indulgence. "Yeah right," she muttered to her-self, feeling foolish.

She took another deep breath and slowly exhaled, letting her sil-liness float away. She thought about her behavior and decided that she shouldn't be upset with herself. She was a clone after all with little to no life experience. Of course she'd behave like a girl with her first crush. She had been made in a test tube, what did she expect? She laughed at herself. Feeling better then thought about where she'd come from and what she has done in her short life.

She walked up to the glass, watching the wastes turn into forest imagining what she'd be like if she was a regular person, free to be whatever she wanted. But in reality, she felt frozen in place by all the eyes watching her, a mold she was forced to exist in.

She followed her line of thought, thinking that she was rebelling against her mold and believed that her desire to be free put Adrian on her path. A selfish motive when she was in a position to help so many. She nodded, agreeing that her feelings for Adrian were designed to topple her position, setting her free to live a normal life around friends who'd be her family.

She plucked at her robes again to give her hands something to do, creating a sense of control over her inner world that seemed to be in full rebellion against her. She thought of Adrian and decided that for the future of humanity, she'd to be cold and aloof. If he tells a joke, she won't laugh and any nice words that flow from his mouth, she'll meet with negativity. And if it turns out that he's the kind of guy that likes abuse, he'll deserve to be kicked to the curb. She smiled at her reflection in the glass and felt the wall around her heart. Her smile told her one thing, but her sad eyes told her another. She consciously put more life in her eyes and reminded herself that it was for humanity and a scandal would give her people enough strength to fight her influence.

She felt the Battle Cruiser stop, slightly jolting her, bumping her forehead into the glass. She rubbed her head, feeling clumsy and unnerved, wanting to punish the window, making her wonder where her good day went. She had a bad feeling. The energy in the air felt dead and ominous. She scanned the forest seeing the Drop Ships, small specks circling, shooting jets of flame into the forest. A white swirling ball formed over the stronghold. She squinted, moving closer, pressing the tip of her nose against the glass. The ball grew, turning grey then light flashed within its center. She clutched her robe over her heart, fearing the new Troll weapon and watched the cloud darken then expand, multiplying over the forest. Beneath, the wind swirled the treetops while a thick wall of rain turned the forest grey.

The experiment was over and her people were in trouble. She waited a second to feel the Battle Cruiser lurch forward to rescue the troopers, but nothing happened. She spun around, planning to rush the bridge and make it happen, but saw something. She stopped and looked out the side window at the trees rising from the forest. She rushed to the window. In the distance, seven Troll Battleships scattered throughout the valley facing the stronghold hovered. Trees still on their backs, the long black lumpy cylinders floated high over the forest.

Sarah had only seen them once before, at night over the Arctic. They were ugly ships. She uttered a string of profanity and was glad no one was there to hear it then watched the Battleships rotate, dumping the trees, rocks and dirt into the pit below. Trolls were terrifying enough, but to witness their decades old plan, frightened her. They must have known someone would come, but didn't know who. They had buried their forces and let the forest grow over them, telling Sarah that it had always been a trap and that the life signs were false, tailored to attract the race the Trolls wanted.

Three Battleships on the other side of the valley advanced into the storm, firing at the Drop Ships, shooting them down with ease. The others turned to face the Battle Cruiser. With a flash of light and a series of loud thumps, the guns on the Battle Cruiser came to life shooting at the two closest Battleships, igniting impact flashed across the surface of two of the closest ships. The Battleships powered on, bellowing black smoke that quickly dissipated in the wind. The bumps on their surface flashed green, streaking bolts of energy that pelted the Battle Cruiser.

Sarah braced herself, grabbing the windowsill a second before the barrage struck, but she barely felt it. She wanted to laugh thinking that they'd win and deliver a painful defeat to the Trolls then chunks of the Cruiser rained from above sobering her thoughts. The Cruiser launched its Fighters that attacked the weakest ship in a co-ordinated dance, strafing the Battleship, but it didn't fight back. The Battleship fired again, but that time Sarah felt it. The other Battle-ships who were closer to the fighters, fired at their companion, de-stroying some fighters and turning the Battleship into flying scrap metal. The wounded Battleship exploded, showering black streaks of smoking shrapnel over the forest. Through the mess, Sarah saw the fighters and was glad some had survived, but was surprised that the Trolls were willing to sacrifice their people on the off chance that they'd kill the enemy. But then remembered that the Trolls re-generate and obviously didn't care if they tore their friends to bits, it would only make more of them.

The door opened behind her and looking concerned, Adrian rushed to her side saying, "We need to get you out of here." He grabbed her wrist and gently pulled to get her moving.

She twisted her wrist and pulled back, lining the side of her wrist up with his thumb then dug in to use his momentum to break his own grip. He fell back a step creating a space between them. Her body took over. No one had ever touched her like that, not even the Slavers when she was on her way to their camp. She stepped in and brought her knee up into crotch. He collapsed against her, grab-bing his knees to brace himself. Seeing the surprised and hurt in his eyes made her regretted what she had done right away. She didn't have to be so cruel. She could have broke free then stepped away and not hurt him. She smelled his pleasant scent then pushed him away. She had to make sure that he'd never come between her and humanity. He staggered back then looked up at her with fire in his eyes startling her.

"I shouldn't have grabbed you like that, I'm sorry," he said then straitened, standing tall, but she could see his pain. "But you also shouldn't have done that, it was uncalled for."

A nearby explosion shook the Battle Cruiser, shattering one of the observation windows, scattering glass across the floor, but she couldn't pry her eyes off him. She thought he was angry, but his eye shone with determination, telling her that he could be dangerous, somehow making her feel safe. "I'm not going anywhere," she finally said over the howling wind.

He calmed then smiled, showing the charming face everyone knew. "From these windows you can't see that we're surrounded. I was ordered to get you out of here before none of us can get away. But, I can tell that you're determined to stay, so I've decided to protect you the best I can before we're both eaten."

Sarah cocked her head, seeing through his passive sarcasm. She didn't like this version of him, or the face he showed the world. She liked the passionate and determined man underneath. She wondered what else he was hiding.

"What's it going to be Sarah? Are we going to stay and risk being lunch, or are we going to leave?" asked Adrian then waited for what he thought was going to be the correct answer.

She turned her back to him and looked toward the stronghold, but couldn't see through the lines of rain. "What about the men on the field?" she asked. She felt the Cruiser shift, pulling away from the closing Battleships.

"They've lost and we can't risk losing everyone to save them."

She faced him then reached into her robes. She pulled out her com and data pad, linking them to the Cruiser's system. The Captain's profile appeared on her screen. A round faced, white haired gentleman glanced at her. "I don't have time to chat right now," he said, dismissing her.

She allowed her power to flow in her words and said, "We are not retreating. Push forward and fight your way to our troops. Once there, land in the forest and call them to us. We are not prey. We do not run from predators who'll take us down from behind."

He turned to face his screen. His eyebrows furrowed over his dark eyes, doubting her. "If we retreat, we might be able to meet up with reinforcements," he said then shook his head. "I'm not going to risk my crew going in there, I'm not Admiral Ashwood."

She almost had him convinced, but his fear took hold brushing away her influence. She tried again softening her tone, playing into his fear saying, "We won't make it with so few troopers. They'll hunt us down, but if we could gather our forces and fortify our position, we could wait for rescue."

His face went slack telling her that her words had sunk in. "Your right," he said then disconnected the call.

Sarah looked into her black screen at her reflection waiting for confirmation that her words had struck home then felt the Cruiser stop. She looked out the windows and watched multiple missiles launch, racing towards a Battleship and explode, lighting up the front of the ship. The Cruiser then fired its forward guns and through the Battleship's bellowing smoke, Sarah saw a cascade of explosions erupt across it. The smoking Battleship fell then dove into the forest, leaving only three more between them and the surviving troopers. The Battle Cruiser lurched forward unleashing its full power. Sarah's jaw dropped. She turned back to Adrian and allowed her anger into her voice. "He was holding back!" she spat.

"That was his orders."

"He was supposed to hold back and if needed, support our forces on the ground. Not use our resources to make a break for it, leaving our troopers to die!" She clutched her robe, stopping herself from throwing another micro-tantrum. "I want him fired."

Adrian shook his head then said, "Not going to happen."

She gave him her best, I know it's not going to happen look, then said, "I want him placed somewhere where he won't hurt people by running away." She waited for him to say something, but instead he looked forward and stared out the window. She followed his gaze wondering what he was looking at, but saw nothing. She gave up arguing with him and went back to watching the battle.

He quietly walked up beside her then placed his hands behind his back. "I would suggest going somewhere safer, away from the windows," he respectfully said.

The trees beneath them spun and the Cruiser altered course then what was left of its main guns fired at the last Battleship, punching an ugly hole into its deck. The nose of the Battleship dropped then slowly spun, lifting in a wobbly charge. The Cruiser shuddered in an attempt to evade. Its engines whined and the Cruiser tilted away from the Battleship. The motion rocked Sarah and she grabbed Adrian for support, watching the battered, smoking Troll wreck approach. Adrian stepped in and wrapped his arm around her, holding her tight.

The Battleship struck. The two ships' hulls bucked. Metal screamed, pushing the Cruiser, flinging Sarah and Adrian into the air. Adrian wrapped her in his arms, pulling her close, protecting her a moment before they slapped against the ceiling. The momentum carried them. They slid passed the lights then hit the opposite wall. Still holding her, they fell. He released her, pushing her away, guiding her fall and managed to keep her upright. Adrian's shoes slapped hard against the floor. He collapsed, spilling himself then rolled into a bench that was fixed into place, wrapping himself around two of its legs.

Sarah hit the floor and ran a couple of steps before she was able to stop. She couldn't believe what had happened. It was like floating, she wasn't even hurt. She spun around looking for Adrian and saw him curled up under the bench. After what he had done, she expected him to spring to his feet and flash that smile of his, but he didn't move. She ran to his side, dropping to her knees, sliding on her robes. She pulled him onto his back, resting his head on her lap.

His eyes fluttered open. "I hurt my head," he slurred.

"Let's get you some help," she said then helped him to his feet.

He stood then made her let him go. "I need to know how bad I'm hurt," he said then closed his eyes. He fell back and Sarah sprang forward, circling under him, catching him before she collapsed under his weight.

While he lay in her arms, she felt the Cruiser list. She couldn't see much out the windows from her position, but knew they were crashing. She had no regrets. She slipped her arms out of her robe then secured Adrian, using her robe to tie him to the legs of the bench. In her white tunic under robes which felt like underwear to her, she lodged herself under the bench then hooked her arm around the bench's legs. Holding her wrist, she waited.

She closed her eyes listening to the quick cascade of trees snapping and brushing against the bottom of the Cruiser. Then with a loud bang the Cruiser slammed into the ground. She bounced, sliding the inside of her elbow up the bench leg, hurting her arm then smashed against the bottom of the bench, breaking her grip on her wrist. The force flung her around and dropped her onto Adrian's chest, knocking her knees against the floor. Her painful cry was lost in the hull's haunting metallic moans. She grabbed onto Adrian's uniform and held on tight. Alarms sounded and rivets snapped. The Cruiser slid across the ground, shaking her with each bump. Her hands moved to her robe, glad it still held Adrian then felt the nose of the Cruiser dip. Then with a crash, the Cruiser rocked back, stopping.

Sarah pushed herself onto her knees, she knew she was hurt, but didn't feel anything. Her hands went to work untying Adrian. She roused him then helped him to his feet. "Don't close your eyes," she said, not wanting him to land on her again. She wasn't sure if she'd be able to push him off her and get him to his feet again. He wasn't light and she was feeling weaker by the minute.

He leaned heavily on her and together they walked into the hall. The alarms blared in the halls and Sarah could hear running footsteps across the metal grates. She spun them around trying to remember where the med bay was. Adrian flung his hand pointing in the correct direction. "Down two decks," he murmured in her ear.

She pulled him along encouraging him to walk. His breathing labored, his step grew short. He reached out, running his hand along the wall for support. Seeing him degrade right before her eyes made her want to cry. She could've been the one hurt. He saved her and she had been so mean to him. "Do you want to rest?" she asked, more to alleviate her guilt than to help him. A kindness returned for kneeing him in the crotch.

"No," he grunted. "I'll cool down and hurt more. I have to keep moving, or I'll never get better."

She wanted to yell for help, but there was no one around. The alarms screamed in her ears and she doubted she'd be able to yell louder than them. She was afraid for Adrian, hot tears streamed down her cheeks. She wanted to set him down and run ahead, but knew he'd continue without her. Fear clutched at her. She imagined the med bay empty, everyone evacuating and leaving them all alone, forcing her to watch him die. She wondered if anyone would miss her, or if James would crack open another vat and manufacture a new one of her.

She kept walking, pulling along a man who risked himself to save her. In a way she was immortal like the Alchemists, or so she thought. If she died, she'd be replaced, ensuring the survival of humanity. She was sick of the same old argument she had with herself, but in the end she had to look at the truth. She may look and feel Human, but she had been made by James, who used his perception of life to mimic the real thing. It wasn't about a question about being real. She wasn't part of the energy of life that flows through the Universe. She was a watered down version of the real thing like the other races.

She felt Adrian's body against hers, bumping into her with each step. This was as close to love as she'd ever get. What could she give him? He's a good man who deserves a good and full life. She was far from normal and not destined for that type of life. She decided to get him to the med bay then abandon him there, giving him the only loving gift she could, a normal life without her.

She needed to get to the command deck and find out what was going on. She wanted to make sure that the Captain hadn't fled and was busy organizing their defenses. She also needed Kole. The flickering lights in the hall worsened, threatening to strand them in the dark. They made it to the half opened med bay doors that sat crooked on their tracks. Together, leaning against each other, they pried the doors open.

The staff hustled, treating burned and broken people. The first thing that repulsed Sarah was the rich smell of blood, but it was the unique scent of burnt flesh made her gag. She helped Adrian to a bed then explained to a nurse what she thought had happened. She looked into Adrian's half closed eyes. "Thank you," she said then rushed back into the hall. She made sure she was alone then wept. All of her stress came rushing forward choking her. She felt awful for ditching Adrian and not making sure he'd pull through. For all she knew, his brain was swelling and he'd be dead soon. Her spirit plummeted. She felt so alone and when she went to wipe her tears away then realized that she forgot her robe. She wiped her cheeks with the sleeve of her under robe then cleaned her face up.

With a renewed determination she rushed up a couple of decks into a dark passageway. Wires and light fixtures hung from the ceiling while inured technicians worked to restore main power. She slowed, walking on the warped deck, careful not to kick tool bags, or step on the workers.

When she made it to command and squeezed through the doors, she found the Captain dead. An explosion had torn open half the ceiling, shattered the windows and washed half the room in fire. The unlucky ones were still laying where they had fallen, burned beyond recognition. The Captain in his blackened and bloody uniform sat in his chair under a large curved piece of ceiling debris. The damage to the ship was more substantial then she thought. It turned out that she had been in the safest place after all, feeling lucky after she heard about the fire that ravaged the lower decks and the explosions that devastated the upper decks. After Command took a hit killing the Captain, the second in command had no other choice but to power through and make it to the ground troops.

She stepped back, getting out of the way and watched her people push though the day's tragedy, working together as one for their survival. She felt proud to be there without having to quell their fear, or bolster their courage. Perhaps she had been wrong the whole time and all that her people needed was to be reminded of where they'd come from and who they were. She was wrong to have worried about humanity for it was the energy of the Universe that flowed through their veins. They may have been beaten down, but once the seed hit the soil, they could only be who they were meant to be, Human.

She felt quite obsolete, but free to finish what she started and choose a new path. She finally understood James' desire to flush away the other races. They were smears on the Universe's lens, defusing the light needed for the humanity growing around her.

Chapter

4

Kole ran. The new legs of his suit punched deep into the mud slowing him down. In the cockpit, he struggled against his restraints, chafing his skin. His shield could have prevented the strain, but he needed the other troopers to see that he went through the same ordeal they had. The storm had worsened, blowing the rain sideways, drumming on this armor, softening the ground. In the mess, he managed to gather one cargo container's worth of troopers, swapping their damaged parts for better ones, getting them ready to follow the Trolls to the other side of the battlefield. The gigantic Trolls did their job, thinning their numbers and destroyed most of them in a matter of minutes then left the wounded behind. Kole thought there'd be a second wave to kill off the survivors, perhaps those little buggers that had killed off most of the Elven women in the Troll's Capital, catching the troopers in their weakened state, but to his relief, no Trolls came. The troopers that he repaired aided in his struggle to collect parts, working beside him, fighting the elements and together they were now ready.

The gigantic Trolls had left a wide path of stumps and broken trees to follow, but the rain washing over the armor's optic lenses and mud sucking their feet, slowed them. The rain created a ripple effect to the darkness, reducing their visibility. Kole pushed on, guiding the troopers over the debris to the tree line that faced the Troll's stronghold. He stopped and directed his men to move into the trees.

His paranoia clawed at the back of his mind. It wasn't like the Trolls to leave fresh meat on the field and he was expecting something bad to happen. Other than the first burst of Troll mayhem, he hadn't seen another Troll. He crawled up to the tree line to get a better look. The long grass in the clearing lay flat, trampled by the rain. He stretched his awareness over the field, feeling the buried landmines then further over the stronghold's wall. He didn't feel any life within the courtyard. He expected to feel the energy of a swarm of eager Trolls ready to clash against him, but was more puzzled than relieved at the lack of presence.

"What are we waiting for?" asked a woman, who he called Serge.

Their com channel was quiet. A grim determination settled over his crew but before Kole answered, he changed the channel and merged with Eric's, trying to hear his status. His electronics weren't fully functioning and between the bursts of static he could only make out people's garbled yells. He turned back to his channel. "I don't like it," he said, answering her. "Where are the Trolls?"

"My sensors detect small metallic shapes in the ground closer to the wall," a young trooper said.

"Are we continuing?" another asked. "It'd be good to regroup with the others."

"My com is malfunctioning," Kole said then asked, "Are there any Drop Ships left?"

"No, they went down right away," Serge said.

"This new equipment sucks!" a man spat.

"Shut your mouth!" ordered Serge.

Kole's smile soured. He could've uses his abilities to deactivate the mines and lay waste to the stronghold, but then they'd question how it happened. He needed help. The Drop Ships could've shot up the mines then covered them while they ran in the open, but that was out of the question. Running in single file behind those who could detect the mines was also a stupid idea. "I'm thinking," he said. "This isn't like regular Troll behavior and I've killed plenty of them to know."

The com went quiet again. He considered the one trooper's suggestion. They could regroup with the other force, but that's not why they were there. On the bright side, there weren't any Trolls around and they were free to rescue the Human captives, getting them to safety. He stretched further into the stronghold feeling for life, but again felt nothing, but the hollow expression of the Ripper Rounds located in hidden wall turrets and grenade launchers on the roof. "Can anyone detect their sensors?" he asked, feeling frustrated that he couldn't turn everything off and save people. He had to gamble with their lives because they couldn't handle what he was.

Troopers along their line spoke up reporting their findings. Serge gave Kole some technical information that he didn't understand, but listening to her explain her idea and hearing the excitement in her voice made it sounded good. Even though he wasn't part of their chain of command, but based on his experience, they looked to him for leadership. He gave the order for her to proceed then waited for the troopers to reroute their power and link their sensors to trace the signals from the Troll's sensor suites.

Kole waited calming his mind. He thought back and remembered not feeling any life within the walls of the stronghold which included Human life. He stretched out again pushing his sensed deeper into the stronghold and even under it. All he sensed deeper underground was a massive machine that used the outer wall of the stronghold as an array. Within the stronghold he sensed automated defense systems along with abandoned laboratories. Not seeing anything to risk the lives of his crew over, he returned to the idea of regrouping with Eric's people, but what excuse could he give his crew to justify his decision. He could order it, but they were getting ready to defeat the stronghold and if they did it right, they could bust in and reprogram the strongholds defenses to pulverize the Trolls.

Kole liked that idea much better.

"Were ready," Serge said, interrupting Kole's daydream of Trolls being blown to bits by their own weapons.

"You're going to disable their sensors?" asked Kole, trying to recall what he had tuned out.

"That's the plan."

Kole studied the stronghold's wall once more then said, "Once done, we charge. Those that can detect the mines go first. Shoot them out and clear a path." He felt eager then added, "The new plan is to take the stronghold and turn its weapons on the Trolls in the field. Let's save some lives."

With that his crew charged, filing in behind those who ran shooting. Their rounds splashed through the mud into the ground to set off the mines ahead of them. Kole followed, thinking that taking down the Troll's sensors would be more spectacular than hitting a button. He on the other hand would've sent his mind along the signal, following its vibration into its circuitry then into its programming before making the trigger, making pushing a button more intimate. He imagined what could have happened if they had wandered onto the field, guessing that all the hidden weapons would've popped out and finished them.

Ahead of then the ground erupted in series of explosions that cascaded across the minefield flinging mud and rocks into the air. Kole's com filled with cheers. He charged through a small crater then fought his way up the slick side when the flung mud fell, splattering across his back. The trooper's cheers turned to curses, having to run half blind to the stronghold's gate.

Kole caught up and joined the troopers at the gate. Serge backed up and passed him. "My sensors tell me that the gates are more fortified than the walls beside them," she said. "That's bad craftsmanship."

Kole laughed at her joke. Soon they'll be in the stronghold. He used his senses to probe the wall, feeling a soft spot then lined up with the wall, making sure he was clear before using his new limbs.

He opened fire, emptying his arms into the wall and made a hole big enough for the other troopers. Once done, he gave the word and they stormed in, securing the courtyard. Using their sensors, they found the computer terminals and quickly armed the strongholds weapons. They then went to work and targeted the Trolls on the field.

Kole listened to the thumping of the stronghold's gun and found the cube shaped building's front doors. He turned on his suit's low light vision and walked across the shale floor tiles through the dark halls, disturbing the small layer of dust that rest on the otherwise clean floor. The dust and lack of black veins running over the natural brick walls of the hall made him wonder how long this structure had sat undisturbed. Too many questions flooded his mind and as he wandered, he habitually searched his surrounding, sending his awareness into the floors and walls. He stopped, feeling a thick false door and a hidden room behind it.

He checked his sensors to make sure he was alone and heard one of the troopers manning a computer terminal announce over the com, "I just cracked their server." He cheered then said, "This place is a giant weather control platform. I shut it down and from what I can read, the weather is returning to normal."

His report set off a series of commentaries about what others have found while searching for the captive Humans that Kole knew didn't exist. "Those gigantic Trolls were part of the experiments conducted here," another said.

Kole ignored their chatter, tuning out their discussion as to why no one had ever seen the gigantic Trolls before. The answer didn't matter to Kole. He was sure they'd see more and sought the trigger to the hidden door.

"I got something," the original trooper who started the discussion said. "The Trolls experimented on their own people to create those things. They trade intelligence for accelerated growth and healing. It also gave them all kinds of tumors and degenerating diseases, but they didn't seem to care about that, being able heal in all."

"That's fascinating," Serge said, exaggerating her excitement, quieting the chatter. "Does it tell you how to shut off their ability to heal? I'd like to that knowledge and turn them all into piles of cancerous crap."

Laughter and agreement erupted over the com.

Kole smiled and found the hidden door's trigger then pressed it. A door opened in the wall, but Kole's suit was too large to walk through. He bent over and looked down the plain duracrete hall, thinking that he'd be able to force his way through the frame, but the hall beyond was too small. "Serge?" he asked over his com.

"Here," she said.

"I found something that I have to check out, but I have to leave my suit."

"Do you think it's wise to be running around unprotected?" she asked. "Do you need protection?"

Kole face the right way then sat against the wall. "I don't think there's anyone home, I'll be fine."

"Well, we're almost done here anyway. The Trolls are in retreat. We're heading out to help with the clean up, we won't be here if you get into trouble," she said, warning him.

"Noted," Kole said, undoing his restraints. He hit the release button unlocking the hatch, but it failed to open. He maneuvered himself around his seat pushing off his view screen to get enough force to pry open the layers of battered metal. He tried pushing off every surface and even curled into a ball against his seat to use himself as a wedge, but couldn't attain his freedom. With the new Human sensors, they could now detect alchemically altered materials stopping Kole from tweaking his way out, bending a piece here and there. Now tired, he hugged the head rest of his seat then laughed at himself when the solution hit him. He slipped back into his controls then used the battered fingers of his suit to pull open the hatch. He cheered with delight then cringed when the cold stale air that flushed out his warm cockpit.

He crawled out of his suit shivering. The air felt hurtful smelling dead and dusty. His body trembled and his teeth chattered. He couldn't remember feeling this way. He released a series of sneezes that forced him to reach for the wall for support. It was an uncomfortable and yucky moment, but the thought of sharing every gruesome detail with Enora made him smile. He cleaned his face with his hand then walked into the hidden passage. The door closed behind him, cutting off his com with a sharp squelch. A series of recessed lights in the ceiling turned on, casting the hall in a dim buttery light. He thought about how long he was going to play being normal, walking around on the cold duracrete floor then gave up and erected his shield. His body warmed and the air freshened, bringing instant relief.

He followed the light spiraling deeper underground, walking on the soft pad of his shield to an average sized door. He hit the glowing mint green button beside it, sliding open the door. He walked into a large square room and onto the light brown, fluffy carpet. The walls were covered in green vine printed wallpaper and adorned with ancient movie posters. The gas fireplace mounted in a brick fireplace at the other side of the room came to life with a loud woof and soft jazz played from a stereo system along the side wall. Kole walked across the carpet to the middle of the room then stopped under the mirror ball that hung from the ten foot ceiling.

He turned on the spot looking at the room's decor. A high end computer consol sat against one wall while an off red dusty heart shaped bed and the wall mounted peg board covered in pictures sat against the opposite. Curious, he walked to the pictures. Above them written in red paint over the wallpaper read, "Wall of love" which was a collection of pictures taken from hidden locations, behind bushes and outside windows. His eyes washed over the collection that focused on one subject, a young blonde woman in a city setting. Most of the pictures were of her opening her front door, taking out the trash and walking down the street. She didn't look happy and her body language was closed, walking with her hands against her chest and the occasional bag tight against her body. Kole doubted that she consented to the pictures.

He found a couple of pictures taken through a window capturing a reflection in a mirror of the girl getting changed, standing in her underwear. At the very heart of the love board were pictures of the girl in the bathroom. But one picture caught his attention. The girl stood naked looking into her mirror pulling something out of her hair. The way she stood made him think of Enora. None of the pictures were clear shots of her face forcing Kole to lean in and look at her reflection. The girl wasn't as tall and had a slightly different body structure, but she looked like Enora.

Kole stepped back. He thought back to the Troll Capital and remembered the amount of power coming up from the hole that Enora had made when she went to face the monster hidden underground. She clearly had a deeper connection to the Trolls than he realized and the thought that some greasy pervert was stalking her, made him want to smash they guy's face in. He looked at the pictures and stretched out with his power, mingling with the grimy energy of perverted intent held within the images. He then waved his hand incinerating the board. A torrent of emotions crashed within him and for a second he wanted to seek out the closest Troll and talk to him about the pictures, asking why he violated her innocents.

Kole took a couple of beep breaths. "Talk, yes. That's what I'd do," he whispered to himself, trying to find the sanity in his emotional storm. He understood Enora's crazy when it came to the Trolls and telling her about the pictures would only darken her spirit. He had to keep it to himself. He looked at the computer consol and part of him didn't want to turn it on. He didn't want to know how far the pervert went.

He calmed down, pushing the red out of his eyes and realizing that what had happened didn't happen to him. Running off and joining Enora's crazy wasn't going to help anyone. All he could do is listen and be there for her. The power of the small would prevail. He would be there, standing quietly then one day she'll talk about it and he'd listen, keeping his opinions and thirst for revenge to himself.

He felt deeply for her and reminded himself again that it wasn't him that went through her trauma.

He walked up the computer consol, a solid piece of wood four inches thick and arched into a desk. Kole sat in the chair and watched the desk come to life. Two slots near the wall opened then two rods decorated with naked women climbing over each other, rose up to project a holographic screen between them. In front of him, art of the table tilted down lighting up a holographic keypad. The screen flickered and had a line running across its middle asking for a password.

Kole groaned, thinking he'd have to go in and hack the computer, but took a stab. He touched a holographic key. He shook his head and his anger tightened his chest, thinking he knew what the password was. The holographic keys clicked as he typed, "Enoralovesme." He hovered his finger over the enter key and waited. Enora had been put in a jar and was long gone from the world. No one but him would know her name and what she looked like. He pressed the enter key and was accepted.

He lost it and thrashed the consol, taking all of his impotent rage out on the holographic keyboard then after he calmed down he worked his way through the system, deleting videos of Enora. Later he found a video labeled "Never Forget" in an unrelated file. At this point, Kole wanted to forget everything he had seen, but accessed the video anyway. It played, showing an older man in a lab coat standing in front of a white board. The man ran his fingers through his white hair, brushing his bangs out of his brown eyes. "My name is Frank Wekser and I'd like to say that I'm very proud to be to be the head of this project," Frank said with a slight accent that sounded Elven.

Frank continued saying, "I work for the Forever Young Corporation and we usually deal with beauty projects, but now we're branching out. We've taken on a military contract to see if we can use our skin rejuvenation technology to create a soldier with rapid wound healing. We suspected that there'd be moral consequences and brought forward the suggestion of using convicts for testing. The military agreed and supplied us with enough people to make progress. One man in particular who we named Stalker John." He chuckled then said, "Not his real name. We don't know any of our subject's names. It's better this way. It helps us distance ourselves from feeling for them while they're going through the mutations." He cupped his hands together then licked his lips. They may not have known his name, but Enora had told him enough about Stinky Fingers and the look in Frank's eyes told Kole that he enjoyed his work.

"We don't know any of their names, but we did find something out about Stalker John, the serial rapist. Knowing what he has done made him number one for our experiments and to our surprise he reacted well to the treatments. Others died, where he survived and... " he pointed his finger at the camera then finished saying, "no one was allowed to be left alone with him."

The video skipped to an operation room where Stalker John was strapped to a table. He lay naked with a sheet across his waist in the middle of the room. Three people in light blue scrubs walked in wearing disposable gloves and took position around John. One doctor faced the screen and by his eyes, Kole knew it was Frank. "Subject Stalker John is ready to undertake our most advanced treatment. We're very excited," Frank said left the screen and returned with a small rolling table that had an injection gun and assorted tools resting on it. Stalker John turned his head away from Frank. His body gently shook against his restraints making Kole think he was crying. He tried to feel for Stalker John, but after seeing all the pictures of Enora, he had a hard time sympathizing.

Frank grabbed the injector and examined Stalker John, turning his head to the camera. John looked like a normal person, someone who could be passed on the street and not noticed. John pled for mercy, but Frank didn't respond or physically show a reaction to the man's begging. Frank grabbed John's forehead then turned his head away, pressing it down before injecting him in the neck. There were so many ways the doctors could've treated John better and at that moment Kole could see the hate behind Frank's actions. Frank pushed off and the placed the injector on the table. He stepped back and waited.

John shook fighting his restraints then screamed a cry that made Kole cringe. Kole leaned closer to the screen watching the greenish colored veins bulge across John's skin. John clenched mouth groaning then convulsed, frothing. Kole touched the holographic screen, clicking ahead to different experiments showing John's slow and painful progression into the Troll he knew. Kole leaned back into the chair wondering how he should feel about Stalker John. He was a prisoner for a reason, but didn't deserve to be tortured. The physical pain and the violation of his already twisted consciousness made him the way he was, but that was no excuse. He could've got help at any time before he became a Troll.

But Kole didn't know if John had gone to a professional for help. Maybe he had, but it didn't help. Only Stalker John knew those answers and Kole honestly didn't give a crap. Stalker John was evil and has filled his belly with too many people. Kole deleted the files then went in alchemically to wipe the drives. No one needed to know about that freak.

Kole pushed himself off the desk and stood. He looked around again and realized that the desk was made for a person his size. He walked to the bed, and though it was heart shaped, a Troll wouldn't find it that comfortable. With everything around the room being Human sized, Kole suspected that there was more to this stronghold than a man's smut collection. He closed his eyes and stretched out with his awareness feeling another hidden door which had a special trigger. He followed the trigger's trail and walked to the record player. He put the jazz record away then picked up a thin rectangular sleeve and pulled out the LP labeled "The Breakfast Club." He played the theme song and the second secret door across the room opened. He listened to the song, thinking about Stalker John and what he put Enora through then shook his head, wishing he could slap John around, but didn't think more violence toward the man would help.

Kole continued through the secret door then down a narrow passage to a small lab. The dark room was filled with equipment covered with bed sheets. Before stepping in he wanted to look around and found the light switch. He waved his hand over the switch then slapped it, thinking it was a button, but nothing happened. He flicked the switch then a series of florescent lights came to life. Their sound bothered Kole and the light hurt his eyes. He ignored his discomfort and went to work uncovering the ancient medical equipment. He balled up the sheets then threw them in a corner. He thought about dissolving them, but a pile of bed sheets in the corner would look more normal if anyone came looking for him.

He grabbed the last sheet draped over a large piece of equipment leaning against the back wall. He looked at his hand and could see that some of the dust in the air had settled on his shield and made a mental note to collapse his shield and make a new one on his way out. It was hard work being normal. He had to watch everything he said and did, over thinking the consequence if someone thought the wrong thing. He missed his old transport and the goofy kid Eric, but more his transport. It didn't argue with him all the time, questioning everything he said. He pulled the sheet down and was taken aback. It was a first or second generation hibernation pod with a flash frozen occupant. He was so shocked that he forgot what he was looking at. Inside the tube resting at an angle was Stalker John who looked partly restored. The large curved panels of glass that made up the tube's door had frost around its edge and inside John looked asleep with a thin layer of frost coating his skin. He looked like the original copy, more man than Troll and Kole couldn't believe his luck. He had a chance to slap the man around and punish his for terrorizing Enora. He laughed at himself for the first thoughts that went through his head. He calmed down and pushed the violent thoughts out of his mind. He tried to forget about the pictures featuring Enora. It wasn't easy and he had a difficult time convincing himself not to open the ground and send the man into oblivion. No one would know.

He turned his back to John and casually picked through the medical equipment. He quickly came to the realization that John was trying to cure himself. Kole found carefully documented experiments that John had performed on himself in the hope that he'd return to normal and find someone like Enora to love.

Kole looked back at the tube and saw a subject that could be used to reverse engineer the remaining Trolls, halting their regenerative qualities. As much as he hated how Frank had treated John, he was about to do the same, but for a better and enlightened reason. He could use the original template to stop the monsters and save the world. He made a list of all the tools and equipment he'd need to transfer the sleeping man. He didn't want to wake him until John aka Stinky Fingers was in a secure location. Once thawed, Kole doubted anyone would care about how, or what John felt. The Trolls had consumed too many people and with the treat of extinction, Kole's moral compass seemed to be malfunctioning.

The thought of ending the Trolls without bombing the planet excited him. He had to tell Enora the good news, but worried about her reaction. He doubted he'd be able to stop her from ripping John's head off and considered not telling her. But she had the right to closure. He didn't like weighing the odds and even now, John was a problem. And no matter what avenue Kole's imagination went down, none of them boded well for John. Where would they put John after they were done with him, in a prison that doesn't exist? They would have to build one, but someone might try to remake the Trolls and that uncertainty put fear and paranoia into Kole's mind. He didn't want to succumb to his fear and remembered Eric. The whole time he had been encouraging Eric to embrace his humanity and find a balance within himself to govern his budding power, he was about to lose his. Fear was humanities true enemy.

He left John undisturbed and went back to the record player, turning it off to reset the door. He put the record away then remade his shield, shaking off the dust before returning to his suit. He stood outside his suit that looked uglier to him and after all the problems he had using the thing, he didn't even want to touch it. Reluctantly he climbed back in then strapped in. The stronghold lay empty and his com channel was quiet. He expected to hear some chatter from anyone nearby when he powered up, but there was nothing. He assumed that he broke his com when we threw a tantrum trying to get out of his suit, but when he left the stronghold his com squelched again, hurting his ear. He was then blasted by frantic overlapping voices. He fiddled with the com trying to select a channel, or find Eric's then came to the conclusion that he had indeed broke it. He couldn't even turn it down. He grew to hate his suit.

He climbed through the hole in the outer wall and saw what everyone was panicking about. The Battle Cruiser that was to be their backup had crashed in the forest. In the distance, back the way they came, Kole could see several Battleships in a holding pattern, circling the forest, using the crash site as its center. Kole couldn't see any immediate threat and watched the Battleships slowly circle, floating above the valley walls. The Trolls had more than enough power to turn all the Humans here into paste, making Kole wonder why they were sitting back. His first thought was that the Trolls were full then he became serious, putting his mind into theirs. He came back with one conclusion, that the survivors were bait. They must know that Sarah, the heart of Winter Haven was here. There was no better bait to coax their army away from the city. He remembered Sarah's influence of the Human population and wondered what would happen to them in her absence. He shook his head, feeling the restraints of normality. He wanted to be the Alchemist and crush the Trolls, saving lives and getting Sarah home to keep her people's fear in check, but that wasn't going to happen.

Distracted by what had had happened, Kole didn't notice that the storm had vanished until he broke into a jog, running through the large mud holes on his way to find Eric. He followed the wide path that the gigantic Trolls had made, passing troopers torching Troll bits and fractured trees that lay strewn across the partly dislodged tree stumps. It didn't take Kole long to find the first gigantic Troll. Kole walked around its pale body to look at its ugly face. Frozen in agony, half of its face lay embedded in the mud with its eyes rolled back and a grey substance mixed with blood oozing out its nose. Kole circled around to the top of its head, finding a huge opening and empty brain cavity. Fragments of skull still attached to the scalp, lay pushed outward telling him that someone was eaten then fought their way out through the Troll's skull.

Kole stepped closer, looking into the hole in the Troll's skull at the brain matter that was regenerating before his eyes. He stepped back and looked for any other signs of regeneration, but didn't see any, which he thought was odd. He looked around at the troopers who were busy and was relieved that he hadn't been noticed and felt free to investigate. He stretched out his awareness into the brain matter wondering if it'd regenerate a mindless beast or a functional troll. The cells moved, building off each other and following the Troll's genetic memory. He shifted his awareness to the regenerating Troll bits scattered around the field and could see that the bits wanted a body before brain, but the gigantic Trolls wanted a brain before body. Kole compared the pattern of regeneration and could see that the gigantic Trolls were an experiment, a knock off. After seeing the different mutations of troll, Kole felt better about experimenting of the original Troll. How could he feel bad when the twisted man experimented on himself, altering his own clones to further his transformation?

Kole followed the trail of destruction of broken trees and crushed Power Armor. Arms and legs lay scattered in the foliage, specks of white in the greens and browns. Seeing the amount of dead still inside their armor, made Kole regret listening to the engineers. He knew better, the suits were garbage and he should've said no to their slick talk of versatility. It was their barrage of techno babble that he didn't understand that pushed him into a yes. If he could've touched the suit, he would've felt its potential and weaknesses, but he had to gamble and trust their knowledge. Still more people slipped through his fingers and fell to their deaths. All the time he had spent trying to bring balance to the world and live with his humanity intact had been a fool's quest. Living like a Human had shown him how different he was. The way he thought, perceived the world and existed was completely different. He may walk, talk and act human, but he wasn't. Now, all he wanted was to stay sane and not hurt anyone, but walking by the dead who trusted the suits that he had recommended made him feel not so sane.

The second gigantic Troll he found lay stretched out on the ground with bloody entrails hanging out its torn and misshapen bottom. Kole walked around the body and found another empty skull pointing to trend. Kole suspected that he knew the person responsible for killing the Trolls in that manner, but didn't know how to feel about it. The method worked and saved lives, but was revolting. He continued on, finding the trail the last gigantic Troll made, arguing with himself over what method of killing was okay. He remembered his quest to preserve his humanity and the desire to stay sane, but looking inside a gigantic Troll's empty skull made his question personal reality.

He found the third gigantic Troll in the same condition of the second and decided that he wouldn't mention it to Eric. He'd let his mind pave over the whole thing and forget about it. But knowing Eric, he'll mention it to annoy him and be very proud he had thought outside the box, dropping a fast regenerating creature. For once, all Kole wanted was for someone else to do the strange things and for Eric to be the normal person who'd be glad they didn't think of it. Though people will thank Eric for saving their lives, the way he did it will set him apart. He remembered Pine View and how Roy treated him after he killed the Werewolves. But the only thing that'll save Eric from the same reaction is the fact that Eric used the same tools as everyone else.

Kole wondered where Eric was and sped up looking for his hot pink bowel covered Power Armor. Part of him didn't want to see Eric looking like the way he imagined, but with Kole's com malfunctioning, he needed to know what happened to him. He expected to see Eric around the next tree drinking ale with his new berserker friends, joking that he had killed those Trolls Dwarven style. He ran toward the downed Battle Cruiser along the landing zones, passing battered, but more capable Power Armor outfitted with flamethrowers, running back to the battlefield. He followed their trail to an opened hanger. The Battle Cruiser lay at an angel spilling unsecured tools, gear and heavy equipment out the open side hangers.

The trail ended at a crooked metal ramp that had been twisted to lay flat on the ground. Kole walked up the ramp, feeling the metal on metal vibration through his seat and into the hanger. A man in a reflective vest and two coned flashlights directed him to a spot where two young mechanics in dirty grey coveralls rolled an orange painted staircase against his chest. Kole reached up then opened his armor almost ripping off the outer hatch. His suit was shot and broke down on the spot. His screen turned off and all the small noises whined down leaving Kole in a hollow darkness. The mechanics pried open the inner hatch freeing him to the cool fresh air. He took the mechanic's greasy hand and climbed out.

"Have you seen Eric?" he asked the mechanic.

"Who's that?"

Kole didn't want to say it, giving Eric credit for his bad behavior, but he had to. "He's the kid in the hot pink armor."

The mechanic laughed then said, "That all everyone's talking about, the leader of the Berserkers. That's his name?"

Kole cocked his eyebrow feeling his patience thin. This was the opposite reaction he was afraid of. It'd only encourage his bad and reckless behavior, pushing the limits of normality. But he was a Berserker and spent time with the Dwarves. Those facts might deter people from looking too close at his odd behavior. But with all this adulation, Eric will be intolerable.

Kole glared and the mechanic's smile faded. The mechanic

cleared his throat then said, "He was carried in. We had to cut him out of his armor."

Kole pictured him half dead on a stretcher. "What happened to him? Is he okay?"

"He's fine. His suit only had one functioning limb and had to be carried in."

Kole wanted to verbally slap the mechanic for worrying him, but asked, "Where is he?"

"He was told to get changed then was sent to see Mother Sarah to give his report. We're also looking for Agent Kole. He was in the second battle group, but got separated. We lost contact with him," he answered.

Kole nodded, putting it all together. "I'm Kole. Where do I go to get changed?"

A short time later he was given a new set of dark blue coveralls to wear then was escorted through dark crooked passageways with flickering lights hanging from the ceiling into burned out sections that reeked of chemical soaked soot. At first he didn't know why he was being escorted then the gruff older man in similar coveralls and a graying buzz cut told him that with all the damage, there was only one passable route to get between the two sections.

After walking into a nicer section with clean walls, he knew Sarah was close. She wouldn't be in a wrecked section. The older men stopped and pointed at a door. "Here we are," he said then continued on, leaving him there.

Kole hit the door control, but nothing happened. He groaned in frustration. He was tired of everything around him malfunctioning. It was supposed to be the future where everything worked. He placed his finger on the door control then leaned in, pushing all his frustration into the button. The tip of his finger turned white then the door popped open a crack big enough for his fingers. He was about to lose it and blast the door open, sending it flying into the room, but managed to calm down. For self gratification, he revisited the idea of blasting the door open before jamming his fingers into the crack, using both hands to prying the door open. He pushed with all his strength and when the door was half way open, its mechanics kicked in shooting the door open. Kole's arms shot out striking the door frame. Surprised, he spun then fell onto the deck, banging the back of his head against the floor. He sat up, wishing he had blown that door apart then rubbed his temple in an attempt to alleviate the pain that was reaching around the back of his head to plunge into the center of his brain. As a child, a person learns how to fall properly, but over the years he'd got used to his shield and forgotten how to protect his head and not bounce it off the floor. He shouted a curse in frustration then heard Eric laugh.

Kole sat on the cold floor letting the pain in his head drain away, taking his frustrations with it. He wanted to be emotionally fresh when he looked at Eric incase he added more tattoos and piercings to his body. He could only imagine what his tats would look like after the way he had killed the Trolls. He shuddered at the thought then pushed the image from his mind, remembering that he wanted to forget about how the Trolls died. He got off the floor then walked into the small conference room. His steps slowed allowing him to take in the onslaught of colors. The decorated walls had hand painted flowers of all types that crawled up the walls to the light blue ceiling. A large circular domed light with flames painted around it hung from the center of the ceiling.

"It's a happy room," Eric said, pulling Kole's attention away from the bright green floor.

Kole didn't know he was holding his breath until he sighed in relief. Eric didn't look like he anything new added to his body. Six root woven chairs with flower patterned cushions sat around a wood table. Kole sat beside Eric. "There's way too much pattern in his room," Kole said, averting his eyes from the shot gunned color on the walls and focused on the table.

Eric seemed happy. He hummed, sitting in his chair rocking back and forth, swinging his legs. Kole wanted to sit quietly and enjoy sharing space with Eric, but his humming wouldn't let his mind settle. He looked sideways at Eric then asked, "What do people think about your yellow eyes? They can see them. Has anyone said anything?"

Eric kept rocking and puffed out his lips then said, "Nope." He went back to humming.

It had been a stressful day and Kole didn't want to take Eric's bait, but couldn't let it slide. He couldn't let Eric's behavior pass, or he'd get worse. "Nope what?" he asked then said, "You didn't answer my questions. People aren't stupid. They must have seen your eyes and asked you."

Eric stopped rocking and humming. "I thought we went over that. It's old news, everybody knows about them. Why are you getting mad?"

"I'm not mad. All I want is for you to answer me when I ask you a question."

He huffed then said, "Fine. When people were interested in my eyes, like forever ago, I told them that it happened when we were with the Dwarves. If people pried, I told them it was a chemical accident that dyed my eyes. That shuts them up."

Kole thought back and couldn't remember talking to him about it. It would've been the first thing they would've spoken about to get their lies strait. "I'm glad people don't ask anymore," he said.

"It depends on the person, but all I have to do is say one word and people leave me alone. Guess what it is."

Only one word popped into Kole's mind. "Dwarves?" he asked.

"Yupperdoodles," he said the flashed a grin. "But this isn't about my eyes is it? You want to know what I did to myself, don't you."

He really didn't want to know, but a small part of him worried about Eric. He knew that Eric was old enough screw his life up if he wanted to, but a part of him still wanted guide Eric in the right direction. That small part was curious and wanted to see, to make sure that it wasn't harmful to him. He shook his head and stomped on the small curious voice in the back of his mind. "No, I don't want to know," Kole said.

"You sure, you must have seen what I did those big bad Trolls?"

"I saw, but I was hoping that someone else did it."

His smug expression soured. "I thought you would be proud. I saved lives in a creative way," he said then his eyes narrowed. "You're pulling a Roy. I did a good job and now you're pissing down my back for it."

He raised his hands trying to stop an argument before it started and to get the imagery of him and Roy out of his mind. "I can see his point," he said.

Eric twisted in his chair and stared at him with his freakish yellow eyes looking less like the boy he had raised. "Tell me how what I did makes Roy right?"

He didn't know how else to say it, but said, "What you did and the way you look, makes you appear crazy."

He laughed. "You have no idea what's going on. You're so out of touch. Stop being so aggressively passive and look around. Mingle a bit. Isn't this what you wanted for me when we went to Pine View in the first place?"

He leaned back and his root woven chair squeaked under his weight. He could've easily argued with him, but he wanted to hear where Eric was coming from. "What do you know that I don't?" asked Kole.

Eric relaxed. "For starters, I started a trend. People don't believe that my eyes are yellow and have make fake eye lenses to alter the way they look. People want to look like me. See, I told you and Enora that people will like the way I look."

On one hand Kole was happy that Eric was fitting in and safe from scrutiny, but on the other he saw only one direction for his fad, escalation. "Promise me that you'll think things through and not forget who you are and where you came from," he said, trying to reach him and show that he cares about what happens to him.

Eric opened his mouth, but before he could say anything the painted door on the other side of the room slowly opened, scraping the paint. Kole rolled his eyes then hissed, knowing that they had added too much paint and that's why his door had problem opening.

Sarah carefully walked across the slanted floor struggling with her tea tray. Kole moved to get up and help her, but she glanced at him then shook her head. He sat back and watched her awkwardly place the tray on the table. The three tea cups slid. She let go of one side to stop them, allowing the tray to pivot away from her then dropped her elbow onto the tray stopping it. She then reset the cups before letting go. "Sorry about that. Normally I'm more graceful," she said.

Kole nodded sympathizing, thinking about his day.

"I didn't know clones could age," Eric said.

"What?" she asked.

Eric pointed at her and said, "You have a grey hair."

Her eyes widened. She grabbed at her hair searching then stopped. Her eyes shifted between Eric and Kole then she slowly lowered her hands to straighten her clean robe, returning to a serine state. "I've been under a lot of stress lately. I guess it's starting to show," she said sounding sad.

"You could always shave your head," Eric said, examining her. "I think you'd look good."

"I'm sorry to hear that you've had a bad day," Kole said. "It must be in the water. I don't think anyone's had a good day."

Sarah smiled. "I suppose not," she said then poured them tea.

The tea smelled good and Kole found himself looking forward to the ritual of relaxation. He smiled to himself at the thought then took his cup, letting it warm his hands. Eric took his then blew on it before sipping.

"This is good," Eric said. "What is it?"

"It's a Dark Elf blend that no longer exists. A friend of mine gave it to me," she said.

"That a really good friend."

She poured tea for herself then sat across from Eric. She turned to Kole then asked, "How did you find the Power Armor?"

Kole took a sip and was stunned at how good it tasted, brightening his mood. "They're not good for combat, or anything involving the elements. They'd be good on a clear perfect day, or for asteroid mining."

"I thought mine was good," Eric said then explained, "Mine took a beating and I switched out the limbs several times, but I couldn't see most of the time."

Kole took another sip then said, "What you're saying is that you cannibalized the dead and lucked out."

Eric frowned then grumbled, "Fine." He shifted in his seat, giving Kole his shoulder then said, "Kole's right, they weren't that good. I thought they were tested for the weather."

Sarah took a moment and sipped her tea then said, "You know how it is when the higher-ups push their product wanting results."

"Things get skipped," Kole said finishing for her.

Eric leaned close to Kole then said, "I noticed something. Whenever she's about to give bad news, she pauses and takes a sip."

Kole chuckled then explained saying, "She's clearing the air and letting us return to a neutral state, so we don't explode."

Eric looked to Sarah for her answer, but she said nothing, returning his gaze. "Whatever," he said.

Kole took another sip then remembered their situation. "I don't know what's going on. I'm so absent minded that I forgot about the Troll army circling us. What's the plan?"

"What's on your mind?" asked Sarah. "There must be something chewing at you to forget our impending doom."

Eric threw his arm over the back of his chair. "He's upset over how I killed some Trolls."

Sarah smiled. "I would if you were my child."

"What, you heard about that?"

"You are the talk around the ship," she said. "If there's a dirty job that needs doing, give it to you." She shook her head disapproving. "You're first on their canary list."

"What list now?"

Kole cleared his throat then paused to take a sip when he had their attention. "It's a list of people they'll send in first to make sure it's safe for the rest of us."

"Oh, like the Berserkers," Eric said nodding. "Yeah, I can do that."

"Did you not see me take a sip before I delivered my bad news? The canary list is a bad thing. It shows you what people think of you," Kole said, reminding Eric about what he had said earlier.

Eric tilted his head and opened his eyes wide, exaggerating boredom. "Again, we went over this. You're old and you don't know anything."

Sarah sighed. "I can see that you two have a lot to talk about. Let's take a sip and clear the air. We can talk about the Trolls when we're calm."

"Oh I'm clam," Kole said, tightening his grip on the warm tea cup.

Eric rolled his eyes.

A silence passed between them then a solution popped into Kole's head. "I assume the Trolls are jamming us?" he asked.

"No," Sarah said. "We have clear communications and have relayed our situation to Winter Haven."

"That's weird," Eric said.

"Nothing today made sense," Kole said. "The Trolls would've won if they had followed through."

"That's what I was thinking," Sarah said. "We believe that we're bait." She took a sip of tea then said, "Our people back home think it's a trap and decided to leave us here."

Eric laughed then slapped the table. He pointed his finger at her. "See I told you, bad news."

"It's all bad," Kole said thinking it through. "If the Trolls don't get what they want, they'll add pressure to Winter Haven by attacking us. More people are going to die."

"I guess we're all canaries," Eric commented. "Kole, relax about that whole Troll in the bum thing. No one's going to be around to remember it."

Kole sighed then said, "I was saying that we could contact Enora and have her use the satellites to blow these bastards apart. That way it won't be a surprise if we have to bomb the planet."

Sarah placed her tea cup on the table then offered a refill before filling her cup. "I thought about it and I don't want to go down that avenue. If the planet dies, we'll soon follow."

"I'm glad to hear that," Kole said then decided to trust Sarah. "I found something while I was in the stronghold, but I wanted to tell Enora first."

He had their attention then Sarah gestured for him to continue. "I found the original Troll in a stasis pod," he said.

"Why do you need to tell Enora first?" asked Eric.

Kole shrugged not wanting to say things no one needed to know. "She has a slight revenge thing against them and I'm afraid that she'll kill him without thinking it through. But I want her to have closure, but I'm afraid of the quality of closure she's looking for."

"Perhaps you should ask her. I think it's sad that you think that way about her. She might surprise you and do the right thing," Sarah said and Kole wasn't sure if she was joking.

"The way you said that makes me sound bad," Kole said, feeling a bit hurt that she'd think he thought badly of Enora.

"You just need to change your mind and think warm thoughts," Eric teased.

Having enough of Eric, Kole raised his hand to quiet him then said, "This is important and I'm not sure how she'll react to the news. I think we should take the first Troll or John or as Enora knew him, Stinky Fingers and experiment on him to find a way to destroy the Trolls before we tell her. But we also can't have anyone else remaking the Troll, so we'll have to be put him down afterward."

Eric took a breath then held it before asking, "How many names does that guy have?"

"Too many, but that's his fate, to be a nameless monster in the night. The doctors called him Stalker John to dehumanize him so they could hurt him without feeling bad. But Eric, that's all you got out of that? I want to experiment on a person then kill him and you're hung up on his name?"

Eric grunted uncaring.

"I think what Eric is trying to say that it's hard to find mercy for a Troll especially after you've personally given three a colonoscopy," Sarah said, surprising Kole with her humor.

Eric crossed his arms then asked, "What does that mean?"

"It doesn't matter," Kole said then looked at Sarah. "You have a twisted sense of humor. I like it."

"I'm glad we're in better spirits," she said. "But your idea is very interesting. We could develop a poison that turns their regenerative ability against them. If we could apply it to their food source we could spare the planet from the bombing."

Eris shook his head disagreeing. "That's not fast enough. Once one gets sick they'll toss their GMO food and start again. And on the other hand, airborne might not get those underground, it may also come with other problems. I think the best thing we can do is make the poison and attach it to a disease that mosquitoes can carry."

Sarah's eyes brightened. "The Trolls will fight off the disease, but be poisoned and they won't know what's going on until it's too late," she said, liking Eric's idea.

Kole visualized the plan, afraid the disease might attach itself to Human DNA and be with them forever, threatening to manifest again, like the regenerating brain cells the Troll carcasses. "No disease," he stressed. "I only want the most trusted people to work on the poison. All the research must be destroyed after. I don't care what advancements can be made. I don't want to take any chance that'll bring the Trolls back. I'll be so mad to have to do this again."

"Agreed," Sarah said. "We won't tell Enora until we've killed off most of the Trolls. She can decide on what she wants to do with, who was it again, John? She can kill this Stalker John and bomb the Trolls underground, if the poison hasn't spread to them. We don't know how it'll move once it interacts with their regenerative ability. It might become a slow acting contact poison, spreading through their race."

Eric smiled then said, "I like the way you think and how you talk. I still think you'd look good bald. A tattoo here and some piercing there would totally make you pop, think about it."

Kole tuned out Eric's wooing and thought about mosquitoes and the fun fact he knew about them. When the Pixies were at their peak they used to cultivate mosquitoes, locking people in small rooms with them to be fed upon. Once the mosquitoes were full, the Pixies would catch the bugs and eat them as delicacy. Things like that used to make him angry, but now it was like everything else weird in the world. He watched Eric's body language. Eric leaned on the table closing the distance between him and Sarah, attempting to be suave, becoming another weird thing he'd seen. Sarah placed her tea cup down and backed away, leaning against the back of her chair. The conversation felt over, but no one took the initiative to end it, or Sarah was being too polite to axe Eric's advancement.

Kole stood. "That's enough Eric, she's not buying," he said. "Here's the plan. Sarah, I need a group of people that you can trust to get Popsicle John. After we have him we'll get Enora to kill the Trolls surrounding us. We'll then need pick up, maybe get James, the Hero of Humanity to rescue up. I'm not sure what he's been up to, but if you can get him out of bed, that'd be great."

Sarah chuckled then said, "That won't be necessary. I can arrange for a retreat."

"But don't tell anyone about Popsicle John, we don't know if the Troll can hear us," Eric added.

"I won't," she promised.

"Excellent, let's get this going," Kole said.

Chapter

5

Frustrated, Enora swiped her hands over her holographic modeling table, turning the light blue image of a satellite into a blur. The table wasn't like the one she had used before the Purge. Its slow and clumsy interface made it hard for her to use, but it came in many styles and colors. She didn't ask for much, a quiet room with a plush chair to relax in while dreaming up ideas, a small round table to put her drinks on and a design table. She didn't choose her table, shiny black surface with silver trim that ran around its edge and down the legs. It wasn't her style and clashed with the light brown wood floor and optimistic yellow walls. Its masculine presence was a sliver, tipping the balance of the energy of the room, but it functioned. Her satellite design slowed then stopped, hovering in front of her. She stuck her finger into the image then slowly turned it. She could have easily used Alchemy to make the satellite. She didn't even have to think about how to make it. All she'd have to do is touch the part of her mind where her consciousness couldn't go, the vast ocean that's connected to the Universe. Her idea, intent and will would bring the creation into existence and it would be perfect for the situation.

Using the table to create the satellite made her think and exercise the part of her mind that had collected dust. She was forced to problem solve and use the computer to run scenarios to see what'd happen to her project in the real world. She started off wanting the best materials technology could offer, but was rudely awaken to the fact that those materials no longer existed. When she gave the engineer her list, he laughed then told her that he'd never heard of those materials. Instead of arguing and creating more questions, she took her list back then apologized for being confused. She asked the engineer to provide a list of materials he did have then went to work.

She had big dreams for her project. She wanted to use drones to collect space junk and have a replication matrix on board the satellite to break down that junk to make new missiles and keep it fully armed, but had to scrap her dreams. She settled for the standard box design with missile pods and a bank of solar paneling as back up for the power cell. She didn't like being limited by current technology. Eventually her satellite would run out of missiles and the power supply didn't have enough charge to feed a beam weapon, but what if she cheated. Given the types of material, she could use Alchemy to create what she needed then use the table to scan and produce a blueprint. She would then destroy the original.

Her mind flooded with ideas on how to torch each Troll using beam weapons. The thought quickly filled her head with imagined Troll screams, putting a pleasant smile on her face, but as fun as it'd be to set each individual ablaze, it didn't fit her needs. She needed something fast, but not devastating. The world had to be habitable afterward.

She left the light blue satellite projection hovering over the table and sat in her cozy chair. She relaxed her mind, thinking about what she wanted the weapon to do. It didn't have to be a one and done deal, it could be layers of devastation. The first bombardment could vaporize their flesh, killing everything organic in the area. Depending on where the Trolls were, the second could superheat the ground, turning their hole into lava. But those ideas bored her. She wanted

to think beyond the punch to the face and chest ripping heart ex-
traction. She let her mind drift away from the standard destruction
to search for an idea that she could run with, something to make her
proud.

She thought past making satellite to the future and what might
be made with her weapons. She didn't want her blueprints, or her
idea to fall into the hands of anyone willing to use them. She was
crazy enough to contemplate creating a devastating weapon to use
against the Trolls and the thought of someone else out there as insane to use it again, frightened her. She'd have to protect her knowledge and tell no one, on the off chance that someone would
overhear and pass along her idea. After the Trolls were gone, she'd
then destroy everything related to her project. She looked at her design table and realized that she'd have to destroy it after her plans
had been made. Nothing deleted is ever really gone. She'll also have
to separate the components, build everything separately on automated production lines. All to protect an idea that she hadn't had
yet, but felt it'd be too powerful to be left on the shelf.

After deciding to protect her knowledge then destroy the
weapon, her mind opened to an idea that both excited and frightened
her. It was no longer about hate and revenge, though she had enjoyed dreaming up way to hurt the barista Stinky Fingers. It is now
about the thorough destruction of the Troll population. Burning
them wouldn't do and having them come back was equally bad. Her
idea was in a way, simple. She remembered a story she once had
heard about a man, who used a device that shook a building apart.
She imagined sending a signal deep into the planet that excites the
cells of the Trolls to the point where they come apart, disintegrating
them. She visualized the weapon and envisioned harmonic compli-
cations, but decided to use the signal in bursts long enough to do
the job.

She then saw the chance of other people misusing her weapon
and shaking the planet apart, making her hesitate. But the weapon
was a long ways off. The first test was to build a sensor that could

detect the troll's cellular vibration. If she was right, she'd be able to detect the precise location of all the Trolls around the world. She smiled at her brilliance and was happy that she wouldn't be destroying the world to get at the Trolls. It wasn't a brutal death for the Trolls, but it was on the level of getting to know someone's cellular makeup before killing them.

She struggled with the simplicity of her plan, wanting to bring justice to the Trolls for all the evil they had done. If she was right then the Trolls wouldn't get the chance to contemplate their deeds before death, but even if they could, they'd end up justifying everything they had done. The Troll's special kind of evil couldn't be reasoned with. For them, therapy and incarceration wouldn't do. She released a heavy sigh believing that the Troll's relished the consumption of the innocent. In her heart she wanted the Trolls to pay and to be the one who'd look them in the eyes before incinerating them. She knew that hatred was on the verge of consuming her and was having a hard time putting her anger away. Destroying the Trolls had to be done, without question and she was happy that she's the one who decides how they should die, but she couldn't let hatred sever that last string of her humanity.

Hatred pulsed through her veins clouding her mind. She wanted to blast apart the walls around her, make her satellites in orbit and blast apart the Trolls then flatten anyone who'd come against her, but that was her hate talking. She wondered when her upset took on a life of its own. She looked back into her life, remembering being stalked then later, having her body dissolved and her brain jammed into a jar. She thought she had gotten over being stalked, but meeting the Troll in their Capital showed her otherwise. All her anger came bubbling to the surface and setting that lowly creature ablaze rendered that anger into hate. She used to be calm and relatively level headed, but now it didn't take much to trigger the furnace within.

She closed her eyes and focused on her breathing. Her hate was developing, growing and justifying the destructive tirade screaming in her mind. She needed to wait it out and allow it to pass without touching any part of it. She felt the air travel in and out of her lungs and when enough calm returned for her to look at herself, she admitted that it wasn't her place in the cosmic scale to personally bring painful death to each one of them, but it was too late. The cancerous hate had penetrated her core, slapping its blackened fingertips all over her being.

The blast of hate fatigued her mind, making her want to take a nap, but she didn't want to sleep. She wanted to figure out a way to remove the black drop in her white paint. She now had a monster within that only needed the hint of a reason to spring forward and take over and if she ever saw James, it'd be a devastating event that she's rather avoid.

Looking within, she explored her being and decided that she didn't need hatred in her life. It was normal to feel and be upset with things, but overindulging in a negative emotion was catastrophic. She visualized another self then felt the power of her Alchemy flow into her, embracing her like an old friend. Feeling her connection to the Universe overwhelmed her with joy and she quietly wept. She dried her cheeks and wiped her eyes. She closed her eyes again and focused, visualizing a second self. Her power enveloped her consciousness allowing her to look within and find her hate. Her mind translated the image showing black vine coiled and draped across the white strands that were her.

Her hate spoke to her, telling her that she needed it to make things happen and that together they were stronger, but Enora knew the truth. When her hate reared its ugly face, her mind clouded over, making her dumb and violent. She could no longer see friend or foe. All that existed in that moment was the desire to spread the hate and infect everyone around her. She felt her hate for her hatred rise within her and chose a new approach, abandoning her emotion. She knew that it wasn't her hate that spoke to her, but her subconscious mind that was trying to talk to her and show her the proper path. She knew that she couldn't touch her hate. It was black sticky tar that gets everywhere. But thinking back to what her hate said, pointed her toward its roots.

Hate would say that it protects you from violence and allows you to do what's needed, but that was another lie. The only place that she found she could touch was folded within that lie. She didn't need anger to defend herself from harm. She just needed to take responsibility for doing so. In a sense her hate told the truth. That it would act on her behalf, flood her mind with clutter and do what she was afraid to do, thus making her stronger without feeling the consequence. To defeat her hate and rip its roots from her consciousness, she had to face a true part of her that was fully capable of violence and become one with it. Her hate didn't give her much of a choice. Live with the anger and take the chance that it'll be triggered, or take responsibility for her survival instinct. Within her visualization, she reached into the fold at the base of the vein of hate and pulled out its roots. Though the problem was solved, she had to continue, or she'd end up contaminated again when another seed finds its way into her fertile soil. She opened the fold then allowed it to become part of her.

Light headed, she felt a cool energy coated her body and as the vein of hate died. She could still hear its little voice telling her that she still needed it and in a way it was telling the truth. She realized that she was addicted to the feeling of hate. She opened her eyes to allow reality to straighten her mindset then absorbed the knowledge that entangled her in a symbiotic relationship with her own hatred. She laughed at the thought than emotion had the power to blanket her mind and make her feel good while doing it. She relaxed into her chair and forgot what she was contemplating. A quiet confusion made her sleepy and she knew something within was different, but she didn't seem to mind. If she was transmuting herself, she trusted that it was for the better. All she had to do is allow the transformation to take place.

She opened her hand and held it out, manifesting a warm mug filled with coffee into her grip. The smell of it brought her back to the time before the Purge when she and her friends would visit their local coffee shop. She smiled, remembering the good times she had listening to the shop's music and reading books with the people who were now long gone. She thought of Colin Stinky Fingers and tried to remember his real name, but couldn't. The Trolls still had to go and her plan was solid, peaceful. She didn't know what had driven Colin to be the way he was, perhaps nothing. He may have been born that way and what happened to him after was between him and the Universe, not her deal. All she could do is help him pass quietly into whatever happens next. She took a sip of coffee and cherished the memories of her friends, thankful that she had spent the small portion of her life with them.

The com channel in her design table beeped disturbing her fond memories. She stood, cupping her mug in both hands. She strolled over to her table and pressed the com button. A projection of Kole's face appeared, replacing her plans for her satellites.

"Hello," she said, feeling her love for him fill her.

The flash of surprise on his face faded. "Hello, back," he said. "I'm glad to see you in a bright mood."

"Did you secure the stronghold and free the Human captives?" she asked, hoping to hear that he was on his way back.

His face saddened. "No, things have gone sideways and we need rescuing."

"Again?" she joked then became serious adding, "That should've been the first thing you said to me in case the Trolls jam the com channel."

He shook his head disagreeing. "We're bait. We're surrounded by Troll Battleships. They want Winter Haven to hear us and if no one comes, they'll keep hitting us until someone does."

"Oh, they want to thin out the city's defenses," she reasoned. "That would mean that their forces have quietly gathered close by. This is bad news."

"I thought it was bad before you added to it," Kole said. "Wasn't falling into a trap and having our forces raped by the Trolls bad enough for you? I guess its perspective."

"No need to get testy. I'm trying to help."

He sighed then ran his hand through his hair. "You're right, we're safe for now. I guess I'm not in the right space for playful banter."

"What's wrong?"

"Eric's getting worse. People around here are actually encouraging his bad behavior and I think he's enjoying it. And no matter what I say, he does the opposite. We were attacked by three gigantic Trolls and instead of burning, shooting, or hacking them up, he crawled up their butts then scrambled their brains before busting out of their skulls. Does that sound normal to you?" asked Kole, looking worried then continued without giving her a chance to answer. "And to top it all off, the Power Armor I signed off on was total garbage. I got a lot of people killed, picking that design."

She smiled reassuringly. "You may have picked the design, but why did they test it in battle without thinking it through? That part isn't your fault. Do you want me to find out who pushed for the test then give them a slap?"

Kole laughed. "No," he said.

"As for Eric and that Troll thing, I wasn't there. I'm sure Eric weighed all the factors and came up with the best plan to take care of the problem. Remember that his choices were limited. What he did might have been the best way to do it with all the other people running around. Did you ask him if it was his first choice?"

"He didn't give me a chance. He used it to push my buttons then hit on Sarah, telling her she'd look hot bald with tattoos and piercings."

She remembered the coffee in her hands and drank. "It sounds like you've had a rough day. Did you manage to save anyone?"

"This is where the story gets interesting. After my team was obliterated, I gathered up the survivors and we attacked the stronghold. It was expecting the Trolls to send in reinforcements to finish the job, but nothing happened and when we got to the stronghold, it was empty. My team did really good getting through the mine field and disarming the stronghold's automated defenses," he said then studied her. She wanted to say something to prod him along, but the serious look in his eyes told her to wait. "I have to tell you something important and I need you to stay calm."

She raised her hand stopping him. "This sounds serious, should we be talking about this over the com?" she asked, worried that the Trolls were listening in.

"Well if you're here and I tell you, then there's a greater chance that you'll go off the rails. I'd rather tell you now and risk it, besides the transmission is encrypted."

"It must be something bad to make me…" she said then made a quotation mark with her free hand, "go off the rails."

Kole laughed again. "All right, honestly if you decided to do something rash, there's nothing I can do to stop you."

"How about you trust me? Do you think that I'd hurt you to get what I want? Your mind really isn't in a good place. You should look at that," she said, feeling sad that he thought she felt so little of their love.

"It's not that," he said then explained, "When it comes to the Troll's you're not yourself. You get a little cranky when we're dealing with them. It's understandable, who isn't upset with the Trolls right now? So, what I'm saying is that you're not alone in your feelings."

She chuckled. "You're sweet for not wanting to hurt my feelings, but you're babbling. You still haven't told me what you've found."

He studied her again and Enora could tell that he was choosing his words. "When we were in the stronghold, I went off on my own and found a stasis pod with the original Troll in it."

"Oh," she said, seeing all her memories flash in her mind. "I can see why you thought I'd lose it and do something rash, but I'm fine with it."

He leaned back. "Are you sure, because we secured the pod and plan to move it to a lab in Winter Haven? Sarah thinks that with having the original template we'll be able to map their evolution and formulate something that'll stop their regeneration, making them easier to kill."

"Oh," she repeated. "Then you'll be keeping him asleep and experimenting on his tissue. I could use a piece or two for an idea I've been playing with."

"What's your idea?"

She shook her head then said, "I'm not telling." The disappointed look on his face broke her heart. "It's nothing personal. It's too destructive, I can't tell anyone."

"More destructive than creating implosions that suck up cities?" asked Kole then became serious. "We've killed a lot of people haven't we?"

"If I said that they all deserved it, would that make you feel better?"

"Not really. But, what are you going to do? Put them in stasis and wait until there are prisons and a judicial system in place?" He said then laughed at his mirth.

She smiled and waited for him to calm down. He was in a mood and she didn't want to sidetrack him. "How do you feel about finding the man who terrorized me? You're worried about my reaction, but I'm thinking about yours."

"To be honest, it was a struggle. I thought about dropping him into a hole and burying him alive. You see, he experimented on himself to try and reverse what the some company did to him. He had some successes and removed his regeneration ability."

"That's strange. Why did he want to remove that? Wouldn't that be a keeper?" she asked, curious to hear his answer.

"It was the first quality that he had to break, so his reversions could take place. Sarah is right. His flesh holds the key to neutering the Trolls."

"That's crazy. And the Trolls left him there?"

"When you say it that way, it sounds suspicious," Kole said then rolled his eyes and groaned. "Do you think it's a genetic bomb?"

"You don't know what Stinky Fingers has been up to. There

could be a virus that attacks the genetic code and turns everyone into a Troll."

Kole cocked an eyebrow. "And I thought I was paranoid. If he had that technology, he would've used it. I don't think it's trapped."

"People do make mistakes, maybe this was his, but if they are listening in, they should be there soon," Enora said, feeling nervous. She wanted to finish their conversation and rush to his side.

"What if the Trolls don't know? Not all of them are split from the same tree," he said sounding hopeful. "Regardless, we need to be rescued."

She thought of something funny. "Do you want me send James?" she asked then snickered, envisioning running up to James, grabbing his arm, batting her eyes at him before asking him to please rescue her man.

"What, no," Kole said, repulsed. "I don't want to see him. That guy is such a blowhard I'd never hear the end of it. Wait, why did you say that? I thought that if you ever saw him, you might snap."

She finished her coffee then dissolved the mug. "I'm sorry for making you think that I'd go to the extremes for revenge. I don't want to be that person."

"After what you've been through its understandable if you were."

"Yeah, I'm bored with revenge. Now, it's just an excuse to be angry and it's hard to let go. And if you do let it go, you feel that they got away with hurting you, but if you hang onto it, it dominates your life. Sometimes to save yourself, you have to cut all your crap loose."

They looked at each other then Kole said, "Fair enough. If you mean that, I'll give you the room to change. Your internal struggle is hard enough without other people sticking their fat thumbs into your wounds."

She smiled, happy that he has ways to make her smile. "Thank you for that. In the long run Stinky Fingers and James will get what's coming to them. Some say that what we do echoes into our next lives. If we dwell in darkness now, we'll be born into it later, trapping a soul into a never ending cycle of pain."

"Ew, that's dark," Kole said then laughed. "Since they're hanging off a cliff above the never ending abyss of pain, why don't we step on their fingers and send them on their way?"

"Silly man, be careful not to sully your karma standing next to them," she said playfully warned him.

"I know. It was a pleasant fantasy I indulged. You never know they could surprise us and work on their stuff."

She thought about James, Stinky Fingers and all the things they've done then said, "Not this life. They're committed to their path. Can you imagine the weight of a soul that would align with the vibration of becoming a Troll? That's lifetimes of evil made manifest."

Kole shrugged. "Maybe he's happy."

She raised an eyebrow, wondering if he was poking fun. "Indeed," she replied.

"I'm serious. For all we know, life is an amusement park where we're trying out the rides," he said then joked, "I think this life I'll be a murderous, rapist, cannibal. What are you going to be James?"

"Oh," she said playing along trying to sound manly. "I'm going to be a megalomaniac bent of world domination. I'll even collect brains and put them in jars. That sounds fun."

Kole laughed. "Okay, enough of this. We got sidetracked. We still need rescuing. Do you have any ideas?"

"Let me layout the variables. You need it fast, but you can't use Alchemy. Whatever force we send to get you will be met to weaken Winter Haven and create more hostages. If we do nothing, the Trolls will snipe your people to get a reaction from Winter Haven."

"Yup, I think you've got it."

She didn't like the option then decided that they needed Alchemy, but in a way that couldn't be proven. Her mind filled with an idea that made her laugh. "I got it," she said.

Kole cringed. "You have quite the evil laugh going on."

"No," she disagreed then argued, "That was my normal laugh."

"Whatever. What's your plan? In some way it's twisted, isn't it, to make you laugh that way."

She shook her head feeling the full complexity of her idea slip away. She raised her hand and said, "Stop. I'm going to make a satellite higher than any other and arm it with my weapon. I'll say I found it and it was used to defend the planet from asteroids. Since Sarah's people have been scanning the planet, they haven't looked up. I'll tell them that there's a network up there, but right now, I can only access one. That'll buy me time to make more and when I'm ready, I'll end the Trolls."

"Yeah, I can see where you got your evil giggle from. It's a good idea. Can you fire your new weapon with precision? I'm asking because you won't tell me about it."

She could see the focus and diffusion of her weapon in her mind, believing that she could target the Trolls and used the hull of their ships in her calculations, but was unsure about what would happen if she misses, or screws up her calculations. "Yes, I'm sure I can do it," she said, more to convince herself.

"I'm going to pretend that you filled me with confidence and nothing is going to go wrong. That's how much I have faith in you. I'll tell Sarah your plan and we'll get our people ready."

"Maybe, don't send people in to investigate, I'm not sure what's going to happen. This will be a test and if I'm right, you'll have Troll Battleships at your disposal."

"I'll go in alone, take one of their ships and load it with our survivors. We'll be home soon. When will you be ready?"

"If we still have communication, I'll call you when I'm ready."

Kole grinned then said, "We'll be packed and ready. I'll see you soon."

Enora disconnected after they said their goodbyes then sat in her cozy chair. She had never sent her awareness into orbit, but had heard of other doing it. People would sit in deep meditation and sent their awareness to other planets. Once Alchemists admitted to being able to do that, the world's governments hired them to find new habitable worlds and came up with regulations for laying claim to their discoveries, despite having no proof that those planets existence. There was even talk of a multi-trillion dollar scam involving a network of Alchemists who backed each other up in a huge lie, a big joke that sent many colonists to their doom. Enora imagined ships in deep space on their way to new habitable planets that didn't exist. Asleep in their stasis pods dreaming of a new start, only to wake up light years from anywhere. After the joke came to light, the governments couldn't afford to trust the Alchemist and dumped the colonization idea. When the leaders behind the farce were asked why they lied, they said that the human race can't take care of one planet and didn't deserve to ruin others.

Enora closed her eyes and relaxed. She stretched out, shooting her awareness high over the Earth and past Sarah's spy satellites. She felt the stillness of space, the web that connects all life and in that web, distance was an illusion. She relaxed into the quiet that reminded her of a sleeping tree in the winter then visualized being there floating and feeling the pure sunlight touch her skin. She stretched out her hand, but nothing happened. She could feel her power flowing through her body, but the strain was too great. She pulled back her hand and felt her environment sensing the huge gap between the molecules. Back in her chair she chuckled. The strain of her first attempt almost gave her a headache.

She focused again visualizing her place above the planet then looked down, manifesting a tunnel that drew up what she needed from the atmosphere far below. Her satellite slowly formed, putting more strain on her. The front of her forehead throbbed with each heartbeat while she held her attention of on each component. Her brilliant idea became a bad one with many more satellite to go.

Chapter

6

Kole stood in the middle of Sarah's quarters smelling the faint scent of paint. The grey walls and light green floor made him feel cold. When she had offered her room to make his call to Enora, he expected to see a luxurious room filled with the comforts of home, but when he first walked in, he thought he was in the wrong place. Bare walls, a cot and a com system decorated the room. Though the sheets on the cot looked clean, the mattress itself had someone else's body grove worn into it. The sad room made him chuckle and he wondered if Sarah had seen it, or would complain in their given situation. He believed she would suck it up then made a mental note to ask her how she slept in the morning.

After Enora had disconnected the call, he crossed his arms thinking. It was possible that the Trolls didn't know of their frozen guest and that his call was intercepted, spilling the information. If so, they'd be stupid not to attack. Kole then thought about making tea to settle his nerves and recognized Sarah's influence on him. Instead, he looked around her sparse room wanting to raid her tea stash, but stopped. She didn't even have drawers to place her things. He chuckled at the thought of being petty and stealing Sarah's tea then realized that Eric had got his bad behavior from him.

He initiated another call and Sarah's face appeared on his screen. Her face wasn't centered and sat crooked, telling him that he was on her handheld com. "I have news," he said.

"By the strange look on your face, it must be a mixed bag."

"No, it's not that, I was enjoying you decor. Have you seen your room?"

Fatigue pulled the brightness from her face. "No, I haven't," she said. "You have news?"

She was right to move him along, but he was avoiding the bad news. "I'm going to sandwich the news, what do you want first?"

"The good news please, I can use some."

"First, Enora doesn't care about our frozen friend. You can do whatever you want with him, but the Trolls may not have known he was there."

"Until you called to Enora telling them," she said, deducing his bad news.

"Yes, we might get attacked soon, but Enora in going to make some satellites with her new secret weapon. She's going to get us out of here and all you have to do is tell your people that she discovered an old network that used to defend the planet from asteroids."

Her eyes widened. "Asteroids?" she asked then her expression flattened. "Why not, what's her new weapon? You know what, it doesn't matter. We're still going to experiment on the first Troll. Right now, he's here and in my hand. If Enora's weapon is better, she can race me to the finish line. Besides it's better to have more than one way out of this."

"I agree, just make sure you get rid of him after, I'll sleep better knowing he's no longer in the world."

"Will do, is that all the news? I was expecting something more than the Trolls are coming. We're prepared for that, it's not a surprise," she said, sounding a bit snarky.

Kole looked over at her sagged mattress then back to her.

"Maybe you need to take a nap, but when Enora attacks, she wants only me to check out the damage. She did promise that we'd be able to claim their Battleships."

"I don't need a nap. Now, that's good news. I can't help but wonder what she's working on."

"She didn't tell me, but I don't mind. Knowledge has weight and if her weapon gets into the world, it might topple things, so I trust her judgment and can't wait to see what's going to happen."

"I'll see if I can spare a Flyer for you," she said.

Sarah looked away and Kole could hear another voice through her com. He waited knowing what she was going to tell him then when he had her attention, asked, "Good news?"

"No, you dork. You know exactly what I'm going to say, but maybe I'll surprise you. I hope Enora's ready because the Battleships that have been circling are attacking."

"Oh, we're under attack," he said to simplify her answer. "Where do you want me?" he asked, feeling the stress in his shoulders.

She looked away, worried and Kole could see unfocused people frantically moving in the background. "I have to go," she said then disconnected.

Kole instinctively wanted to shield himself and rush into danger, but remembered his Anti-Alchemist surroundings. He then thought of Eric and placed his com into his ear. He waited, expecting Eric to reply strait away, but Eric didn't answer. His second impulse was to find Eric and throttle him for not answering, but it was time for him to let Eric do his thing.

He opened Sarah's door into a bustling passageway. Crew-members ran, passing each other in front of the hatch, almost plowing into him. Kole waited then caught a mechanic carrying a portable welder. "What's happening?" asked Kole, surprising the man.

"Trolls have infiltrated our ship and we're sealing the decks," the mechanic said then quickened his pace.

Kole followed him running toward the damaged sections where he guessed he'd find the Trolls. He felt heart pounding in his chest.

Without his shield, he felt exposed, running toward danger and with each step he imagined a Troll stepping out from a hatch to shoot him. A new sense for freedom coursed through him, lightening his steps. He felt pumped, wanting to yank off his mittens, flood his body with his power and feel his shield again, but first he needed get away from the Human population. He hit a stairwell and almost tripped dragging the top of his foot down a step to regain his balance then ran into two mechanics about to seal a hatch.

Kole dipped around them then and darted through the hatch into darkness. "What are you doing?" one of the mechanics yelled, but Kole didn't answer.

Kole brought up his shield, feeling it reinforce and strengthen his body then altered his sight to see in the dark. Earlier, the mechanics had cut power to all the damaged decks to conserve power and to stop the power drain from severed conduits. Kole slipped on debris and stumbled into a wall. The passageway had been twisted in the crash, bursting the overhead pipe and shattering light fixtures. Kole ducked under a cluster of stretched wires hanging from the ceiling then shifted his power to push his senses outward, feeling for the Trolls.

Kole was right, but didn't take the time to enjoy it, feeling the hoard of Trolls moving through the deserted decks around him. He knew he had made a mistake telling Enora about his frozen friend and felt that every death that happened afterward would be his fault. He closed his eyes, focusing on his surroundings, seeing white and black silhouettes of everything around him, like static forming pictures. He could see three Trolls running toward him. They stopped, raised their rifles then Kole felt the hurtful pressure of Ripper Rounds. He spun, moving to the other wall, feeling the rounds pass by. The Trolls opened up. Kole could feel the regular round mixed in with the Ripper's and ran toward them. He ignored what his shield could handle and danced around the pressure, ducking under the rounds, sliding across the deck then sprang off a wall to close the distance.

A Troll seeing his end, charged passed the other two carrying something in his hands. Kole couldn't see what he held, but could feel the Ripper core grenades. Kole's world slowed and he wondered why the Trolls brought Rippers into an Anti-Alchemist ship. Humans weren't affected by the rounds and judging by the nasty look on the Troll's face, Kole came to the conclusion that they were expecting him.

That knowledge cheapened his experience making it personal. He wanted to be the fluttering butterfly in a hurricane, but now he had to be serious without leaving an alchemical trace for the Humans to detect. Although he could blame any alteration in the ship's plating on the Rippers, running unarmed into danger didn't look good.

An Elven war chant coursed through his head, reminding him of his lost music collection. Embracing the song, he danced sliding under the path of another Ripper Round then stepped into the mouth of the closest hatchway. He saw his plan, a flash in his mind and shot out his shield, stretching it into a long blade that reached for the advancing Troll. The Troll charged. His feet pounded the deck and his arms pumped the air. Kole timed his blade then sliced through the Troll's fingers into the grenade. The grenade exploded shattering his shield, sending a wave of pain cascading over the surface of his body. Kole stiffened. He clenched his jaw and his body shook. He lost his balance and fell through the hatch, landing hard on the deck. His watering eyes watched the massive bluish explosion rolled down the passageway passing by, washing heat over him. The smell of burnt rotting flesh and dirty chemicals filled his nose making him cough through his teeth.

His stabbing pain lessened, turning into hot prickles, reminding him of when he was a boy when he was shot at by his teacher for the first time, but this time it was worse. He had been grazed before, collapsing his shield, hurting him, but somehow the Trolls have purified the gel, increasing its hunger.

Kole reformed his shield then slowly stood fighting his numb body. He limped to the hatchway then slowly edged his way around the corner to peek down the passageway, incase more Trolls waited to blow his face off, but it was clear. He took a deep breath then ran, kicking out his rubbery legs, doing his best to make it to what was left of the two Trolls. They lay on their backs, horribly burned and gutted by the explosion. Looking at the smoldering mess, Kole wondered why the Trolls were using Rippers at all then remembered that they were there to kill Alchemists. He bent down and grabbed one of their rifles. He didn't expect to find it intact, thinking that the grenades set off secondary explosions, but the large rifle looked almost new.

The rifle looked heavy and without his shield, he knew he's have a hard time carrying it. He readied the rifle then knelt, balancing it on his knee. If the Trolls were there for him, they'd soon find him, but the rifle intrigued him. He brushed his senses across along the rifle's smooth exterior and felt the Ripper Gel reach for him like the clawed rancid hand of a Troll. He recoiled not wanting to go through the pain of having his shield collapsed again and got the sense that the gel had been grown then manipulated by the Trolls. Somehow the gel felt famished, desiring to feed on him. He ignored the gel, but could still feel it reaching out to touch his mind. The rifle felt like a haunted lover aching for his caress. He shook the image from his mind and tightened his grip on the oversized handle, barely able to get his finger on the trigger. The thought of using the rifle sickened him, but using it would allow him to wipe out the incursion without using his own Alchemy.

He stretched his sense outward, feeling the Trolls converging on him. He couldn't use Alchemy to slaughter them, missing the chaos he could create by using the walls to shoot spikes into the gel, making it do his work for him. He looked down the passageway, feeling them getting closer. He needed to rob them of their advantage and surprise them. His power flooded through him and with his skin still sore, he felt like a tightly packed sausage on the verge of busting and reached out, careful not to brush his awareness against his rifle. He heated the air in the passageways well above his body temperature to confuse their Troll sight then began his hunt.

He moved quick and quietly avoiding the debris, letting his adrenaline stoke his fire. The Trolls stopped and when he found the first group, the five of them knelt in a stairwell whispering complaints that they couldn't see. Kole aimed then fired into them, grateful that they had clustered together in their discussion. At the last second they saw him in the light of his muzzle flash, but couldn't react. Blood and chunks of flesh sprayed the walls. The odd Ripper Round found its target turning pockets of their flesh into gooey tendrils that sought Alchemical flesh to consume. The sight of the modified Ripper Gel at work sickened Kole. He never knew what the gel was, leaving it at something that destroys Alchemy, but it looked alive, with purpose, seeking out new material to corrupt until nothing was left.

The Trolls were down and Kole could still see the Ripper Gel spreading across their bodies. Kole instinctively reached out to sense what was happening, but the presence of the void repulsed him. He wanted to laugh at the Troll's stupidity for evolving a horrific weapon, but knelt, waiting for the gel to die. Kole felt movement below him. The Trolls slowed their advance, spreading out and when the gel finally died off, Kole moved down the steps to the landing. The gel hadn't consumed all their parts leaving chunks to regenerate. Kole rummaged around the corpses and found what he was looking for, a couple of grenades. He grinned and mocked a prayer for the fallen Trolls then pulled the pin on a grenade, dropping it into their gore.

He jumped down the rest of the stairs and ran, ducking into a side passageway. The explosion drummed the walls and rolling fire shot clanking debris down the passageway. And as quickly as the bluish light came, darkness fell upon him, turning his vision back to static. He leaned against the wall listening to movement, a quiet scuffing and knew the Trolls were closing in. The explosion, gunfire and screams told them where he was. It baffled his mind that they hadn't pulled back to reequip or run away. He had the advantage, but in the past it was rare that they retreated, throwing waves of bodies at their enemy. There was no love of self there, or the Trolls were possessed by another mindset.

In his quiet contemplation, a sneaking Troll crept by. Hunched over with his weapon pointing in front, the Troll's shoulder passed inches from the top of Kole's head. Kole stopped breathing and didn't move. He thought about mowing the Troll down then running away, but chose to trap his friend. He stretched out, feeling for the closest group of Trolls, gambling that they'd come running to the noise. Finding the Trolls behind him made him realize that the Troll that had past him was bait while the others waited in ambush. Kole planned his escape then pulled the pin on his last grenade. He tossed the grenade down the passage then stepped across the passage and through the hatch, bumping into the sneaking Troll's back. The sneaking Troll spun with his elbow leading the way, brushing across Kole's shield, knocking him back into the passageway in time to see the explosion rip apart the ambushing Trolls, their black silhouettes trapped in a pose against the light.

Kole didn't have time to admire his work. He rolled backward and onto his knees, meeting the sneaky troll's gaze. The explosion rolling up the passageway behind him lighting the Troll's face and in his eyes, Kole could see the flames. The Troll sidestepped trying to dodge while bringing his weapon to bear, but Kole fired first, punching a Ripper Round into the Troll's chest. The Troll fell back. Its chest erupting in gore that painted the wall as it fell. It hit the deck hard with a fleshy thump, but before Kole could move on, he turned to see another Troll come through the hatch beside him.

It thrust its meaty leg forward, kicking him, sending Kole sliding over the dead Troll's chunks. The Troll in the hatch brought his weapon up, but Kole rolled onto his back, spread his legs then fired. The recoil bounced his rifle, blowing apart the Troll's knee. The Troll fell, twisting, firing his weapon passed Kole's shoulder into the wall behind him. Being unable to dodge and feeling the Ripper Rounds reaching for him, kicked Kole's mind into survival mode.

He pulled his rifle in close, pressing it against his chest and fired again, running his rounds up the troll's torso, blowing the Troll apart. The Troll's severed arm fell still holding his rifle, pulling the trigger. Its meaty flesh jiggled with each round that fired into the ceiling, arching away from Kole. Kole didn't wait for it to stop firing and kicked his legs out, spinning onto his knee then sprang onto the Troll's corpse, sliding on its guts. He didn't know why he did it, instinct controlled him. He hit the floor then sprang to his feet running.

He didn't know why he ran and couldn't stop. He was the copilot in his own body, forced to watch his escape from an unperceived threat. His oversized rifle swayed with each step throwing off his balance making him compensate with longer strides then felt the pressure increase behind him. His rifle slipped out of his hands, crashing to the deck, allowing him to run harder. Through his shield, he could feel the deck shake beneath his feet. His static vision faded, replaced by a bluish light. The void made by the Ripper Gel sought food, coating the walls, pushing deeper into the passageways. Kole leaped into the air and kicked an unsealed hatch open then sprang in, grabbing its handle. He slammed the hatch shut sealing it, but the rumble intensified. Panting, he looked around the cafeteria. He could hear the rumble and felt the void intensify. He couldn't think straight. Somehow the Trolls have sent the void after him. He envisioned his flesh and soul being ripped apart, devoured by gooey tendrils then ran, charging into the kitchen.

Unsecured pots, pans and dishes lay strewn across the floor. Kole didn't stop. He charged in and felt his shield shoot out, sweeping the floor in front of him, sending the pots and dishes crashing out of his way. His shield gave him a hint to where he was going. The path back freezer lay clear. He slammed into the freezer door, grabbed the handle then pulled it open. He spun in and for a second he saw what his body knew, but he didn't. Through the serving window he saw the wall of bluish flame rolling through the cafeteria. From ceiling to floor, the flame raced toward him. He had felt the void and knew it was coming then saw its light around him, but for that second before he slammed the freezer door shut hoping he'd be safe, he could hear its voice in his mind. One voice with many mouths, the void knew he was there, calling to him. It wanted him to stop, to feed its hunger, promising a quick, but painful death.

Kole backed away to the freezer's center and felt the void reach for him through the door. He knew the void itself couldn't hurt him, but it brushed against his shield sending a chill up his spine. The rumbling intensified, shaking the freezer. Kole braced himself watching the freezer twist, severing the bolts fastening the shelves to the walls. The shelves fell, spilling boxes of partly thawed food across the floor over his feet and up to his knees. The explosion pushed passed the freezer leaving Kole in the void. The void touched him. Through the walls it was drawn to him, immersing him in its presence and for the first time he understood what it was. For all of his life he hated the Rippers, never trying to understand the gel. To him it was a tool of pain that his teacher used to train him to survive. Nothing more than weapon to destroy his kind, but it had been made by an Alchemist, an altered material in itself. Kole knew that James had created the Rippers, but thought the gel was part of the balance, nature's way to return the world back to normal. But now Kole could understood what it was. The void whispered to him, showing him James' fingerprint. James made the gel as well and with him being so powerful, no one could see his work. The whole belief of Alchemical balance came from the thought that the Universe had made the gel and someone else weaponized it.

The void touched his mind showing him pictures of James working on a bacterial culture, altering its state to feed on Alchemical energy and in the right environment, the gel would grow. More pictures flashed in his mind of the Trolls manipulating the gel's environment, making the bacteria hungry and being alive the alchemically altered bacteria exists in a state of starvation. The void that he felt wasn't a void, it was the living song that the bacteria sang while being shot out of a Ripper. If the gel wasn't alive and didn't have a living song, he would've been dead a long time ago. The old gel sang a warning that they were coming, but the new gel was trapped in a state of perpetual hunger, singing a song that wants you to stop while it devours you. The pictures in his mind stopped and the voice faded. Kole's mind returned to the freezer and his trembling body. He had come close to death and his body knew it. He remembered a couple of times when he was a child where his body had taken over, moving when it shouldn't have. An odd feeling, but only lasted for one action, not running for its life.

Kole felt the strength of the void weaken and the rumbling stop, but his body refused to move. He was still scared, imaging the gel was wasn't gone, that it was sitting quietly on the other side of the door. He tried to take a step and lift his hand, but it didn't happen, making him wonder if he was sleeping, trapped in a picture the void had left in his mind. He bit his tongue feeling pain, but he had felt pain in dreams before. His dreams had never been nice. He'd been shot, stabbed, blown up, electrocuted, disembodied and drowned, but his dreams were always disjointed with blackened out areas. The freezer looked normal making him think it was real and that he was okay.

He raised his trembling hand to his forehead and wiped the sweat away. He breathed a deep nervous breath then took a step. Surprised, he dropped his shield, bent forward then threw up over the boxes, feeling the cold air of the freezer. After his stomach had emptied, his body gave a couple of extra heaves to make sure the job had been done right. Feeling terrible, Kole dragged the back of his hand across his mouth then remade his shield. He stumbled over the boxes and slipped, falling onto his back. Somehow he felt comfortable and wanted to take a nap with his head and arms resting on collapsed boxes.

At first he was angry with himself for being afraid and acting weird then used his disappointment in himself to smack the stupid out of his head, but calmed remembering that he was a person who almost died in his most feared way. He patted his shoulder, thanking his body for running and felt that it was a strange thing to do, but he was still alive.

He fought with the crumpled boxes and pushed himself up, then kicked his way on the way to the door, spilling the thawing food stuff. He placed his hand on the door release then closed his eyes and reached out with his awareness, feeling for the void on the other side of the door. Within the gel the bacteria could life forever, starving, waiting for a chance to feed, but once fired the bacteria spends its last moments of its life seeking food. Kole was sure that the gel was dead, but worried that the Trolls altered that too. He thought of what the bacteria had shown him. James was responsible for its initial creation and all that the Trolls had done was alter the bacteria's environment, affecting its behavior. He pushed the doors release, confident that the Trolls didn't have the power to rewrite James' work and was relieved, the gel was dead. He stepped out of the freezer into the cafeteria. Through his static vision he could sense the chemicals coating the singed walls, floor and warped tables that were still bolted to the floor. He stretched his awareness outward feeling for Trolls, or any other living thing that wanted to eat him, but found only silence. He thought the void had hurt him, somehow damaging his mind then stretched out further, feeling the people far above him. The Trolls in his area were gone, but he still didn't trust his senses. He didn't want to get caught strolling through the corridors whistling a sweet song and twiddling his thumbs and went back the way he came to find the rifle he had discarded.

Kole found the rifle, not where he'd dropped it, but down the passageway torn asunder. He guessed that the explosion had picked it up and thrown it, bending its barrel, rupturing its power supply which blew it in half. Kole was happy that the modified Ripper was destroyed. Rippers were bad enough, but this new gel freaked him out on a whole new level. He calmed, remembering being lost in the Elves Arctic stronghold. He then followed Enora's example and closed his eyes, searching with his awareness to find a way out, one that would get him outside. Going around the long way would avoid curious guards and sealed passageways.

The thought occurred to him that these weren't the only Trolls and that the ones who tried to kill him regrouped to go after Eric. Kole tried his com again, but there was too much interference, blocking his signal. He searched for Troll one last time not finding any then touched the com resting in his ear. He pulled his senses in turning off his static sight then amplified his com to reach Eric. The com chimed, but Eric still didn't answer. Frustrated, Kole slammed his hand against the wall and shouted a vile curse. He sensed his environment then marched down the corridor on his way outside to find and throttle Eric.

Chapter

7

Eric lay stretched out with his hands behind his head sunbathing on the outer hull of the Battle Cruiser. He closed his eyes and in his mind's eye, he went back to meeting with Kole and Sarah, wondering if Sarah was playing hard to get, or truly didn't want him in that way. He had made the mistake before, throwing his affections at a woman who wasn't attracted to him, but why Sarah? She was older, job orientated and a clone. She'd have no time for him, but he smiled at the last part wishing she had said yes to his advances. The sight of the veins pulsing in Kole's fore head would have made it worth it, plus with her on his arm, he'd be the envy of Winter Haven. After the meeting he wondered why Sarah had rejected him, but decided that she was free to be with whomever she wanted.

He decided to go for a walk and found himself outside. The air and sun felt good on his skin and in the short time that he'd been using his shield, he thought wouldn't quickly forget the feel of the sun's warmth, but he did. His instinct called for his shield becoming his safe place, beating his primal need for daylight and fire.

He suppressed his survival instinct and enjoyed the sunlight. He ripped the arms of his coveralls off, sure that the mechanics who gave the coveralls to him wouldn't mind, but the arms weren't enough. He then ripped the coveralls up, making a pair of shorts using one of the discarded arms for a belt. He felt better, washed by the light then walked out to the highest point he could find near the edge, overlooking the forest, a quiet place where everyone in the control room could see him. He was sure that if Sarah saw his free spirit and firm his body, she'd swoon.

He lay down embracing the warmth of the deck and cast thoughts of Sarah out of his mind. He wondered if it was her rejection that spurred his compulsive behavior, or if it was her unavailability that made her sexy. She was too skinny for his taste and didn't have tattoos, or markings. She was dull and pushed tea on him. He didn't even like tea. It confused him because even if she cut off all her hair and got piercing, she still wouldn't do it for him. Maybe it was to irritate Kole. He loved doing that most of all. Pushing Kole's buttons and making him choke down his fatherly advice made him giggle. It was payback for all the times he had said no. But he had really liked Kyra. He even focused real hard and made flowers for her and ale for Nick, but no one other than Nick noticed and he wasn't going to go anywhere near Nick. No means no, he heard himself say to Nick.

Sarah and Kyra said no, but why was he obsessed with them? All that was left was their unavailability. They are safe to love from afar. He'd never have them, never be loved by them. He gagged then forced the mushy feelings out of his mind. He was a man now and men aren't mushy. He wanted to be rough and tumble like real Dwarven men, the Berserkers. Crazed and full of spunk. He liked who he was becoming, his evolution into manhood. He smiled at the thought and let the thought of Sarah go.

Someone blocked the sun casting a shadow across his face robbing him of the sun's warmth. He opened his eyes thinking that it might be Sarah. She could've changed her mind, but it wasn't her, it was someone better. The young woman around his age stood, leaning over him with her hands on her knees. Her lovely smile brightened her yellow eyes. Eric blinked meeting her gaze. He tilted his head to get a better look and take in the view. Even in her blue coveralls, Eric could see her strong shoulders and curvy body. He thought he was dreaming. He liked her dark eyebrows, bald head and her multiple ear piercings.

"Hi," he managed to say.

"Hi back," she said then asked, "Do you mind if I join you?"

He quickly sat up and spun on his bum to face her then heard his com chime in his ear. He turned his com off then gestured beside him saying, "Please."

She smiled again then sat across from him, intriguing Eric. She wasn't there to please him and sit beside him. She was there for something else, perhaps something special. He watched the way she moved while she sat, liking how she commanded her movement. A sloppy mind drives a sloppy body and he planned to watch her a lot. "I like your eyes," Eric said, complimenting her choice, wondering if they were real like his.

"I saw yours and liked them. Of course mine aren't real, but they are nice. Do you like them?" she asked then tilted her head and blinked at him.

He smiled. "Yeah, they look like mine." He examined her face and liked her cute little ears then remember passing by her in training. She had brown eyes and was fair-haired. He wanted to say something witty, but was having trouble and the silence between them was growing.

She looked away and her pleasant face turned to worry. Confused, Eric followed her gaze turning around. The distant Troll Battleships had changed course and were now advancing. Eric stood then tried to decide on what to do. His armor was junked and there were limited resources to use. Even if he ran, he wouldn't make it to the hanger in time to commandeer a Flyer. He then remembered the com, knowing that Kole must have tried to warn him. Eric was about to turn his com on when the distant clouds high above the Battleships opened up. Eric didn't know what had happened. Seconds apart, large holes appeared in the clouds. He couldn't see missiles, explosions, or any sort of munitions, but watched the Battleships list, rolling then dive into the forest. Balls of flame and black smoke erupted over the crash sites before he heard the first explosion.

"We need to get out there and kill the survivors," the young lady said.

"Wait," he said stepping forward to gently clutch her arm. "What's your name?" he asked.

"Sophie," she answered. "What's the plan?"

"Well, I thought I'd ask to see if you wanted to sit with me in the mess hall tonight."

"Not that," Sophie said then pointed to the distant columns of black smoke. "That."

"If you have a functioning suit, go get it. I wrecked mine and there's not enough to go around."

"I thought you were a Berserker," she said looking confused then flashed a wicked smile. "We can go down to the hanger, strap some guns to a hover-lift and mess some Trolls up."

Eric laughed seeing her plan. "Yeah, let's do it." He grabbed her hand and together they ran across the deck to the hatch. Inside it was chaos. Eric and Sophie shoved their way through the crowd who ran in the opposite direction. Alarms echoed down the passageways and voice over the intercom informed them that Trolls have entered the ship. Eric smiled and tightened his grip on her hand, careful not to squeeze too tight, but just enough to keep from losing her. He'd just met her and she was perfect. He hoped she liked him back, but remembered that she had changed her eyes to get his attention. No one had ever tried to get his attention before and it made his feel special.

They ran down a couple of stairwells and into the hanger. He was right, there was nothing left for them to pilot. The Flyers and Fighters had taken off and most of the Power Armor was in the forest. Eric had no idea where the Trolls were, but he had Sophie's plan.

"We need to find out what's going on," Eric said.

"Use your com."

"It's a closed system, we need others."

She nodded and her look of determination assured him that she was with him. They parted and Eric looked around the hanger, spotting the hover-lift and a large bin filled with limbs that had been salvaged after their first fight with the Trolls. He wanted to impress Sophie with his ingenuity and build a poor man's tank. He saw the plan in his mind and went to work. He ran to the hover-lift, jammed his foot into the step and leaped, landing his bottom on the driver's seat. He fired it up and stomped on the throttle spinning the lift around. He sped over to the bin then slammed on brakes, initiating the inertia dampeners. His rear lifted out of his seat, pressing his guts into the controls and almost rammed into the bin. He had grand designs for the lift, armoring and arming it, but that'd take too much time. He frantically searched finding chest pieces then slapped them on around his seat, securing them with wire. He created a rear gunner's position, attaching four Power Armor's arms to a swivel that rested on the cab's roof.

Sophie returned, running up to him and handing him his new com. "This looks great," she said.

He slipped the com in his other ear and watched her check out his rig. She tugged on a chest piece testing to see if she could pull it off. Eric smiled at her enthusiasm, watching her test the layers of armor. The rig looked like a floating trash heap of discarded parts held together by twine, but he'd been in worse. He thought of Nick and Kyra's Battle Barge. They loved that flying heap and if Eric loved his rig half as much, he was sure it'd see them through the day. "You really like it?" he asked.

"Yeah, I'm driving," she said then opened the loose flap used as a driver's window, climbing in. "There's a lot of weight. I'm not sure how fast this thing will go, but let's give it a try."

Eric climbed up and jumped into the rear gunner's position then banged on the roof twice.

"That was loud," she said over their com, reminding Eric he could talk to her, but before he could apologize, she punched the throttle, shooting out of the hanger. Eric grabbed onto the frame, stopping himself from rolling over the fastened armor and falling out. And despite the extra weight, the hover-lift still had speed, but he could feel that it struggled with the turns.

They tied their com into the Power Armor com channel, hearing that the fighting was at the front of the ship, but there were new reports of explosions coming from the rear. Sophie turned hard, dipping the side of the lift close to the ground, heading to the main battlefield. "No wait, let's go to the back," Eric said.

"It's been sealed off, there's nothing back there."

"There's going to be a lot of shooting up front and as fun as it'll be, we'll get in the way. Besides if I was going to attack, I'd send some in the back when everyone's occupied."

"You got it," she said then cranked her control, but this time Eric was ready.

He didn't know which way she'd turn and braced himself equally, wondering where she learned how to drive. He wanted to complain, but didn't want his whine to drive her away. She impressed him with her daring and he didn't want to her to run away.

She sped up the slope dodging the trees, flattening the underbrush, bumping overhanging branches and all Eric could do was hunker down and wait for the ride to be over. The pitch in the anti-grav dropped daring Eric to look, but the last time he'd thought about seeing where she was going, a tree limb almost took his head off. He then decided that for now, he'd keep his mouth shut and not complain until they got to know each other better.

She came to a stop. "We're here and you're right, the Trolls have cut their way into the ship."

Eric raised his head high enough over the top of the lift to look down the slope and see a large mass of Trolls lining up and entering a hole they'd cut into the hull. "Let's get down there and divide their forces," he said.

"Are you sure, there's a lot of them and only one of us," she said, sounding hesitant which told Eric that she wasn't stupid.

He chuckled then said, "There's a difference between bravery and stupidity, but I can't tell anymore between the two, but we need to get down there before they're dug in. People are counting on us to protect them."

With that, she cut the rest of Eric's speech off and punched the throttle then charged down slope. Eric grabbed his gun's controls and opened up. The guns blazed and the recoil shook his arms enough for him to worry that the guns would come lose. He watched the four trails of his rounds cut through the underbrush, punching through large leaves, rotting logs and into the line of Trolls. His barrage was perfect. He sunk his rounds into the legs then backs of the Trolls closest to the hole. He owed it to the Dwarves, re-membering their song about firing a heavy machine gun, but he got confused, mixing the lyrics with another song. Their songs were all bad and sounded the same, but he remembered to aim low to hit high.

Sophie turned, putting trees between them. Eric turned and re-membered another part of the song that told him to control his burst. "Clack, clack, clack," he yelled then fired another burst at the Trolls who dove for cover.

Sophie banked striking the side of the ship. The armor screamed and some of the plating came off, but Eric didn't noticed. He could feel the Trolls on the hill regrouping up the hill while the ones in the ship had moved on. The Troll weren't stupid, they hid from him, but there was something else lingering among them. The lift jolted, knocking Eric against the frame as Sophie ran over the Trolls Eric had gunned down.

"Did you see that?" she asked, yelling. "I want to spin around and do it again. Keep shooting."

Sophie turned again circling, climbing the slope. Eric ignored the branches and underbrush scraping the sides of the lift and fo-cused, feeling the Troll's position. His awareness brushed against their weapons and knew what the presence that enveloped them. They carried Rippers, but they weren't normal. He had felt that presence before, when he was trapped in a vortex with the Lollypop King. A chill ran over him and triggered another memory. In the vortex, his perception of time had been warped and moments before it all came apart, he felt something else had joined them. A void, like the one in the Rippers penetrated their power, reaching for them. He had forgotten, but now remembered that void consumed parts of him, pulling out pieces of him that he could never get back.

He tightened his grip on his jury rigged handles and aimed his guns. He could tell that the Troll's Ripper Gel still wanted him, but also was repulsed by him. Pictures in his mind flashed before his eyes reminding him of being in the vortex. He had opened every conduit of power within his being, adding everything he was to the vortex in an attempt to kill the King. He refused to let the King win then right before his victory, something happened. He had felt the King's attention wane, it wasn't much, but he took the chance and thought he had delivered the killing blow, when the void punctured their bubble. Their power inverted, crashing upon both of them. Eric struggled to keep the pressure from killing him and felt the void seeking to touch him. Like being submerged in water, it followed the vortex's currents, latching onto and consuming the exposed parts of him, the parts that he had used to attack the King. He could feel an itch in his skull and see the tendrils of the void wrap around the energy of his mind dissolving him. He was trapped in a moment, watching his mind being consumed and unable to do anything about it without being killed by the pressure. The void inched closer and when he thought he was going to die, he was blasted out of the void.

The memory of the void and the presence of the Troll's Rippers pushed his mind into a dark place. A thick energy welled within him, flooding his mind and pushing against his skin. He couldn't think strait and knew that his weapons also had Ripper Rounds, but there was a difference between the types of weapons and the only logic available to him was that void had come to finish what it started. It had found its way out of the Ork Lands and hunted him down to finish him, but he wasn't going to let it.

The rage within him built to the point of bursting. He screamed and squeezed his triggers, firing low into the ground then up into the trees. Sophie still circled and Eric planned to use his Alchemy to ignite the rounds embedded in the trees and ground, blasting them into the next life, but then felt the pressure. He instinctively ducked. Eric had been focused on his memories that he didn't realize that the Trolls had come out from their hiding place.

Pinging metal rained against the side of the lift. Sophie pulled away and without looking, Eric spun his guns to face the direction of their incoming rounds. Through the rage, he felt as if he was standing next to them then opened fire.

Sophie cursed then said, "We're coming around for another run."

Eric had enough. He wanted to kill the void like he had killed the King, making it suffer like that pervert did. "Go straight at them," Eric ordered. "We're going to ram this rig down their throats!"

Sophie let out a whoop then cranked her controls, spinning them around and to Eric's surprise he expected her maneuver and braced himself. He remembered stumbling across a group of Trolls in the forest who proceeded to shoot up his armor and hoped that the lift's armor would hold. Knowing that they'd be charging the lines, he made the front three times thicker with a crap load of wiring to keep it all in place, but there were a lot more Trolls he expected and they were the only target. He needed to thin them out without using Alchemy, but he wanted to. It would've been easy to transmute the barrels of their rifles closed, blowing them up, or turning the air around them into a corrosive and combustible gas, but he'd just met Sophie. He needed to do something lucky and create an event that would give him what he wanted and not upset his new Anti-Alchemist friends.

Under the strain, the hum of the anti-grav engines changed pitch and the lift shuddered. "That's not good," Sophie said then reported,

"We're getting close to overheating. This wreck wasn't built for doing this."

"I put my love into every chunk of armor I strapped to this, she'll hold together."

The Trolls advanced, running between the trees and Sophie charged. Eric fought to control himself. He wanted to jump out and gut the Trolls with his bare hands then destroy the void within their weapons to find peace, but instead focused on the Dwarven songs and fired short controlled burst, not at the Trolls, but at their weapons. He will make the void work for him. He reached out feeling it, envisioning it to be a humanoid ghost that he was going to thrust his hands into and consume its very being. He owned the void, it was his to kill, his to devour. The Trolls returned fire and in the noise Sophie released her war cry, the scream of her soul as she struck two brave Trolls who stepped out from behind their trees to fire at her eye slot. She sped through the group and Eric spun, taking his shot. Each burst that he fired tagged a Troll's rifle setting off their gel. The gel sprayed against the Tolls then erupted into fleshy explosions and with a meaty pops, spreading to those nearby.

Eric didn't hear the screams of the Trolls being consumed by the gel over the gunfire punching through the first layer of armor into the second. He had forgotten about the other side to charging and put less armor on the back to keep the weight low. He ignored the pinging and pressure from their Ripper Rounds at his back and focused on where to shoot. He released a couple of quick bursts, sensing his rounds bite into trees and logs to find his target. The void reveled in its short term freedom and fed on the closest Alchemical material then died out. Sophie changed direction, circling the opposite direction, forgetting that she had side swiped the Cruiser and had lost some armor.

"Circle the other way," Eric said, but was too late. Rounds shot through into the engine and cab. Sophie cried out in surprise then jerked her controls. Eric felt the nudge then heard a bang, reminding him of the junk heap they drove into the Ork Lands that fell apart.

The hum of the anti-grav waned powering down. Eric could feel it lose speed then braced himself a moment before it plowed into a tree. The force of the collision broke his grip slamming him against the cab, knocking his head on the frame. He cursed then clenched his teeth fighting the pain shooting around his skull into his eyes. He felt light headed and sleepy. He wanted to jump up and check Sophie then remembered the Trolls, but before he could ask her if she was hurt the tree creaked, twisting then fell. In his mind's eye, he saw the tree flatten them, but with a thundering crash, the tree landed beside them.

Before the gunfire, Eric felt the pressure. He was stuck again, sucking up their rounds like before, but this time he wasn't alone. It was time to be a hero and save Sophie. He pushed through the pain then sprang forward and grabbed his gun's controls that broke in his hands. He held the two halves and yanked one to turn the guns, but they didn't respond. He dropped the two pieces, leaving them hanging then forced his guns to turn. The gun track had broken in the crash, but was still movable. He grabbed a handle, readying the trigger in one had then forced the guns to move with the other. He could feel the Trolls coming and wasn't able to shoot them fast enough.

"What are you doing? Get out of there."

The fuzzy buzz in Eric's head didn't allow him to recognize Sophie's voice. "Who's that?" he asked then shot through the side of a tree into the Troll hiding behind it.

"It's me. Get out of there," she repeated.

Confused, Eric asked, "Me who? Who is this?" He yanked on the other guns then pulled, trying to line up another kill.

He heard a deep sigh in his ear. "This is Sophie and at any moment the Trolls are going to be on you. Get out of there."

Relief washed over Eric. He though she was still in the cab pinned against her controls, or worse. "I'm so glad you got out. I thought you were still in there," he said then fired another burst, but she was right. The Trolls were getting closer and Eric could feel the voids they carried. He didn't want to leave, get hunted down and shot in the back. He couldn't let the void go. He wanted revenge. He wanted to reach into the void, take back what was stolen from him and become whole even though he had forgotten what that felt like. He wanted them all to pay. "Run Sophie. After they're done with me, they'll be looking for you," he said, but she didn't respond.

Eric glanced down at the armored paneling and could see bullet dents, telling him that he was running out of time. Sophie was right. One way or another, he needed to get out of there, but he couldn't let go. He needed revenge. He pushed the guns with his sore shoulder, then aimed and fired. The Trolls stopped and he heard a large thump. His instinct screamed and he moved in time to avoid a rifle barrel being stabbed into his chest. The Troll didn't fire. Eric sprang up, using the Troll as a shield and thrust him forward, sliding across the Trolls arm and into his face. Eric kept his fingers closed with a gap between his them and his thumb. His fingers met the Troll's face, hitting the bridge of his nose and he allowed his fingers to slide into the Troll's eyes. The Troll's head jerked back then moved his hand to cover his eyes while Eric brought his other arm down, breaking the Troll's grip on its rifle. Eric wanted to shoot the Troll, but didn't want the Ripper Gel to splash on him. That's not how he wanted to die.

Eric grabbed the Troll's arm and pulled, climbing out of the box while the Troll rubbed its face. He balanced himself and stood on the edge of the frame, worried that the other Trolls will shoot through their buddy to get to him. He wanted a quick retreat, deciding to do a back flip. In his mind eye he imagined everything working out perfectly, landing on his feet, he'd then run for cover behind a tree, but that's not what happened. His stiff back and sore shoulder didn't move right and the weight of the Troll's rifle throwing him off. If he had his shield on, it would've compensated for all the variables giving him what he dreamt up. He also forgot about the extra lip his armor made when he tied it to the lift.

He sprang into the air seeing sky and tree tops then a flash of red before black. Pain shot through his other shoulder and knee. He forced his eyes open, refusing to become a Troll's snack then still holding the Troll's rifle he pushed himself to his feet. Somewhere in his fall he scraped his face and filled his mouth with dirt. He moved the terrible tasting gritty stuff with his tongue, pushing dirt, small rocks and blood out of his mouth. He was several feet away from where he thought he would land and tried to run, but his swollen knee wouldn't allow it. With everything going wrong, he thought he was going to die there, but he was going to make them pay for their dinner and he wasn't cheap.

He readied the troll's oversized rifle, tilting it sideways to get a better grip and fired at the squinting Troll, blasting a hole in his chest. The Troll fell back, splattering the gel across the lift's armor. Eric limped on, sensing where the Troll were going to be and firing when he saw a piece of them. It didn't matter what he shot. Some rounds blasted chunks of meat off, while the dreaded Ripper Rounds turned them to pudding.

His senses gave him a moment's advantage allowing him to stay ahead of their rounds, but his body stiffened and his steps shortened. Pain pulsed in his head and down into his body. His body cooled, clamping up, but his movement kept his pain at bay. He limped through knee high grass to a tree and fell against it to rest. He was still outnumbered, but had thinned their numbers, shooting the gutsy Trolls. All that were left were the planners. Eric knew that all the Trolls came from one source, but they all developed different qualities. Some planned while others rushed in. Some shot their friends while others saved them. He never knew what he was dealing with and at the moment he wanted more to rush in.

The pain increased and he needed to move. He tightened his grip to fight his shaking arms then pushed off the tree. A round grazed the back of his shoulder, spinning him, he then felt the pressure. He could've caught himself, but the Ripper Round would have ended him, but instead he fell with style. Adrenaline coursed through him numbing his wound and allowed him to focus. He embraced his second wing, mentally thanking the Troll for shooting him then using his senses he found the shooter and before he hit the ground he returned fire. He squeezed the trigger until he felt the pressure then tucked his other shoulder in to soften the fall.

He rolled away and over the noise of snapping twigs, grass bending and crunching underbrush, he heard the Trolls storm toward him, taking advantage of his weakened position. And they were right. In his rolling he had moved away from cover. His balance was off and somewhere he thought that rolling to safety was a good idea, but in his heart he knew it was over. He just wanted to focus one last time and spun around on his back stopping himself with his good leg. He dropped the rifle between his legs and noticed the size of his swollen knee. Seeing that, he wanted to keep moving so his body wouldn't cool and stiffen up, hurting him more.

He kicked his good leg under the rifle and used it to elevate the barrel then laid himself flat, using his Alchemy to feel where the Trolls were. The rifle was heavy and he thrashed his hip to kick then fired short bursts at those in the open. They returned fire. Their rounds tore up the ground around him, showering him in dirt and clumps of grass, but Eric, accepting his death and kept firing. Then he ran out of bullets leaving only the Ripper Rounds. Hearing his rifle whine down and feeling the constant pressure from his Ripper Rounds, he couldn't help but laugh. It wasn't his normal laugh, it was the wide eyed laugh of a mad man and he couldn't stop. His mind opened up and he was again standing over his body. His body looked awful, battered, bloody and bruised, but it was his crazed look that worried him.

In the past he had fallen out of his body when he needed to get up and was too tired to move, but was immediately pulled back after he took a couple of steps, confusing him. This time he was able to stand there and take it all in. The pain, fear and stress was gone leaving him feeling peaceful. He wasn't sure if he could get back, but wasn't worried. He was enjoying the break from the pain. He didn't want to try and move in case he triggered his body to call him back and looked into the forest. He could see the Trolls and wondered if he could tell his body where they were, but his body jerked then fired responding on its own. He turned his head and noticed the couple of Trolls circling around to flank him and Eric was glad he was out of his body. His hurt leg pushed, kicking out, allowing his body to flop and point the gun in the flanking Troll's direction. Eric watched the Trolls explode, but didn't feel the pressure. His body flopped around like a possessed meat puppet freaking him out, but he forced himself to calm down. On one hand, his body was doing better than he would've been, but on the other, he'd been shot in his good leg and had a couple more grazes. He was bleeding out.

He didn't know how long he was going to be standing around, watching his body fight for his life and decided to try something. He was going to die and move on, or return to his body then die, either way he didn't like his options. He had nothing to lose and in his peace, he opened himself up, feeling his power fill him in a way he'd never experienced before. He could feel the life around him in the soil, air and around the planet. He looked down at the rifle and wondered when the Ripper part of the rifle would run out of power. He then felt the area around his body and understood that he was surrounded by the void, a side effect to his crazy body not letting the trigger go.

It was an interesting sensation to feel Alchemy outside one's body and wanted to explore it, but he had work to do if he still wanted to live. A piece of him enjoyed the quiet and wanted to venture into the Universe to experience its mysteries, but the larger part told him that he'd eventually die and do that anyway. For the first time in his short life, Eric didn't have a problem focusing. He sent his awareness into his body and stopped his bleeding. It was as easy as waving his hand. He replaced some of his blood to keep him conscious when he returned and dissolved the waste in his bowels, so it'd be days before he'd use the toilet again, creating undisturbed healing time.

He felt connected to the world, the life around him and a deeper sense of love for everything, bringing understanding to his life. He was on the verge of uncovering something huge and life changing then the last Troll fell. His flopping meat puppet of a body managed to kill them all then out of the light of love and peace, Eric fell into darkness and pain.

Eric heard an annoying voice calling his name. The voice was close and getting louder, pulling him out of sleep. "Eric, wake up. Come on, wake up," Kole implored and gently smacked his face.

A moment ago Eric loved Kole with all his being and felt Kole's love for him, but in a flash, old habits took over pushing the love away. "I'm sleeping!" he growled, hurting his throat. The anger of being woken up caused pain to pulse in his head.

"Open your eyes."

He listened and could see a fuzzy Kole in his dirty coveralls kneeling beside him. "I thought they were open. I thought it was night. I had a dream I was in a warm place with lots of light and you were there, but now we're here. I'm confused. Help me up, I can't move."

Eric could feel Kole probe his body with his Alchemy finding his injuries. "How do I look?" he asked.

"You're not getting up. I'm going to find something to put under your knee then I'm going to get help," he said, looking worried. He ripped his sleeve then found a clean spot to bandage his beg.

Eric wanted to argue, but the thought of being alone and napping appealed to him. Kole propped his swollen knee up then assured him he'd return, but Eric barely heard him. He remembered more of his dream. He was outside of his body and something told him it was real, but it still felt like a dream. He wanted to remember more and pressed his memory, increasing the pain of his throbbing headache.

"Eric," Sophie said then collapsed onto her knees beside him.

Eric squinted up at her and wondered why she was breathing so heavy. "Sophie, you're alive," he slurred. "I could've used your help."

"I did what you said and ran. I was so scared and I wanted to come back, but I couldn't stop running," she said with tears flowing down her cheeks. She placed her trembling hand on his arm then said, "I'm sorry for abandoning you."

Her tears dropped onto the grass and Eric couldn't help but wonder if she was trying to manipulate him. As far as he could remember, Kole pounded paranoia into his head and he was having a hard time deciding if she was for real. Sure, he told her to run, but no one ever listens to him, but what if she did. What if she was telling the truth and he was going to wreck it with mistrust? Not everyone was out to get him even though at the moment it felt that way.

He decided to trust her and said, "You did good and I'm glad you came back. I like how you handled the hover-lift and I don't think anyone else would've gone with me."

She smiled then wiped her tears. "I was having fun until they almost shot me and when we crashed. Other than that, I liked running them over. It was satisfying."

Eric couldn't help but chuckle. He picked a crazy one, but realized that they might balance each other like Kole and Enora. And Enora was right. Sophie isn't the kind of woman that'd want to hear his poop jokes. He was going to have to grow up if he wanted to keep Sophie around. He wanted to touch her in a reassuring way without making her think he was making a pass and lifted his hand, placing his finger tips on her knee then said, "Everything is going to work out. Kole has gone to get help and with all the Trolls gone, we'll be out of here soon. Winter Haven has good hospitals."

"I know we're going home and that you'll be taken care of, but when I saw the Trolls coming, I panicked. Suddenly I was the girl who ran when her village was slaughtered. Very few of us made it out that day and I thought I had put it behind me, but I was wrong. Their faces and screams came back and warning you to get out of the lift was all I could do. To tell you the truth, I was relieved when you told me to run and that's what I did. I didn't even look back. After I fled my village, I went to Winter Haven and joined the military thinking that I could face them. I wanted revenge and teaming

up with you was how I was going to get it. You Agents have a rep-
utation for killing Trolls and I thought I could be one of you, but I
can't."

Eric's heart sank. He'd heard this type of talk before ending with
the girl asking to be friends, or she thinks of him like a brother, but
this was a new one. She used him to kill Trolls and he could understand that, revenge was a powerful motivator. "And your eyes and
hair?" he asked, hoping she did it because she liked him.

"I shaved my head and got the lenses to make sure you'd like me.
I'm so sorry."

He slid his fingers off her knee. All his dreams for change joined
his dashed hope for companionship, but on a bright side, he didn't
have to grow up. He had plenty of time to bug Kole and pester
Enora before someone new crossed his path. "You did good Sophie.
I really thought you were into me, but thanks for telling me the truth
before I bought you flowers and took you out for dinner."

She smiled then wiped her eyes. "I'm sure you'll find someone
your speed. You are crazy and I thought I could match your level
of madness, but I was fooling myself. This isn't who I am, but I did
hear something. It's a secret and if old people find out about it they'll
shut down," she said sounding secretive then gave him the look that
told him that she wanted him to promise not to tell anyone.

"I won't say anything."

"Do you remember those drones that were used to broadcast
Mother Sarah's sermons?" she asked.

"Yeah, but there isn't anyone out there anymore to hear it. Well
not on this continent anyway."

"But the drones are still out there and some tech figured out a
way to use their network to store data. Since no one is watching
them anymore and the Trolls ignore them, the tech modified them
to stay close enough to each other to maintain the signal."

"You made a data network using the drones?" he asked, seeing
its potential, but worried that the Trolls would hack into it and infil-
trate Winter Haven electronically. "Won't the Trolls figure that out?"

"The guy who thought it up is a super tech and rumor has it that the setup layers of security to stop anyone who hasn't set up an account from accessing it," she said, assuring him that it would never happen.

"Why are you telling me this?"

"For safety, the drones move the information around between them and someone made a site where people can meet people. They post pictures and talk about their day. It's all secretive. Nobody uses their real name unless they choose to privately give it out."

Eric still couldn't see why she was telling him all this. He wanted to say that no system is impenetrable even if her super tech ghost was monitoring it, the Trolls can find a way in. It was bad news, but it was a good way to connect the world and bring people from across the planet together. He could tell by the look on her face that she wanted to make things right between them and by giving him this information it made them even in her eyes. "You're using it?" he asked, wondering if she had a secret boyfriend.

She nodded then said, "I found a support group that focuses on healing instead of revenge. I didn't understand what the others were talking about until I went on this adventure with you. I should have listened and not sought revenge. They warned me, but I thought they were being fluffy in their impotence. My last post was kind of mean. I told them that the only reason why they were in the forum was because they were too cowardly to grab a gun and put a bullet into a Troll's head. Once we get back to Winter Haven, I'm going to post an apology."

Eric chucked, but the shooting pain in his ribs made him flinch. "I have a feeling they'll forgive you," he said, understanding that emotional pain makes people do funny things. "You just called them names, it's not like you ate their children." She didn't laugh. She just looked at him with sad eyes and he thought he was being funny and put things into prospective, but somewhere his joke fell short.

Eric watched her eyes look around the forest. "You did very well here," she said. "I wasn't expecting to see you alive and if I didn't see you all messed up on the verge of death, I'd think you were an Alchemist."

Eric chuckled again then held his ribs to ease the pain. He was cold and it was getting dark, but was too tired to be miffed at Kole for taking so long to get back. He studied her expression, seeing the hint hate and mistrust in her eyes. She was never meant for him and if they got together, how long could he keep the secret that he's an Alchemist? She'd eventually find out and be very upset for not being told the truth. "No," he lied, "I'm not an Alchemist. I have no idea how I survived. I got lucky when I ran out of regular bullets. Those Ripper Rounds saved me. I'm so glad that someone had the foresight to make those, or I'd be in a Troll's stomach by now."

"Yeah," she said. "You're very lucky. Take care of yourself because one day your luck might run out."

He almost gagged, thinking that way could create a negative manifestation. He wanted to say something to cancel her curse, but thought that she might be testing him by making him say something an Alchemist would say. Instead he said, "I know. I thought I was dead, but at the last moment I came through." Silence fell between them and he could tell that she was about to bail then added, "You never told me how to access the drone network."

She stood then smiled down at him. "There's a coffee shop called Brews on the ground floor. Near the washrooms in the back is an old computer that looks broken. Hit the spacebar and when the screen activates type a happy face then you'll be able to create an account."

He half smiled at her. "Maybe we'll meet on a forum and connect without knowing it's us. Who knows, maybe we're meant to be together," he said to make her uncomfortable enough not to look back. He knew what he said was bogus, but wanted to burn his bridges so she wouldn't come back.

"You never know," she said without feeling then left him in the cold and coming dark.

Chapter

8

Jas hadn't left her hidden lab in days and felt gross. She ran her hands down the sides of her lab coat, feeling the bumps of her dress clothes underneath, making sure they hadn't bunched up then leaned, resting her lower back against the table. When James arrived from Europe, she expected him to contact her, but he didn't. She had been working hard on her virus and hit a couple of snags. Licking her finger to pick up James' hair did ended up confusing the computer after all. In her frustration, she went for a walk and decided to check in with James then found out he'd run off to save more people. Sarah had even left to attack a Troll stronghold. She didn't think there was anyone left to save, but people were still out there.

She took at James' absence as a sign that her virus was close to being completed and returned to her hideout with a renew vigor. It hadn't been easy for her to get as far as she had with the computers. She thought they knew what they were doing, but was wrong. They needed input, forcing her to learn things that she never needed to know. She was an Alchemist and could rearrange matter to suit her needs, but the virus didn't like her doing that. On her way back from her walk, she thought of something new and when she got back, she put it to the test.

She waited, leaning against the table with her arms folded across her chest. She closed her eyes, resting her mind. Numerous failures and troubleshooting had worn on her patience. There were times when she wanted to throw the computers through the wall, but stopped herself remembering that greatness came at a cost. Then the tester dinged instead of buzzed, she hated the buzz, it was part of the trigger that set her off. Her eyes shot open, but she didn't move. She wanted to enjoy the idea that the virus was ready and she no longer needed to mess with it. She let the good feeling soak in and filled her head with pleasant dreams of the future to shield herself from any disappointment. She didn't think she could take a negative result and believed that the computers knew that and were conspiring against her. That idea dominated a good portion of her thoughts wasting energy that should've been used to complete the virus. She ended up having to tell herself that she was being ridiculous, but her paranoia was so loud in her head, she had to yell at herself to shut it up. Her outburst and screams at nothing made her grateful she was alone.

Before she pushed off the table and checked her test results, the com in her ear went off. Her first thought was that James has returned in time to stop her and destroy the virus. She froze. Panic gripped her, bringing back the paranoid noise in her mind. Her head filled with stupid scenarios on ways to fight him, but she managed push away her fear. The com chimed again and her hand moved to answer it, but the noise in her head didn't subside. "Shut up!" she screamed, he voice reverberated off the walls silencing the noise. Satisfied that she'd put the voices in their place, she then answered the call.

"Hello, Jas," Sarah said sounding exhausted.

"You're back. How was your mission?"

"It was a complete failure and I'm very upset."

Surprised, she asked, "About what?" Somehow Sarah's upset superseded her test, telling Jas that she was expecting a failure, but the test dinged. That must be a good sign.

"It was a trap and we lost most of our forces. The Power Armor doesn't work and I was shot down."

Jas became interested in her story, putting the test in the back of her mind. "A trap, do you think someone told them you were coming?" she asked, thinking that it was impossible to find out. People could be using laser light and code from the top of the wall to convey information.

"No," she said, defusing Jas' escalating treasonous scenarios.

"How do you know, we could have a spy."

"Trust me, we don't have a spy. They had their people buried there. Trees grew over them. Now that's planning, but they were probably there to protect the stronghold and our presence woke them."

"But didn't you detect people there?" she asked, unable to move passed the idea of a traitor among them. She'd get her virus working then take over and soon have her empire up and running, but she couldn't tolerate traitorous scum lurking around her, striking from the shadows.

"It was biological material that confuses our sensors," she said getting more frustrated. "It doesn't matter. I'm upset that the Mayor and our military leaders refused to rescue us," she said then went quiet. She then spoke with a little heat in her voice saying, "I know I'm not supposed to feel this way because we're all in this together, but they abandoned me. After all that I did for these people, they left me to rot." Jas took a breath to say something supportive, but Sarah cut her off. "I almost died and a lot of people did. And then there's the matter of pushing through the Power Armor without properly testing it. I'm going to have someone's balls for that." She took a deep breath then slowly exhaled. "I'm not sure what I'm going to do, I want to fire them all, but I understand their point. They didn't want to weaken the city, but what are we fighting for, if not for each other?"

"Why don't you have some tea and take a hot bath," Jas said, thinking it'd calm her down so she'd be able to think strait.

"I don't want tea, or a bath," she said, adding a frantic pitch to her voice. "They're a bunch of jerks. When I see them, they're going to spin it in a logical way to justify why they left us to die, but I won't hear it. I've been ignoring their calls and will talk to them when I'm ready."

Jas didn't really know her, but she sounded like she was about to do something she'd regret and wanted to derail her frenzy before things worsened, asking, "If they didn't come get you, how did you get here?"

Sarah's sudden silence peaked Jas' curiosity. Jas waited. "We have access to a new weapon that destroys Troll flesh," she said, sounding oddly calm. "We used it to kill all the Trolls on their Battleships."

Jas could tell Sarah was hiding something. One moment she's off to fight the injustices of the world, the next she's calm. That didn't fit. "Spill it," she said, wanting in on the secret.

"There's nothing to spill. I'm not sure we should use the weapon."

"Why not, it kills Trolls," she said then wondered why Sarah would hesitate. "You said it killed all the Trolls on their Battleships allowing you to get out. What happened?"

"I was told that the weapon would kill the Trolls and leave the Battleships intact, but it didn't. It was a mess. The Trolls were disintegrated, if I can call it that. We're not sure what happened to them. All that was left of the Trolls was residue on the plating, a discoloration around where they stood. The hull also buckled, the metal became brittle and we had to shut down all their reactors. They were all on the verge of breach. I don't know what's worse, bombing the planet of using that weapon and causing something else bad to happen."

"It's the devil you know," Jas said. "Did you take samples for comparison so you can figure out what happened? You might be able to recalibrate your weapon." Jas looked around her secret lab and for the first time felt good about learning all that science stuff.

"Yes, I asked them to take samples. I wasn't going to send them out again later."

"So it's a beam weapon that can pass through walls and strike Trolls. I've never heard of such a weapon. And in order to hit all the Trolls on a ship it'd have to be big and the best place for it would be from above, because on the ground, there's too much in the way."

Sarah sighed. "I have no idea what you're talking about."

Jas laughed then asked, "Did Kole make it? I figured him more of a hammer guy. This weapon sounds like a scalpel, but it's very promising. It does sound better than bombs." She thought of James saying, "You can focus it, targeting one person and blow them apart, it sounds very promising indeed."

"Very promising indeed? You sound evil. I didn't tell you so you can copy the idea."

"I would've found out once all the Trolls are dead. Like me, people are going to wonder what happened and there'll be scavengers looking for lost loot, who'll come across enough information to piece it together. The best thing you can do is perfect the weapon, so it doesn't leave a hint that it exists. How are you going to spin it?"

"What do you mean?" asked Sarah.

"I assume that you have a way to make sure that all the Trolls will be killed and when they are, how are you going to use that information?"

"I was going to tell everyone that they are gone," she said sounding confused. "Their fears will need to be dispelled so they can leave and have lives."

"That's one way you can go," Jas said, thinking of a better way for when she takes over. She could use the Troll weapon and target the Ripper Gel exploding the lot then take over with no opposition. She'll also implement tests to find newborn Alchemists and deal with them then. She'll rule forever. "I have a better idea that'll work for both of us."

"I'm afraid to ask."

"Ouch that hurt. I'm trying to help," she said knowing that Sarah might not like her Idea at first, but thought she would warm up to it.

"I'm sorry. What's your idea?"

"Hear me out. What if after we kill all the Trolls, you don't tell anyone that they are gone?"

"Why would I do that?"

"Your ultimate goal is to take care of the Humans, right? Well, once the Trolls are gone, everyone will want to leave to strike out on their own. There'll be plenty of land to go around and some people might steal equipment and Flyers to go exploring. They'll want to be the first out there to loot, get the best lands, lay claim to mines and set up their little empires. They'll stop listening to you, but don't worry. They'll remember how much you comforted them. But words don't fill bellies."

Sarah was quiet and Jas let her words sink in. Sarah sighed then said, "Go on."

"You're going to need more time to guide the human race and letting them believe that the Trolls are still out there will keep them within reach until you've done your job. Then you can tell them that the war with the Trolls is finally over. You have to make a lie and stick with it. You can tell the people that there's a Human army out there fighting on their behalf, but have become too violent to return home, but in the end they all died in the final assault. Those fake people will be honored as heroes."

"It's true that some people will leave to find rich soil and minerals, but it won't be to line their pockets or to start empires. We will need colonies because this city can't sustain more growth. Locking people behind these walls in a prison of fear is more evil than what the Trolls are doing," she said, defusing Jas fearful manipulation. "People will separate and my work will take time. I had no illusions on that, but let me look at it from your point of view. You wish to use fear to create a society that'll be easy to control. And using my very promising idea, you could kill off all that oppose you. Which leaves another question, where's James in your plans, or is this his idea?"

"We both know that James wants to rule the world and there's nothing we can do to stop him, but what did you think was going to happen? This is James we're talking about. He'll probably set up a utopia and keep you around to suppress rebellion."

Sarah laughed. "If it's a utopia, why would I be needed to suppress an uprising? People will be too happy to do that."

It was Jas' turn to laugh at Sarah's naivety. "Who will do the menial tasks that no one wants to do? Even if they make machines to clear the sewer lines, collect the garbage and maintain the cities, there'll be a class system based on what job you do until not working becomes the ultimate wealth. Regardless of what you do, different social layers will emerge creating barriers, worlds within worlds. People who are last will think they're first with only the people at the top knowing better."

"Jas, I'm going to cut you off right there. The world in your head is too dark for me and quite scary. Let me tell you what's going to happen. James and I plan to rebalance the population by removing the fear and stress of the Trolls. We'll implement mandatory programs for the population to build the social tools to manage future stress and anxiety. If some refuse to manage their internal crap, eventually they will be outnumbered by happier people and learn by osmoses. In a way it'll be a lie. We'll say it's mandatory, but we won't enforce it. What it'll do is collect the honest people, those who want to make a better world and get them to police the rebels," Sarah said explaining then admitted, "Parts of what you said rings true. We'll eventually need automated services, but until then, we'll ask for volunteers to do the less desirable jobs because there are people out there who enjoy doing things that others don't. I want to give everyone a chance to choose what they want to do."

Jas gave her head a quick shake and wondered what drugs Sarah was on. She knew James and had done many shady deeds for him.

There was no way in her mind that James would make a future without him on top then realized that both Sarah's world and hers are one in the same. See could see the future of the human race as a balance of light and dark where those in the light never hear about those in the dark. And those that fall into the dark never return to the light. It was James' style to control what people see, hear and eat. This new vision of the future marked her totalitarian society as a foolish child's dream. Even with him out of the city and faraway, he was still schooling her. "You're right, Sarah," she said, deciding to get back on Sarah's good side because she was at the heart of James' plan.

"Right about what, that you need to learn tools to manage your stress and fear?" asked Sarah. "I can help you with that and together we can build a future based on love and freedom for our people."

Jas almost gagged then held in her laughter until it subsided. She wiped her eyes wondering how James puts up with her, but admitted to herself that Sarah is a very powerful tool. Once again James demonstrated his wisdom, patience and cunning. Her admiration for him almost made her rethink her plan to kill him. "I'm going to pass on learning your tools for now and learn by osmoses when the rest of the population conforms to your idea of what the future should be."

"We always seem to butt heads. You do know that we're on the same team, right? But, your ideas point to a different path of control and domination that I won't help you achieve," she said sounding absolute.

"Sarah, despite what you think, we are on the same path, I'm just being honest about it. The concept of freedom can only be measured by confinement. Everything is perception, vibration and balance and if you want to toy with them, you'll quickly learn that you should've never touched them in the first place."

"If we are on the same path, how would I succeed in building the future that I want?"

Jas couldn't stomach Sarah's bloated arrogance, but chose to focus on something positive instead of verbally slapping her. She accepted that in order to create her totalitarian society, she'd have to crush the will of her people, enslave those who resisted and eliminate all those in her way, much like James did to build his shadow. But Sarah wanted to force everyone into a future of her design for their own good without taking the responsibility of robbing them of their free will. "Your idea of tricking people to conform by forcing them to learn to deal with their crap is a good start. Controlling what people see and hear with your sermons is also a great idea. The power of assumption is an excellent tool and if done right, you can make people believe it their idea to make this better future. You see you have to manipulate their perception, vibration and balance until they gravitate toward the proper manifestation."

"You make it sound as evil as it is easy."

Jas laughed then said, "You have no idea of how dangerous messing with those forces is. James has been playing with them for a thousand years, but he's never told you about his failures, or the side effects he's created. It's easier to wipe the world clean and start again then to manipulate the collective manifestation of the planet, unless of course you're the one who made it. What I'm saying is that it's not easy and as for being evil, that falls into perception."

"You're telling me that James caused all this death so he can gain control of the world?"

Jas was confused, wondering if there was a miscommunication. "I thought you understood that."

"I didn't think he'd take over. I thought he did everything to return the human race to its proper place," she said then was quiet. "No you're wrong. I made James into the hero of humanity he didn't slap that title on himself. We want the same thing. He's out there right now saving people and where are you? You're in town messing with me and I don't appreciate it."

Jas knew that she'd lost Sarah's vote, perhaps never had it and decided that even though Sarah is a fantastic tool to keep the masses in line, she'd have to eliminate her at the right time. But for now, they can be friends. "I'm sorry if I've upset you. I wasn't messing with you. Manipulating the population is a very difficult and time consuming affair that requires a lot of energy. I was trying to give you the right advice and with getting your people to police themselves is an excellent start. You have to watch out for eddies in the flow of energy you're creating. I might sound negative, but I'm worried about you Sarah."

"No you're not, you're lying," she said astounded. "James told me once that the perfect lie is eighty percent truth and you've used that formula on me."

"Oh, pathetic Sarah, I was hoping that you'd follow me instead of James."

"I was never going to follow either of you!" yelled Sarah over the com into her ear. "I serve the human race and will aid whomever they put in charge!"

"It's my mistake," Jas hissed then spoke low and threatening, "I should've done this a long time ago when I had first had the thought, but I'm going to have to remake you. But don't worry, the new you won't have a problem kneeling before me."

Sarah gasped. "You're threatening to kill me?" she asked, sounding shocked. "James won't like that, but I suppose you have a plan to kill him too. You'd never be so bold without having something you could use against him." Her shock turned into a grim realization saying, "That's what you were talking about when I supposedly interrupted your supposed sexual encounter. You've been planning to betray him all this time."

The screaming in her head hurt her mind. "It's too late for you," she whispered then added her chipper tone, "See you soon."

Chapter

9

Sarah eyes widened. A chill run up her spine. Jas' last words had scared her, threatening to kill her. She had done that before, but this time the malice in her voice made it real. Jas went quiet then disconnected their call and Sarah took a moment to let their conversation sink in. She couldn't believe that Jas was coming to kill her. There was no question in her mind as to who she would follow because all of the Alchemist she'd met are a shade of crazy, Jas being the worst. She handled James, Kole, Eric, The King and even Byron with few problems, but all of them had been touched by madness. It was a matter of finding their twisted logic and using it to point them in the right direction, but there was no reaching Jas. She clutched her trembling hands to force herself to calm down then activated her view screen to call James.

His smiling face appeared on her screen. "Sarah, it's nice to see you," he said.

"I have a severe problem," she said, trying to control the fear in her voice.

He became somber then asked, "What's wrong?"

"Jas is coming to kill me."

James chuckled. "No, she wouldn't dare. You're under my protection," he soothed.

"Not anymore," she said then played back the end of their conversation. "When she went weird, I decided to start recording then led her on to find out her plans."

James leaned back, his face darkened on her screen looking sad. "What is wrong with the kids these days? This is depressing news. Maybe I should call her," he suggested, but Sarah didn't think it'd do any good.

"That's not going to happen. She'll tell you what you want to hear then kill me anyway and replace me with another clone. I need you, where are you?"

"I'm across the planet," he said. His eyes darted back and forth, frantically thinking. "Call Kole, he'll save you."

Sarah though of The King and the fight he had that destroyed an Ork city then said, "No, you can't be serious, they'll level the city. Everyone will die and all this will be for nothing. I need you here now, she's on her way."

"I won't get there in time, call Kole. But you might be right, you might have to take one for the team and I'll deal with her later. Don't worry I'll get you up and running again."

Sarah's jaw dropped. "Take one for the team and you'll pull a clone from the tank," she said, making sure she had heard him right. She imagined a room full of clones ready to be taken out of their tanks to replace her and her fear was replaced with anger.

James nodded then said, "That's what I'd do."

"No, you wouldn't," she seethed. "You lying, self centered, bastard, you're no better than Jas. You're wasting my time." She disconnected then placed a call to Kole.

Enora's face appeared on her screen. Sarah had met her before in the Arctic and hadn't seen her since. She had always dealt with Kole and the security system's recordings had her face blotched out when everyone else's was still fine, telling her that Enora wanted her privacy. "I need to speak with Kole," she said.

"Are you well, I can't help but hear the panic in your voice."

Sarah straitened her robe to keep her hands busy. "I have a unique problem that only you or Kole can deal with it. There is a special kind of assassin on their way to kill me and I would like to live," she said with a hint of begging, knowing that her time was running out.

Enora smirked then said, "Kole's in the hospital with Eric and I don't want to disturb him. I'll handle your assassin, besides I need a distraction anyway. I feel bad for not being there for Eric."

Hearing that Enora was going to help her took some of the stress away and she finally was able to focus. She'd been so angry at her people for leaving them to die she'd forgotten to thank Enora for saving them. "You created the weapon that saved us, thank you. I have samples for you to look at so you can perfect your weapon."

She scrutinized her. "You have a sample? Have you told anyone about the weapon?"

She imagined Jas kicking in her door and blasting her into oblivion then calmed, but added stress to her voice to spur things along, saying, "We needed ships so I sent a small group of people over to steal what they could, but the ships were all too badly damaged. My people gave me the sample, no questions asked." Enora stared at her wanting more. She groaned. "Yes, I told one person and now they're on their way to kill me. She went psycho after figuring it out by herself. Now she wants to kill me and James, so she can take over the world."

Enora's face slowly changed from serious to a slight smile. She laughed then said, "That's funny. I have no problem with your friend killing James. In fact, all I have to do is nothing and the world will be rid of his evil. Kole and I can kill your friend later, one evil at a time, you understand."

She could feel the heat in her cheeks. "You Alchemists suck, no wonder the world ended with you self centered morons in charge. Fine, I'll die, but it's your inaction that has killed me!"

Sarah didn't want to spend the last moments of her life spitting hate, but Enora raised her hand, stopping her from continuing her rant. "I'm teasing," she said. "I'm sorry. It's Kole's influence on me. I'll save you, but know that you alone put yourself in the line of fire." Enora then tapped her screen, disconnecting the call.

Sarah breathed a sigh of relief, but doubted Enora would get there in time. She decided to be happy and spend the last moments of her life doing what she loved, brewing tea. But if Enora does arrive in time and her and Jas have a short and tidy fight leaving everything intact, the victor can enjoy the tea.

She finished her tea and placed it on an elegant tray then carried it to the coffee table. Knowing that it may be her last tea, she placed her focus, intent and love into it, making it special. She smiled at the teapot then felt Jas' presence. She turned to see Jas looking not herself. Her oily skin and smeared makeup darkened her crazed violet eyes and her wavy dirty hair was pulled back into a loose ponytail. She stood quietly in her ruffled grey trim suit and pink blouse, but Sarah could feel her murderous intent rolling off of her. "Tea?" asked Sarah, hoping to stall or negotiate her way out.

Jas' eye twitched then she reached out, but nothing happened. Instead to Sarah's surprise, Jas levitated off the ground. She floated a couple of feet into the air then spun around before shooting through the room and slamming her back against the wall. Sarah had never seen an Alchemist attack anyone and wondered if this was part of the show then Enora walked in wearing a white robe in a similar fashion to Sarah's. Her long strait blonde hair flowed over her shoulders and her red lips looked stunning against her pale skin. Her bright blue eyes shone with a deep wisdom making Sarah want to know her, to see if she was as mad as every Alchemist she'd met.

"Who is this?" asked Jas in a threatening tone while struggling against her invisible bonds.

Enora ignored her and walked up to Sarah. "Mother Sarah," she said then gave a slight nod. "I know we've met before, but let's count this as a formal meeting."

Sarah nodded back then said, "Enora, please call me Sarah."

"Enora, I've never heard of you," Jas said then threatened, "You better let me go or my teacher will gut you."

Enora turned to Jas. "I've already been gutted by your boss, your threats are meaningless. Now shut your mouth, I want to share tea with Sarah."

Sarah smiled and felt comforted by Enora. She was happy to share her tea with someone who appreciated it and who treated her like a person. She gestured to her sofa. "Please sit," she said then sat. She poured the tea with shaking hands, but was careful not to spill any. She then handed Enora the teacup and saucer.

Enora took a sip. "I've been looking forward to this since the Arctic. You make good tea."

Sarah blushed. "Thank you," she said.

Jas kept struggling against Enora's hold, but failed to set herself free. She then mocked throwing up. "I think I'm going to be sick," she said. "You two are so sugary sweet it makes me sick." She glared at Enora and asked, "Who are you?"

Enora took another sip then quietly enjoyed it before answering, "My answer won't satisfy you. And the truth is I don't want to tell you. I like this tea and you're ruining it." Enora went quiet and stared at Jas then said, "You silly little thing, you've been modified by James."

"He made me stronger."

"Not strong enough to stop me from pinning you to the wall. It doesn't look like you're having a good day. You look crazy and speaking about that, how's your mind been? Are you hearing voices, or experiencing paranoia?"

Jas' eyes narrowed and her lips pressed together refusing to answer.

Enora turned to Sarah then asked, "How's your day been?"

Sarah shifted in her seat to face Enora and ignored Jas. What Enora was talking about interested her, it was the first time anyone has hinted about the source of the Alchemical madness in her colleagues. "I could talk about my day, but what you just said intrigues me. You think she's mad?"

Enora laughed. "I know she is. I can see it. She's still there, but buried under layers of garbage." She smiled warmly then continued saying, "You look confused, let me explain. Your friend has been modified by a stronger person and by looking at the thumbprint it was James who did it. He wove abilities into her, making her think she's stronger, but that's not how knowledge works. Everything we learn takes energy to hold and if a piece of knowledge is too great for us, it falls out and we forget it. Sometimes, a person will have a moment of clarity that gets swallowed up leaving them with a feeling that they've understood something big, but lost it."

Sarah couldn't remember feeling that way, but didn't want to argue and distract Enora.

Enora continued, "Before the Purge, there were experiments to modify people. They wanted to see if an Alchemist could be created, but the subjects went insane before destroying themselves." She looked at Jas and asked, "You look like you're on the path of self-destruction, how do you feel?"

Jas glared, but was listening.

Astounded at the revelation, Sarah couldn't help but ask, "You were around before the Purge?"

Enora nodded then took a sip of tea.

Jas rolled her eyes then looked at Sarah. "She's lying, you idiot," she said. "Do you know how many people have claimed they were around before the Purge?"

Sarah had no reason to doubt Enora and didn't want to take Jas' bait and force Enora to back up her claim. Her conversations with Kole and now Enora has been open and honest, a welcome relief from the other Alchemists she had known.

Enora placed her teacup down then said, "Before the Purge, we called those experiments, alterations. Foreign elements were woven into a person's mind in the belief that the person was being improved. What really happened is hard to explain. When something was added to a person, their mind worked to expel it." She looked at Jas and continued saying, "And since James is stronger than you, your mind ended up entangled in the mess he created. It starts off slow and you have access to greater power, but your mind knows that the alteration doesn't belong there. Because your mind can't remove the alteration, you become a caged animal that's slowly driven mad. In reality, there are no cheats and a person has to earn their power, slowly evolving to be able to purchase greater knowledge. In my time, what James did to you is a crime."

Sarah refilled Enora's cup then sipped hers, not understand the full implication of what Enora was talking about, but knew enough to hear the answer to her question. James made Jas, The King and Byron crazy. He turned them into what he wanted and all their foul crimes were on his shoulders. She looked at Jas, seeing the misery on her face then asked, "Can you help her? And if you can, does that mean you're stronger than James?"

"Unfortunately I'm not as strong as James. Seeing the work in your friend showed me that, but in this case there are two sides to this story. I'm strong enough to help her mind eject his influence. What he built was never meant to be, giving her a way out."

"Don't touch me!" spat Jas.

"I have to," Enora said matter-of-factly. "There's no other choice. If I let you go, you'll kill Sarah then James and I don't have a problem with you killing him, but if he knows you're coming, it's too late for you. All he has to do is undo what he did before you get close enough. Frankly, I'm surprised you're still alive."

Sarah was confused asking, "You mean James could've killed her before she got here?"

"Yes. He has placed his power within her and can remove it at anytime from anywhere. The notion of distance falls under perception and with the Universe connecting everyone, there is no distance when it comes to power."

"What a jerk," Sarah said, remembering how he acted when she had called him. He acted concerned for her wellbeing and pretended he couldn't help when all along he could've lifted a finger and saved her.

Enora gazed at Jas then raised her hand and gently swayed it in the air. Jas grunted. Her eyes clamped shut and teeth clenched. She threw her head back, banging against the wall. Sarah watched imagining the invisible struggle between the two then Enora released Jas, crumpling her to the floor in a heap.

"Is she dead?" asked Sarah.

"No," Enora answered then laughed. "It's more like she's rebooting."

Sarah didn't laugh, but could see the comparison between a mind and a computer. Enora removed a virus on Jas' hard drive and Jas' mind needed to reorganize itself, so it turned off. "Is she fixed?"

"I've restored to who she was before James corrupted her, but for all I know I did more damage. If it were me, I'd be happy to be free, but she didn't give me permission."

She looked at Jas sleeping on the floor in an uncomfortable position and wondered what type of person she was going to be when she woke up, but a frightened whisper in the back of her mind worried that Jas would finish what she started. She turned to Enora asking, "Can you take her with you when you leave? I don't feel safe around her."

"I can take off your hands, but you'll be fine. Do you have a gun?"

"A gun won't stop her."

"Sure it will. She won't be able to use her Alchemy for a while, besides she'd forgotten how to access her power, it's a side effect of leaching off of someone else's power. And I'm looking forward to dragging her away. I'm curious to find out what she's been up to lately. Kole and I will have some questions for her."

"James isn't going to like that."

Enora took her cup and sipped. "I wonder what he thought was going to happen. If Kole came, he would've seen the corruption within her and in the middle of their fight, unplugged her. He's could've done it, so it makes me wonder what James wanted."

She wanted to help Enora, but couldn't see why James wanted

Kole and Jas to face off. "I have no idea," she confessed.

Jas moaned then pushed herself against the wall. She sat with her eyes half closed looking at Sarah. "I came to kill you, didn't I?" she asked then slowly shook her head. "I'm sorry, that's not like me."

Sarah didn't believe her and searched her face for a hint that Jas was lying and waiting for a chance to strike at her.

"Do you remember James?" asked Enora.

"Of course I do. I've worked for him for years, but I feel different now," Jas said then looked confused. "I can't think. My mind is slipping away. What did you do to me? You wrecked it."

Sarah wanted to trust that Enora had helped Jas, but in her heat she didn't want to. She never liked any of James' Alchemists and was happy that Jas was the last one. "Enora, are you sure she can't use her power?"

"Yes, her connection will take time to rebuild, but there's something wrong here. Usually when a person is freed from the alteration, they feel better, not worse, unless she was crazy to begin with."

Sarah didn't feel better hearing that and said, "I'm going to carry a gun. Jas, if you come near me, I'm going to shoot you." Sarah expected a flash of understanding to flicker across her face, but Jas didn't react. She sat there, a mess and looked used up. "I figured out the reason why James wanted Kole to deal with her. It's because he no longer needs Jas and wanted to make room for Kole to join him."

"No," Jas disagreed. "James knows that Kole will never join him. But James also won't hurt him, well not yet anyway. He believes that Kole has helped him in ways he couldn't foresee, making Kole part of his manifestation. I could go into it, but it's too far out there for either of you to believe. And Sarah, I'm sorry for trying to kill you. I feel better now."

Sarah placed her cool cup on her coffee table and chose her words saying, "It wasn't just you. All of you Alchemists are nuts and dealing with your kind had aged me. I have grey hairs. I'm stressed from wondering if one of you is going to level Winter Haven. The thought plagues me at night and there's nothing I can do to stop you. And Kole is no different. He threatened to kill me too. I can see his point though, but the look he gave me showed me his crazy."

Enora smiled. "And me?"

She looked at Jas and said, "You were right. Kole is a hammer and Enora is the scalpel. Enora you look calm, but deep within you is an inferno of rage aching to get out."

Enora leaned closer and placed her hand on Sarah's lap then said, "I hear you and understand that you've been under a lot of stress. It's been a busy week and when you finally made it home, one of your people tried to kill you. That must suck, but don't worry about Kole. He sees James' vibration in you. He might not know what he's looking at, but that's what he has a problem with. We're not going to hurt you. You've done a lot for your people and have sacrificed so much to keep things together. We can see it, that's why we're here."

Enora's kind words from the heart touched Sarah deeply. Her people compliment her all the time, but she was never sure if it was because of her power, or if they truly meant it. Then they left her to die, showing her the truth about her power and that hurt her, making her feel unappreciated. Sarah slid across the cushion and wrapped her arms around Enora in a hug. Warm tears flowed down her cheeks melting the last of her stress, rejuvenating her.

The people she'd left in charge had failed her, succumbing to fear instead of embracing their humanity to fight for those in need. And now she had to rip the command structure apart to rebuild it, placing the right people in the positions of power who understand the value of an individual's life. She understood their logic to sacrifice the few to protect the many, but was miffed to find out that they didn't even look for a secondary Troll force that could've attack once the city was weakened. As far as they knew, they could've rescued the people at the stronghold without worry. She pushed herself away from Enora then wiped her eyes. "Thank you Enora, I needed that," she said feeling grateful for Enora's kind words.

Looking hurt and confused, Jas slid up the wall, pushing herself to her feet. She glared at Enora and hissed, "You had no right to touch me. I'm going to tell James what you did to me and get him to fix it. I'm leaving don't even try to stop me."

Sarah gestured to Jas then asked Enora, "Are you going to stop her? You mentioned questioning her." She sounded petty to her own ears, but was still mad at Jas for trying to kill her.

Jas walked up to Enora then stopped and waited for her answer.

Enora met Jas' eyes saying, "No, I'm good."

Jas left with the muffled sound of a door closing.

Enora smiled at Sarah then said, "Now that we're along. I can see that something other than Jas is bothering you. Come on spill it."

Sarah wanted to talk about it, but didn't have anyone she could trust with what she had to say. She decided to take a chance on Enora and get it off her chest. She took a deep breath then slowly exhaled, stalling, trying to think of something to blame, but decided to tell her the truth. "I have feelings for someone and I treated him badly. I feel terrible, he got hurt and it was my fault."

"All of this stress and anxiety is over your feelings for a man?"

"You don't understand. I can't have feelings…"

"Or society will fall apart?" asked Enora, interrupting her.

Sarah didn't like feeling exposed and said, "Ha, ha, make fun of me, but I'm serious. Part of what I do is to wear the uniform of a spiritual leader. It creates a door in people's minds allowing my words to be heard. Uniforms are important because they put you into a predetermined judgment in another person's mind. Every group has a uniform and part of mine is to be physically unavailable. It puts me onto a higher level. Women won't compete with me and men will want me because I'm unattainable. And if I indulge in my feelings, I'll fall off my pedestal and loose my position. People will stop listening to me. I'll be excluded from the major decisions and punished because they'll think I deceived them. What makes it all worse is that I'm upset because I want it all."

Enora laughed then said, "We all want it all and that's normal, but it sounds like you made up your mind. I do feel for you, but search your heart. You can still do your thing with a man beside you."

"It won't be the same. Sure people will be happy for us, but I'll end up giving up the larger picture. I'll lose footing and won't be able to help rebuild the human race. When I weigh the future with what I want, I feel terribly selfish. I also feel bad because I was deliberately awful to him. I didn't even visit him in the hospital."

"You're pushing him away," Enora said. "But there's a simple way to figure out what you truly want, flip a coin." She smiled then continued saying, "Don't look at me like that. If you flipped a coin right now, heads, you go to him and tails, you don't. Ask yourself, what would it feel like if it came out heads?"

The turmoil in her heart lessened and she was able to feel the answer. She truly didn't want to be with him. She wanted to help build the future and in time when she was no longer needed, she might find someone then. She smiled, feeling peace warm her heart. "Thank you Enora. As much as I hated being terrible to him, I did the right thing. I'll get him promoted then sent to a different department."

"It's hard to choose what you want without feeling that you've missed out on something else, embrace your decision and be happy. You mentioned that you have a sample for me, can I get it from you?"

"I'll be right back," Sarah said then got up. She left the room and went down the hall to her office where she retrieved the sample then brought it to Enora. "I personally held on to it because I know how important it is to your work and didn't want anyone examining it. It'd open up too many questions. I could explain away the satellites and say that they were around since the Purge, but it's the idea of the weapon that worries me. Are you going to destroy them once the Trolls are gone?"

"Yes, I'll dissolve them and add them to the void of space. I can't chance that one of the satellites will survive reentry and fall into the hands of someone who'll use it. I can't let that happen, so what I'm going to do is recalibrate the weapon, vaporize the Battleships then take care of the Trolls. What are we going to do about the people who took the sample and explored the ships?"

Sarah didn't like the cold look in Enora's eyes and felt her gaze burrowing into her. She didn't want to say anything, knowing that it was a death sentence for those she sent to the Battleships, but knowledge of the weapon was that dangerous. "Since I didn't know what to expect, I took the precaution and had them quarantined. You and Kole didn't keep me in the loop and for all I knew, a viral agent was used. I questioned them personally and isolated them to keep the information from leaking."

"I didn't want your people involved. I told Kole to investigate to keep your people safe, but Eric got hurt and Kole forgot about the Battleships. Now here we are."

"Here we are," Sarah echoed. She gave the order and sent her people in, making it her responsibility to silence them. After the Trolls are gone, any story could be told to explain what happened. The Trolls ran out of food and consumed each other was her favorite lie and the most believable one. Or, the Trolls encountered a flesh eating virus from deep with some jungle and it spread across the planet ending them. Those stories were more believable then telling her people that the Trolls were killed in battle. And once Enora figures out what's wrong with her weapon, the war will be over. Too soon for her people to believe that they won by force and without the aid of an Alchemist. "I'll take care of my people," she said. "I'll say they encountered a plague on the ships that had killed the Trolls and infected them. They'll die peacefully then I'll incinerate their bodies. But if there was another way to insure their silence, I'd take it."

Enora nodded sympathizing with her. "I'd love to reassure you and tell you that you're going to do the right thing, but it doesn't seem that way. Knowledge is power and an idea can shape the world. For all I know, my weapon could be used to set off earthquakes creating tsunamis, damaging the Earth's crust to eventually break the planet apart. Or it could be used as a race weapon, which I don't want James to know about."

"Speaking about James, what should I tell him? He will want to know."

A dangerous look crossed her face. "It occurred to me that I'll have to deal with him, not out of hate, but for the same reason that you're going to execute your people for. No matter what lie you tell him, he'll be able to see through it and find the truth. He will be able to feel my weapon's influence in the ground and find traces of the Trolls. He'll connect with the Universe and trace the vibration of my weapon its source then have the weapon that'll end his race war."

Sarah's day went from bad to worse. Jas had come to kill her and now if she didn't play her cards right she knew Enora would finish what Jas started. It wouldn't be personal, but if she defended James, Enora would see her as a threat and remove her. "This has been a really bad week for me," she said and met Enora's eyes. "I've always been on the side of the human race and have chosen to give everything I am to it, but it seems that you Alchemists are destined to collide with each other. No matter who survives, I'll always be on the side of humanity. You are all insane and it's sad that we're at your mercy. Just do me a favor when you try to kill James, make sure you're far away so none of my people pay the price."

Enora cold eyes warmed. "I like you and I'll always know where you stand, it's nice. I'll make you a deal. If you keep my existence and weapon a secret, when we come for James, we'll do it far here."

To her surprise, the thought of keeping information from James felt good. She thought it would've been harder to betray him, but after knowing that he altered Byron, The King and Jas, turning them into monsters made it easy. "For humanity's sake, you have a deal."

"Is James serious about building rockets and launching the other races into space? It's an old joke. Lets launch everything we don't like into space, there's plenty of room out there."

"Honestly, I don't think he was serious, but if he is, he'll need the Trolls as leverage to motivate the others to leave. But since you're going to get rid of the Trolls before the rockets and ships are built, that plan will fade."

"Not if the other races use Alchemy. As far as I know, they still have Alchemists."

She had forgotten that the other races use Alchemy and wondered if they had already left. "Where are the other races? They've all disappeared."

Enora shrugged then said, "Does it matter? They took off when we needed them the most. If they would've come together, we'd all be better off right now." She shook her head, looking disappointed then continued saying, "It's an old argument. We think the Dwarves went underground, but that wouldn't stop the Trolls, so we're not sure that they're still around. We also figured that the Orks went either above or into the ocean and as for the Elves. We think they've made a city and are in orbit, but we're guessing. The truth is that, we have no idea where anyone is."

"No idea? I guess it's safer for everyone that way besides, they'd never trust anything James built for them. I think it was Kole that said that James would fire them into the sun, he's probably right. But the only thing that I'm concerned with is finding the nearby hidden Troll army. With this whole stronghold debacle, it'd be stupid for them to lure us away from Winter Have and not have a way to exploit our weakness. I think they buried their people here when they had first attacked. Can you find them for us?"

"Yes, I'll take your sample, modify my weapon then test it on the Trolls around Winter Haven." Her eyes shifted away, looking distant. "I know that it's not much, but I want to give my condolences for the people you're going to handle. It's unfortunate, but you would've sent them in anyway. Someone had to salvage a ride."

Confused, it took Sarah a moment to back track their conversation then asked, "What are you thinking?"

"Sometimes it's hard to see your individual path. I was going to let everything that James has done to the world slide, but things have changed. If Eric didn't get hurt, Kole would've went alone to the Battleships and you would've found your way home like you did. But our conversation wouldn't have happened and I wouldn't have seen that James needs to be taken care of to safeguard the future. He'll figure out what I did then go after everyone he doesn't like. Here I was, I was going to let it all go and live on the beach with Kole somewhere, but knowing James, he would've wrecked it. In the end, I guess it's a good thing that your people went in."

She thought about her earlier talk with Jas and compared it to what Enora had said. She wondered if Jas would've come to kill her if Eric hadn't of gotten hurt, believing that the talk of the weapon had set everything off then said, "Ripples, I guess."

"Yes, everything ripples outward. You never know, the decisions that we made today might save millions in the future."

It was the guessing game she didn't like. It was a different story when she saw things unfold in front of her than to guess what the future holds. For all she knew, the world is conspiring to kill off the human race and James has been the good guy the whole time. She shut down her "what if machine" and changed the subject asking, "How's Eric doing?"

"Physically he's doing well. Your doctors are phenomenal, they patched him up and he'll be fine with some bed rest. What he did was foolish, but almost dying for it made him look stupid and lucky, but best of all, it made him look normal. His idiocy is collecting quite the following. Kole and I are stunned at the hero worship. Eric's getting get well gifts from strangers. It's all going to his head and we're worried that this behavior will escalate to the point where he'll do something so dumb it'll kill him."

"I heard that there was a woman involved."

"Yes, the vile heartbreaker. The harpy that sang her song and tricked him into doing what he did. Those are his words. When

Kole found out that it was all about a girl, he was so mad it took me all day to calm him down. I'm just glad that the doctors wouldn't let Kole see him until he had calmed down, or the disaster would've kept building. But when Kole saw Eric bandaged up, all black and blue, he didn't do much yelling."

"Eric is lucky to be alive. The vile harpy, Sophie, her report wasn't clear. She did say that she convinced him to act and together they slapped armor onto hover-lift then went into battle. Later she ran away, but returned when it was over. She put in a transfer for a desk job."

"So I've been told. There's a lot of gossip floating around," Enora said then stood. Her robe shifted, cascading down her body to fall into place.

Sarah watched the beautiful flow of her robe and gasped. "What material is that? I'm always fussing with my robe and yours looks like you just put it on."

"I don't know I haven't looked at it. I found it in the front window of a store in the garment district," she said then chuckled. "It was named after you, so I had to buy it incase I'd meet you again." She reached into her robe and produced a business card. "I knew you'd like it, here's their card."

Sarah graciously stood then took the card. "Thank you. Let me show you out," she said then walked Enora to the door. She locked up after they said their goodbyes then to calm her nerves, she wandered her home. She slowly checked all the hiding places and made sure that Jas wasn't hiding in her bathtub, waiting for a chance to murder her.

Chapter

10

Jas closed the door behind her and walked out onto Sarah's landing pad where she'd parked her hover-bike. She felt empty, hollowed
out and confused. She remembered leaving her lab and running
through the tunnels deep under Winter Haven to her hidden landing
pad where she kept her bike, a smaller model of the one she had
seen in the Troll Capital. She was in a hurry to get to Sarah and kill
her, but the part of her that knew why was gone, swallowed up in
the blackened mess of her mind.

She walked up to her bike then hesitated. She didn't want it anymore and didn't know why she had it built. It was a trophy, a reminder of all the pain she'd caused the Trolls. She liked causing
things pain, but everything about her felt off. Her taste in clothes,
hair style and her very skin felt wrong. She thought about her virus
and couldn't place its importance. Earlier, it was the center of her
existence, a means to power that would grant her domination over
the world. Now, global domination was the furthest thought in her
mind.

James had shown her peace, creating order to the growing confusion in her head. She thought back to when she was younger. She

believed she was content and happy in her life, but didn't know truth. She didn't understand what she was and went looking for something to define herself. She found James and he convinced her to join him. That was when he first altered her, bringing clarity. It was something small and simple that had changed her life. After that she became hungry for possessions, love, respect and power. James became her father figure, who she tried to please, but never could. Whenever he'd be happy with her, inside she felt he was humoring her. Something inside her robbed her of contentment sending her into spiral of self-loathing, a festering seed that grew into hate and mistrust, adding to her violent past.

She wanted to be angry and toss the hover-bike off the landing pat, but didn't feel it. A flash in her mind drove the confusion away. She was alive, well and free. She could do anything and go anywhere, or could've without the Trolls running around. She was in such a hurry to kill Sarah that she forgot to check her latest test results. Her virus might be ready then laughed at the thought. It figured, now that she was free she'd no longer need it, but destroying the virus felt wrong. She no longer wanted to use, but also wanted to keep it.

She slung her leg over the bike's seat then started it, but didn't know where to go. She didn't want to stay there incase Enora wasn't finished with her, but knew Enora could find her no matter where she went. In a way she was still pinned to the wall. When her mind had cleared she could see into the depth of Enora's power. It was frightening, but warm. James on the other hand was as cold as his eyes.

Jas shook her head casting out the thought of James' eyes and of what could be then focused on the now. She turned her bike off and watched the colors of the city change with the coming of dusk. The city had grown and Sarah was right, it needed to expand. Hover vehicles flew between the tall buildings and far below the mass filled the streets. She wondered where everyone was going and thought about hanging out with a random stranger to see what life was really about, but didn't want to come off as a creeper. She had met way too many people who had tried to do to her what she wanted to do to someone else. Was she that lonely?

In one moment she knew what she wanted and had plans to get it, even though it was to conquer the world and plunge it into tyranny, the next was confusion and apathy. She wanted to wake from the darkness and please James. It was all the please him, even becoming smarter and stronger than him, so that when he was dying, he'd know he was going to be replace with someone better. She laughed again. She argued with herself. She no longer needed his approval, but wanted closure. She had questions that only he could answer. As sad as it was, the young woman inside her wanted to know why he crushed her soul and turned her into a coldblooded monster. Or was she already that way and he gave her the ability to focus. She could leave and be free never to know why, but she wanted her personal power back. She knew that her connection to her Alchemical power would return, but telling James off would make her feel much better. She then knew what to do. She'd return to her lab and make sure the virus was completed then confront James when he returns and tell him how bad of a father he is.

She started her bike again then took off, dropping to a merge altitude. Getting closer to dinner time, the lanes had thinned out making it easier for her to make her way back to the lab. She needed to know if the virus was ready, but wasn't in a hurry to get there. She meandered her way through the tunnels to her secret lab then slowly went through the data to learn that the virus was ready. She was shocked and had to read through the test results again to make sure her mind wasn't making it up. The virus would indeed strip James of his Alchemy and return him to a normal person, but she didn't want to be the one to use it. She loved and hated James at the same time and decided that she'd hurt enough people. She'd tell James off then disappear, but also needed to tell someone that the virus existed. It was the right thing to do.

Jas thought of Enora and how powerful she was then compared her to James then realizing how foolish she was to ever think that

James didn't know about her secret lab. There was a chance that he didn't, but if he knew that she went to kill Sarah, he'd assume that she'd have a way to try to kill him. He would cast his awareness over the city, searching for her fingerprint and find her lab. She'd never be allowed to leave and didn't want to serve him anymore, leaving only one possible outcome, her death.

She had to be smart and play it right, or he'd find her virus. She took the vial out of the tester then held it to the light, examining it one last time then slid it into a foam lined metal suit case. Since the virus reacted with anything Alchemical, her Alchemical finger print wasn't on any part of the container and all she needed to do was destroy her lab and hide the virus. She shut the case then locked it, leaving it in the middle of the table where the hair originally sat. She raised her hand, reaching out then forced a connection with the Universe, feeling power trickle through her. She focused like she did when she was a little girl, building the power between her hands until she was able to use it. She then pointed her palm at each machine, sending her awareness into them to destroy the information on their drives.

Sweat trickled down her temple and over her cheek. She brushed it away then wiped her forehead with her sleeve. Her exertion reminded her of who she used to be, bringing her back to when she thought she was a good person. She wanted to do great things, but just for her. Everyone else would learn to love what she did, or be used as an example for future generations, she would have no complaints. Looking back, James hadn't changed her too much. She had always been herself, only a different shade of the original color.

Once she finished destroying all traces of information, she doused the room in various chemicals then incinerated her equipment. She returned the wall to normal then walked back the way she came carrying the case. The only questions on her mind was where she was going to hide the virus and how she was going to get there without the video feed tracking her. By now, James would've tapped into the feed and seen where she went. She knew she was on borrowed time and counted on James' arrogance. He has all the cards and power. He'd take his time coming home then deal with her when he saw fit, Winter Haven would be his.

She'll meet with him and get her feelings off her chest then he might kill her, but she'll never tell him about the virus. It was her last trick. She'll have to entrust the virus to someone who'd have the will to use it. She thought of Kole, but Enora was clearly the stronger. She knew Kole, or the type of person he was, but Enora is powerful enough to be unpredictable. She couldn't decide between the two of them, but it didn't matter, she no longer knew what she was doing and why.

Jas grabbed a fist full of hair and pulled. The pain cleared away the darkness clouding her thoughts. She knew that using the video feed, James would follow her every move. He'd know who she gave her virus to. Jas felt her power slowly building, but wasn't powerful enough to knock out the city's surveillance and the fear of James watching her gave way to paranoia. She didn't know what drones he was using to spy on her, so she decided to hide the case in plain sight. She turned around and wondered the tunnels looking for a cubby hole to stash her loot then once done, she returned to her bike then went to the hospital.

Though she had never met Kole, she had seen surveillance footage of him. She passed in through the emergency then asked around and found him asleep in a chair beside his apprentice who looked mangled. She couldn't help it and snuck in, stepping close to Eric, careful not to wake him. He lay there half covered in bandages. She examined the yellowish bruising across his face. He was a mess of art with all his piercings and tattoos. What he did on his exterior made her wonder what her emotional body looked like with all her layers of emotional scars and remade emotions.

She backed away then crept up to Kole who slept with his chin against his chest, dressed in a new set of blue coveralls. Jas wanted to used her com and call him with a delayed message, but with all the drones buzzing around, James would intercept her digital message and kill it before it was delivered. A traditional note slipped into a sleeping man's pocket would have to do. At least she knew that due to privacy, the hospital rooms were surveillance free. She backed away then left the room. She thought about wondering the halls to visit different rooms to throw James off her trail, but all he'd have to do it see the Kole's name on the visitor's list and know who she came to meet, but with not staying long , she could say that she couldn't find him.

Jas took so many precautions, trying to outthink what she thought James would do and made elaborate plans, but doubted James cared enough to be thorough. The whole time she knew him, he barely cared about anything but his precious plan. Even after she had her hand in Byron's murder, he sent an investigator instead of looking himself. Thinking back, she was sure that she would've been caught. Her fuzzy mind believed she was untouchable, but now it was time to pay up and she was okay with that. Now all she wanted to do is get to her bike then ride up the tallest building and watch the sunset. It was a simple want and a beautiful idea that she could use to calm her mind and when James returns, she'll apologize for trying to kill Sarah.

Chapter

11

Eric lay in the hospital bed on the edge of sleep, resting his eyes when a figure darkened his doorway. He was sore, even with all the painkillers and didn't want to move, so he pretended to sleep, peeking one eye at a woman he'd never seen before. She stepped into the room and he closed his eye. He fattened his awareness, pushing it outside of his body to watch her lean her face close to his. She was pretty, but smelled. She needed a wash, but she was good looking enough for him to look past that, for now. He felt her soft breath on his cheek and felt the heat off her skin against his, becoming aroused. He lay still, relaxing, trying to think of anything but the attractive woman whose face was close enough for him to kiss then it ended. She backed away.

Her heat faded and he was sad to feel her go, but watched her sneak over to Kole who slept in the chair beside him. When Kole first walked into the room, his eyes burned with rage. Eric though he was going to lose it, but then his eyes softened, showing him how worried he was. The look reminded him of when he was a boy and he'd scraped a knee. But that was before the Ripper training. Kole got meaner after that. But for now it was a nice reminder that the original Kole was still in there.

After the drugs kicked in, he didn't have a problem relaxing and sharing his feeling about everything including how attractive the nurses were. They were nice, but not into him and he was glad that he could still get up to use the bathroom instead of getting them to change his bedpan. Then the lady came and his first thought was that she was another fan coming to give him a get well gift. The best gift so far was the raisin spice cookies an attractive older woman had given him then told him to come by her shop for more when he felt better. He thought the "more" was something else, but it was just for the cookies.

He watched the lady in her nice fitting suit sneak up to Kole to slip a note into his pocket. He couldn't help but feel jealous. Kole was getting all of the girl's attention, first Enora then Sarah and now this little thing, but if he woke up now before Kole, he could have her all to himself. But he had a better idea. He needed to protect Enora from this new hussy who slipped a secret love letter into Kole's pants. He waited a couple of minutes after she left, confident that he'd get his chance to woo her later then quietly pulled his sheet off his leg and painfully moved to Kole's side, retrieving the note.

"Yoink," he whispered then smiled at Kole.

Kole's eyes shot open, meeting his gaze. Kole squinted moving his head back then asked, "Why are you so close to me grinning like an idiot? Did you fart? If you farted, I'm going to…" He shook his head in annoyance then said, "You're so lucky your hurt, or I'd do something bad to you."

"I need to go to the bathroom," he lied and palmed the note. "I've been trying to wake you up for like five minutes, you must be exhausted. Maybe you should go home and go to bed. But before you come back, take a shower, you smell ripe."

Kole glared then smelled himself. "I smell fine," he said. "I cleaned up before I came here." He studied his face then asked, "What are you up to?"

"I'm not up to anything."

"Yes you are. Your bottom lip twitches when mischief if about. So, whatever you're thinking you can forget about it."

Eric groaned and rolled his eyes. "Fine, I won't fart then," he said telling Kole what he wanted to hear. "Can you help me to the bathroom? My legs hurt."

Kole got up then helped Eric to the bathroom and when the door closed, Eric's grin returned. He planned to read the note and if it was indeed a love letter, he'd drop it into the toilet and poop on it, but when he unfolded the paper, which was too small for someone to express their emotions on and read.

"I'm no longer sure of what's real," Eric whispered, reading the note, "I'm off to face James and I'm certain that I won't return. I made a virus that'll kill him and I trust you to use it. I hid the virus in a metal suitcase in the piping tunnel under Winter Haven. The instruction to where to find it is on the back, good luck." He thought that she had nice penmanship, but it was an obvious trap. He crumpled the paper and was about to toss it in the toilet, but hesitated.

He un-crumpled the paper and reread it, imaging what her voice would sound like. She sounded like she was in a hopeless situation. She was going to meet James who was going to kill her, but she looked so hot. He then had an idea, if she couldn't use the virus on James, he could. And if he got there first, he'd rescue her and maybe she'd hang out with him instead of use him like the other women in his life had. Kole had been right about that, people would use him. He flipped the note over then memorized the instructions. He used the bathroom then destroyed the paper so Kole wouldn't find it and stop him.

He was a hero and now he was on a quest to find the ultimate weapon, kill the evil overlord and save the damsel. It was just like those books he used to read when he was alone in the transport. All he needed to do was get away from Kole and escape the hospital.

Kole helped him into bed then said, "You're moving better. You'll be running around in no time."

"Yeah, they have good drugs here."

"I'm trying to be serious, but you're making it hard."

"I am feeling better. I'm itchy. I want to get out of here and walk around. Movement is really good for the body and will hasten healing," Eric said, hoping to hear that he was allowed to leave.

"You're probably itchy because you're healing, but the doctors want to keep you for a little longer."

"How's Enora?" he asked then remembered coming on to her. "Did I make a pass at her?"

"You remember that? You were having an adverse reaction to the medication and threw up on her, but don't worry, she forgave you. I forgave you too once you messed your bed," he said then laughed. "They won't be giving you that anymore."

He only remembered hitting on Enora, but could see the other things happening. "The next time I see Enora, I'll apologize. What are you doing now?"

"I'm keeping you company. I wanted to be here when you sobered up and came around. I didn't want to hear your complaints if you woke up all alone," Kole said.

"I've woken up before and I've talked to people."

"Yes, you've woken up, but you've hit on every woman you looked at you. You weren't being yourself and I wanted to wait until your brain to return to normal, but that could take a couple of years," he said joking.

Eric frowned. There was nothing wrong with his brain and chatting women up. A person had to try and there was nothing wrong with rejection, it builds character. "Thanks for sticking around, but I think you can go now. I need some rest," he said and crossed his arms.

Kole smiled then said, "I was kidding. You don't have to be offended. I want to know why you went to fight the Trolls with Sophie. You knew that you couldn't use Alchemy in front of her, but you went anyway."

Eric remembered her lies and felt the pain in his body. His knee throbbed and his ribs ached. He looked up at the clock and wondered where the nurse was going to come around with his pills. "I thought we'd be like you and Enora, that I'd hide my Alchemy from her for the rest of her life."

Kole placed his hand on his bed. "I think she would've figured it out when she aged and you didn't." He sighed and shook his head then continued saying, "And when she finally dragged the truth out of you, I think she'd be a little angry that you had lied to her."

"I wasn't going to lie. I just wasn't going to tell the truth."

Kole laughed then raised his hand saying, "I understand. You weren't going to tell her."

He felt dumb. Kole was laughing at him. He decided that he'd wait for the painkillers before he left to look for the virus then remembered he could simply make the pills. He'd been playing normal for so long that he almost forgot that he was an Alchemist. "I thought she'd love me and overlook that, but I think I hit my head."

"Why do you think you hit your head? Is there something wrong?"

"For a minute there I forgot I could transmute."

Kole stood then placed his hand on Eric's shoulder. "We create the reality we want, now get some rest and I'll come back tomorrow. I'll make sure I'm clean. You never know, Enora might come to if you promise to behave."

Eric groaned. "I said I was sorry."

Eric watched Kole leave then waited, feeling the quiet of the room. He didn't like forgetting that he could manifest the pills then discarded the notion, asking himself why he'd make their drugs when he could make his own concoction. He hid his hand under his bed sheet and focused on what his body needed to heal quickly. He opened himself up, feeling his Alchemical power flow through him. He felt the cool energy pulse through him easing the pain then manifested several small pills.

He then made a glass of water and took the pills. He dissolved the glass and waited for his pills to kick in then found his clothes, an awful set of blue coveralls like Kole's. He wanted so bad to make his own clothes, but knew he couldn't. Security would be able to detect the perfections in the material and come looking for him to perform tests on him that he wouldn't like. He slipped the coveralls on then limped his way out of the hospital without anyone asking him where he was going. He wondered if they even knew what he looked like then dismissed the thought, remembering all the hardware his face carried.

The sun had gone down and the walkway lights flickered on. The city had grown and with all the hover-vehicles, the streets were converted into walkways. No vehicles were allowed on the ground floor and had to park overhead in parades, making it nice to wonder around at night when the streets weren't crowded. In the newer parts of town, closer to the buildings they had movable walkways that ended at each corner allowing you to rest on the move while you put in a hard day of shopping.

Eric frowned. He wanted to ride the walkways, but was heading into the older part of town that had been made for the ground cars. He told himself that it was a good thing. There were less cameras and technology to have tracked her, making him feel confident that the virus was still there. Though James wasn't in town, Eric didn't know if he had any minions searching for the treasure. All he knew was that he had to get there before them, but first he needed supplies. It'd be a long journey into the tunnels and he was hungry. He thought of the raisin spice cookies and that a nice lady who was twice his age. Her shop was a little out of the way, but he'd make up the time after.

He picked up the pace, trying to walk normally and stretch out his knee. The pain wanted him to limp, hobbling down the street, keeping his arms close to his body, but that made it worse. His body warmed and what pain his pills didn't take care of slowly subsided. He felt better moving and barely limped. He made it to the cookie shop five minutes before closing, becoming that customer who kept you working when all you wanted was to go home. He looked up at the clock that hung high in the middle of the wall behind the counter and smiled. It was a cute shop that sold everything cookie. Under glass, the main display housed the actual cookies and beside that, the till. The tea and coffee had already been put away and the owner moved around the small venue wiping tables and straitening chairs. Along the back wall, shelves displayed tea and coffee pots, baskets with pictures of cookie arrangements and the list of options that a person could request.

"Remember me?" asked Eric then looked at the woman, but wasn't sure if it was the same person. She had the same features, but he didn't remember her having a scar down her left cheek and crooked nose. He also thought she was blond, but this woman had her grey hair pulled back into a tail.

"Yes I remember you. Did you like the cookies?"

"Yes," he said rubbing his tummy. "They were really good, they inspired me to get better so I could come to your shop and get more."

She straitened, holding the table cloth. "You look flushed. I hope you didn't escape the hospital to get more cookies. You could've used the directory and called me. I would've dropped some off."

Eric grinned. He liked her and she was right, he did like her cookies. "No," he lied. "They released me. It took me awhile to get here and I'm a little sore."

She moved around the tables meeting him then leaned in. "Those cookies are so addictive I wouldn't have blamed you for escaping. They're my best seller."

There was something mischievous in her eye and at first Eric though she was coming onto him, but realized it was again about the cookies. "What's in them?" he asked, thinking she was crazy and had spiked them with drugs.

"The magic of the cookie doesn't come from the ingredients. My friend has a gift and everything she makes tastes angelic. The two of us together have cornered the cookie market in town and that's why I came to see you."

He was disheartened. He found another person who wanted to use him, but her cookies are tasty and doing normal things made him look Human. "I'm listening," he said, encouraging her to continue.

"You're the new in thing among the young people and if they see you carrying around a box of our cookies, it'll increase our sales."

Eric didn't need money, but doing what she asked did more for him. He'd look normal and could use the cookies as a conversation piece, but best of all, he gets to eat cookies all day long. "I don't know. I might eat you out of business and rot my teeth."

A warm smile softened her face. She placed her hand on his forearm then assured him saying, "No, no, no, you won't rot your teeth."

He smiled, amused by her mothering. "You mentioned a partner?"

"Promise you won't freak out."

The image of an ugly disfigured old woman with a hunchback and gnarled fingers flashed in his mind. "I Promise," he said then smiled. "I've been around and seen a lot. I'm sure I won't be surprised."

She locked the door behind him then turned off the open sign which made him think the worst then he remembered that it was closing time. "Mother Sarah has done a lot to help us put away our hate and mistrust," she said. "It wasn't too long ago when we in Winter Haven had a problem with the other races, but Sarah has shown us a better way."

"Yeah, she can be quite persuasive," he said then looked at the display of tea pots. "She makes good tea and would probably buy a teapot off of you." He imagined showing up at Sarah's place with a teapot and putting a smile on her face. Maybe she'd like him then, but didn't know a good pot from a terrible one.

"You've met Mother Sarah?"

"A couple of times," he answered.

"Do you think you can give her a box of cookies?"

"Sure, but I thought anyone could meet her."

"She's very busy. She gets out when she can, but there're so many people who want to see her, she doesn't have the time for everyone."

"Maybe there should be two or three more of her," he said joking.

Puzzled she said, "That'd be weird. I don't like that."

He choked on his mirth then changed the subject asking, "Have you lived here long?"

"I was a slave for a long time and when my friend was picked up, we bonded instantly. I looked out for her and when we came here after the destruction of the Slaver party, we stuck together and built this shop."

Mentioning the Slaver party made him feel awkward. He wondered what she'd say if she found out that he helped kill the people there. Sure they could've infiltrated the party and spent a week freeing the slaves by either smuggling them out or instigating an uprising, but the Slavers wouldn't have waited around for that. "Well," he said smiling. "I'm glad you're free now to fill my tummy with cookies."

She laughed then called out over her shoulder, "Monique, come out and meet our new friend."

He followed her gaze and looked over her shoulder at the door, but nothing happened.

She then explained saying, "She's mute. She'll sign and I'll translate if you don't understand and when you're talking to her, ignore me."

"Sure," he said, not sure what to expect, but when a slender Dark Elf woman walked through the backroom doorway his mouth went dry. Even wearing a hairnet, dirty apron, and splotches of flour across her face, she was prettier than any of the nude Elven women on his old partial set of playing cards that were forgotten in Eric's mind forever. She moved around the display case with the elegance of a dancer, pleasing him.

Monique's hands moved quick and precise showing him her

sharp mind. A sloppy body means a sloppy mind, he told himself, but wasn't sure if was true. Even with the older woman talking for her, Eric was enthralled by her, making him want to learn sign language. Monique signed, "I've been listening to you and it's nice to hear that you've met Mother Sarah. One day, I'd like to meet her. Her words have brought me peace."

He wanted to say something witty and impressive, but all he could manage to say was, "Um, good." And in his head it sounded far better than it was. He wanted to ask her if she liked baking and how people have been treating her in Winter Haven, but couldn't find the words. It felt like he turned right, but his brain went left. Now he was lost in the gaze of a beautiful woman while his brain was running around and having fun without him. He wanted to thump his head against the closest table, but another concussion wouldn't help. Then there was dead air between and with each passing second, he wanted to run away die from embarrassment.

The older lady chuckled then said, "You're not the only man who's become an idiot in her presence."

He cleared his throat then lied, "I'm fine, I was thinking about cookies." He tried to look away to salvage some dignity and self-control, but he couldn't pull his eyes away from hers. On the surface there was peace. A little deeper, pain, but under all that there was a fire, an intensity of spirit that was as attractive to him as it was threatening.

Without breaking eye contact, she stepped closer and raised her hand. Eric didn't know what she wanted and fought his instinct to flood his body with power, creating a shield, but she stopped then touched his arm. She quickly let go leaving the ghost of her warm touch behind. She blinked breaking their connection then moved her hands signing, "I'm sorry. You look like an Alchemist."

"What?" he asked. She freaked him out, but he had enough self-control to play it stupid. He had spent a lot of time honing his disguise, but wasn't sure how to respond. He quickly went through what a normal person would say if they were accused of that then said, "You're kidding, do I look like an Alchemist?"

"She didn't mean that," the older lady said.

"Yes I did," Monique signed. "I can see it in your eyes. You hide it well, but I've seen it before."

She went from hot to creepy in seconds, depressing Eric. He didn't even get a change to hit on her and be shot down. But he couldn't leave unanswered questions. "That's kind of upsetting. You're the second person that accused me of being one of those things."

The older lady stepped between them and blocked Eric's view. "She not from around here and didn't mean to offend you."

"But, there aren't any more Alchemists, they're all dead," Eric argued, committing to the role of an Anti-Alchemist. "Why would she think I was one of them?"

Monique placed her hand on the older lady's shoulder and signed, "James Ashwood is an Alchemist. He lived in the Dark Elf Capital. I've seen him."

Eric shook the surprised look off his face then said to Monique, "You shouldn't be saying these things." He imagined the city's guards busting down the door and shooting the place up with Rippers to see what'll explode. He tapped the older lady's other shoulder getting her attention then said, "Do you like your cookie shop and want to keep it? If you do, you might want to keep your friend from accusing, Admiral James Ashwood the Savior of Humanity of being an Alchemist."

He unlocked the door and was about to leave the shop without any cookies when Monique grabbed his arm again. He wanted to get as far away from her as he could, but when he turned to shake her hand away, he froze. It wasn't the worry that was spread across her face that made him stop. There was something in her eyes that reached in and touched him on a deeper level. No other woman had ever connected with him like that. He held her gaze while her eyes spoke volumes to him and he didn't want it to stop.

But paranoia whispered in his ear. If it weren't for all his injuries,

Sophie would've turned him in and he'd be hunted, having to defend himself from the Humans while he fled Winter Haven. All they'd have to do is shoot a Ripper at him to test his humanity and of course he'd fail and be blown to bits, ruining his new coveralls. He'd gone through so much and dying that way would feel meaningless.

To Eric's anguish, she released her grip then looked away breaking their connection. Eric felt hot and his face flushed. He suddenly didn't care about being accused of being an Alchemist. He felt something between him and Monique that he couldn't explain. And thought the older lady was standing close to him, he no longer could see her. All he could see was Monique.

He forgot about his hurt knee and sore body then slowed reached down hand held her hand. "It's getting dark. I'd be honored to walk you home."

She smirked and Eric could tell that she was thinking about it. He was going to compare the time she was spending in her contemplation to his past failures, but everything about her felt new. He then let go of his past and didn't care about hers. He wanted to be fresh and see her as new, looking at her without judgment.

She nodded a yes which thrilled him. He wanted to squeal with joy and do a happy dance, but instead he opened the door for her, allowing her to pass then joined her on the walkway. He walked with her asking questions about baking and cookies. She gave him rudimentary hand signs answers which he slowly picked up, but he was more interested in observing her subtle facial expressions. He enjoyed his time with her and when it was time to part, he asked to see her again. He could tell that there was a deep sadness in her, making him think that she was going to say no, but she nodded again. He said he'd see her again then with a song in his heart, he started his way back to the hospital before remembering the virus.

Feeling chipper, Eric found the closest entrance to the tunnels, a partly rusted metal door. He could've sent his awareness into the tunnel to find the fastest route to the metal case, but was in a good mood and wanted to explore. The whole adventure excited him. He had found his princess and now didn't know what he was going to find. He let his imagination fill in the blanks, wondering if there was an entire civilization of mutant or disenfranchised people living beneath the city. A hidden world with different laws made up of people who literally fell through the cracks.

Excitement spurred him on, but his imagination took on a darker tone, reminding him of the Zombies, Nick and Kyra came across in the Werewolf tunnels. He cringed at the thought and pushed it away. At the time, he was having problems concentrating and working his shield. He ended up stepping in some of the disgusting mess Nick and Kyra had left on his way out of the tunnels. The rancid smell burned his nose and the floor was slick with gore. The memory was so vivid he almost threw up in his mouth. He didn't remember much after that until they went back to Pine View.

He slowed, imagining Zombies around every corner then slapped himself. He fought his growing fear using logic. People would've seen Zombies, or smelled them, but his fear reminded him that he was going into the bowels of the city where few ever go.

He placed his hand on the door handle and was relieved that it was locked, which was a good sign. Fewer people had access. He pretended to fiddle with his pocket and pull out keys that didn't exist then used his Alchemy to open the door. If he had lock picks he would've learned to use them. But before he opened the door, he gave his head a shake forcing the Zombie Apocalypse out of his mind. He pulled the handle and the door opened with a loud squeak that reverberated down the street. Noise travels further at night and he worried that he alerted the wrong type of people. James might have minions hiding in the shadows, ready to pounce and he gave away his position. He quickly stepped into the tunnel and cringed when he closed the squeaky door, locking it behind him.

The badly lit tunnels looked spooky. Partly insulated pipes clung to the walls dripping condensation onto the duracrete floor. The air smelled stale and moldy. He walked to the top of a small set of stairs, placing his hand on the moist railing then recoiled. The paint on the rail crackled at his touch, leaving tiny flakes of paint and rust stains on his hand. He cringed, feeling dirty then wiped the rust on his leg. Somehow the tactile feel of the rust grossed him out more than ramming his Power Armor up the rear of a giant Troll. He looked at his palm in the dim light thinking that it was the small oddities in life that made things interesting.

His mind was in full out rebellion, imagining scary creatures lurking in the shadows. He was freaking himself out and had to get a grip on himself before he was able to continue, following his damsel's directions, moving deeper into the tunnels. He paused again. Meeting Monique made him forget about the woman who'd slipped the note into Kole's pocket. In the light of Monique, he no longer thought of that woman as a damsel in distress and was able to continue.

His journey wasn't as fun as he planned. All the old tunnels looked the same and when he finally found a marker painted on the wall, he realized that he didn't quite remember the details of the note he had memorized. Sure he could use his Alchemy to stimulate the portions of his mind that held the memory, bring forth the image, but that was boring. He stood quiet, examining the worn paint like a person admiring a painting. He crossed his arms and with a free hand, played with his chin. He wanted to look compelling if anyone was spying on him while he was secretly listening for people. It was a quiet place of dripping water, humming pipes and buzzing lights, but no footsteps.

After finding more steps and descending a couple of levels, he came to the conclusion that he was lost, or in the right place and time. His mind flooded with thoughts of what he'd stumble upon. Maybe a group of Trolls, but that bored him. He was sick of killing Trolls and for once wanted to solve a problem using love, but the tunnels sucked. There wasn't anyone there, they smelled and the lighting hurt his eyes. He gave up then stimulated his mind, bringing the memory of his ex-damsel's instructions to the forefront of his mind. With the image fresh in his head, he stretched his awareness out and found the metal suitcase where she said it'd be. Disappointed that he caved to his boredom, he made his way to the case. He expected an ambush and a massive fight that'd test his very existence, but there was no one. He was glad he took his time and enjoyed Monique's company, but before he grabbed the case, he wondered if it was a trap.

He pulled his hand back then dreamt up way of how he'd trap the case. He looked down the tunnels for any spies then manifested a light cloud of smoke to detect laser light, but found none. He frowned then stretched his awareness out, brushing the case, trying to sense explosives and a triggering device, but felt something else. The void reached out for him touching his mind. A cold shiver ran up his spine making him shudder and lose his balance. He fell backward to slam against the duracrete wall. The pain of his injuries flared and his mind went back to his fight with The Lollypop King. He bent over and retched, but didn't throw anything up. For some reason he thought of Nick and was grateful that he didn't have any of Monique's cookies.

He calmed himself and collected his thoughts. It happened quickly, but in his mind, he was able to rewind his memory and slow it down. It was indeed a virus based on Ripper technology, but not the same. The void within it called for a specific home, rejecting him. He was glad to have that kind of rejection. Half of it was Ripper, but the other half was brown to its blue. It was his mind's way of telling him that the virus would consume Ripper Gel. And though a person had made the virus, it was nature's way to bring balance to the world. It was perhaps the only thing that'd be able to kill James.

His mind reeled at the thought. He had found the most valuable treasure on the planet in the dankest of places. He was afraid to touch the case. The weight of the world rest on his shoulders and his life finally had meaning. He was destined to find the case and achieve what Kole always talked about, balance. He needed to hide it in a better spot. If he had known the virus, he could've easily found the case by sensing the void within it. James could do the same, but Eric had an idea. He would hide it close by, to quickly retrieve it when they go to face James. He'd hide it in the armory under the other Ripper Rounds, but not close enough incase the voids somehow consume each other. It'd be in a place that a person would overlook, unless they knew what they were looking for.

It was now his secret. If the ex-damsel questions Kole about the virus or note, he won't know anything. Eric wrapped his fingers around the handle and pulled the case free from its hiding place. He now held the fate of the world in his hand and wondered why his ex-damsel gave up the case in the first place. All she had to do was get close enough to James to deploy it. He looked at the case not knowing how he was going to do that, but as Enora and Kole had taught him, if all else fails, use a bomb.

On his return drudge through the sad tunnels the responsibility of saving the world weighed heavy on him. He knew he'd only get one shot and didn't know what the virus would do while it was killing James. He remembered the void reaching out to devour all those it could reach, but this void was different. He had time to get to know the virus and probe it with his consciousness to learn how it'd react and how to deploy it. All he needed to do is find a nice quiet place in the decrepit tunnels far from where the ex-damsel had hidden it. James could be back, questioning her right now and of course she'd break, telling him everything, so Eric needed to be quick.

With the treasure in hand, he snuck deeper into the tunnels, peeking around the corners, hiding from the minions he had yet to find. At the bottom of a blocked off stairwell, sitting in the dark, Eric formed a connection with the virus, using his encounters with the other voids as a guide. Each type of Ripper Gel had a different personality. The original gel was made to do its job, the Troll gel is a twisted version of the original, but the virus was something new. It was gentle, uninterested in Eric, but he could see the waiting aggression and power within it. It surprised him. Its power lay out before him like a window to the Universe and Eric could almost hear it talk, asking to be united with James. As Eric probed it, it probed him back. It found out that Eric had met James and knew where to find him.

The virus deepened its connection to him feeling like a warm rose petal caressing his soul and he didn't want to see it go. Through the virus, Eric felt the Universe. He wanted to be the one who'd carry the virus inside him and in a way he loved it like he loved all life. He wanted to help the virus find James to bring balance to the world, the way it was meant to be. Eric learned what he could about the virus then made his way out of the tunnels to hide the metal case on the base.

Chapter

12

Kole woke, sliding his hand under the blankets, searching for Enora, but her side of the bed was cold. He quickly retracted his hand, returning it to his warmth then opened his eyes. He frowned, her tidy pillow that told him that she hadn't come home during the night. After leaving Eric, he went to her lab. She was immersed in her work, building the massive satellites that would rid the world of the Trolls and didn't have time to chat. She was inspired. The samples collected from the downed Battleships helped her perfect her weapon, exciting her and her excitement was contagious. He was happy for her success and hung around, trying to help, but he wasn't strong enough to unite the particles in the upper atmosphere. Discouraged, he got sick of the silence between them then decided to go out for dinner. He offered to bring something back for her, but she declined. He could've called a cab, but decided to walk. He'd been busy for so long he forgot how to relax when there was nothing to do. There was nothing for him to do, no one needed him. The others were busy doing their jobs and when the Trolls are gone, he'd have even more time on his hands.

Deciding that he'd better learn to relax again, he went to a prestigious restaurant to dine alone. Sarah was kind enough to set them and Eric up with two apartments and cash cards loaded with a small fortune as payment for what they've accomplished, but eating alone surrounded by the well off, made him wonder what the future held for him. When he walked into the restaurant they were going to throw him out. He wasn't properly dressed and didn't have a reservation. He didn't think he needed one because there was plenty of seating, but then understood the coveralls. Everyone in the restaurant looked done up, wearing mostly black. The restaurant looked nice, clean floors and art hanging on the wall. The food smelled good and everyone talked in a low murmur. It was a ritzy place, opposite to the greasy spoons he was used to. When he turned to leave, he was recognized by some of the staff. It turned out that he was just as famous as Eric and was given the proper attire to dine. He thanked them then after the meal, tipped heavy.

He changed back into his coveralls then on his walk home he realized that he didn't really know Enora. He knew the person she was under stress and bits of her past, but didn't know her peaceful side. They've been battling evil since they've met. There was no doubt that he loved her and thought they fit well together, but do you really know a person who's always reacting to stress. With the end of the Trolls being near, the world is going to open up for them. They'll have nowhere to go and nothing to do, which appealed to him, but he wanted to get to know all of her. The whole time he had run around the waste, he never learned to relax. He was always waiting for an ambush, entertaining his paranoia. He doubted that he'd ever known peace. He thought he did, but when he really looked at his past, he knew he was fooling himself.

In a way he was glad that he and Enora had met the worst in each other. Any argument without throwing a bomb at it was a mild discussion and now the world will see peace. He thought about how rude he had been to Sarah, threatening to kill her for messing with people's minds, but living in the city she helped build, made him change his mind about her. All the stress he was under clouded his mind and made him do regrettable things, but that was the past. He could've learned to manage his stress better, but its nature is toxicity, corrupting everything around it until that's all you are. Stress was no excuse for bad behavior, but the thought of traveling into the world without Slavers or Trolls made enough of his stress triggers melt away for him to see how crazy he was becoming. But it was more habitual then crazy. With more stress in your life, the shorter your fuse becomes until the first thing that you find to deal with your problems, is a big stick.

Deep in thought, he watched the walkway roll along then felt a person's stare. He looked up to meet Roy's gaze. Roy stood on the opposite walkway rolling along wearing the same cowboy hat, jacket and boots as he did in Pine View. He thought he was seeing things and it took a moment for Kole to confirm that it was indeed Roy. Kole's hand twitched. He instinctively wanted to reach for the dowel he no longer had and blow a hole through Roy's chest. With one blast, he'd avenge all those who died in Pine View and get revenge for being treated like garbage, but peace was coming.

He stepped off the rolling walkway onto the wide brick walkway and Roy did the same. He expected Roy to run, but was glad he didn't. The sun had gone down and the walkways empty giving them privacy. "I forgot you were here," Kole said. "I flew over Pine View after the Trolls were done with it and caught a message. You have a bounty on your head."

Roy nodded then said, "I know. The Trolls were coming and I knew my town would fall, so I made a deal with Winter Haven. I wanted to pay our way in with all of our resources, but they'd only take the Humans. It was a hard choice, but I saved who I could. Those damn drunken Dwarves weren't happy about it and laid claim to the town. They even stole half of our stuff then kicked us out."

Kole laughed at the imagery. "Well, what goes around really does come back to bite you. Now you're known as The Murderer of Pine View. Oddly enough, I find that greatly satisfying."

Roy frowned. "I'm sorry about all that with you and the Were-

wolves. I had to do what I did to keep people calm. When you refused to leave, they thought you were going to take over. They were
on the verge of panic. Those idiots, after all my years of service,
they screwed me when we got here and robbed me. I ended up with
nothing and my woman left me." He took his hat off, holding it between his hands. His hair was matted and dirty and Kole could see
how much he'd aged since the last time he'd seen him. "I saw footage of you and recognized you right away, but didn't tell anyone.
You're one of the good Alchemists. You're still out there trying to
save us after we treated you badly and that's commendable. As for
me, I could use a little help."

Kole's hand twitched again. He reminded himself that peace
was coming and that he needed to learn to properly channel his
stress. "We're old friends, so let's cut the crap. Are you blackmailing
me?" he asked.

Roy took a deep breath and held it a couple of seconds before
saying, "No. You've killed a lot of Trolls and I don't think blackmail
would be a smart play. I want a loan. With you running around, I'm
betting that the Trolls will soon be extinct and I have managerial
skills. I want enough to be able to buy and outfit a Scavenger Hauler.
The influential people in Winter Haven are excited. They feel change
in the wind. And when they feel change, something is going to
happen. There are companies building new haulers and once the
Trolls are dead, it'll be a race to secure the finest salvage."

He'd heard a similar speech from Nick, before Nick blew all their
money on drugs, gambling and hookers. The paranoid voice in his
head warned him that Roy had staged their meeting and was going
to betray him for the Alchemist bounty after he'd squeezed whatever
he could out of him. But the logical part of his mind argued that
Roy could've turned him in ages ago, besides killing Trolls was one
thing and murdering an old defenseless man in cold blood was
another. "Let's start out friendship over," he said, letting his past
grievances fall away. "Make a company and I'll be your silent partner
with a chance of buyout." He pulled out his cash card and held it

between them. "I'll loan you what you need and you can pay me back or give me a cut of your profits, choice is yours."

Tears welled in his eyes. "I knew you wouldn't let me down," he said, blubbering then with hat in hand, he threw his arms around Kole and gave him a big hug.

Kole gently pushed him away when the hug lasted too long and together they went to the closest bank terminal to transfer funds. The truth was that Kole never cared about money, or what it brought, but everyone else did, making him think about it and Sarah didn't scrimp. He wasn't expecting much, a little allowance to get him by and when he saw how much she'd given him, he thought it was a mistake. He did the right thing and told her about it and she smiled, telling his that it was his reward for helping to save the world. Eric and Enora were also rewarded with their own cards. Eric hadn't seen his card yet and Kole worried what he was going to do with it. All he hoped is that Eric wouldn't follow Nick's example.

After parting with Roy, Kole expected never to see him again. Contracts weren't signed and the money was transferred, but paying him off and planting the idea that Roy could use him later was better than killing him. Even if Roy turned him in to collect a reward, Roy knew that he won't go without a fight, destroying whatever he needed to survive. Sarah wouldn't like that either and probably come to his rescue, but he hoped Roy would disappear into the background of Winter Haven.

He arrived at his apartment, a spacious corner loft that over-looked the city and was loaded with nice furniture. Another gift from Sarah and for the first time in his life Kole felt appreciated by someone outside of his group. It wasn't the apartment or the money that made him feel appreciated. It was the care that she took to provide for them that touched him. He took off his shoes and walked across his open living room to stand next to the full sized windows. The only thing that the apartment didn't come with was clothes because Sarah wanted them to have fun shopping. He hated to shop, preferring to hit one store, go directly to what he wanted then leave, but Enora loved to explore, making him think that Sarah had given that extra gift to Enora.

He wasn't surprised that he beat Enora home, but expected her home before he turned in for the night. He didn't like missing his kiss goodnight, but being alone inspired him to want to change their relationship for the better. He wanted to show her the real him that slept under the layers of stress. The calm person within that acted without anger, having peaceful thoughts instead of the torrent of angry paranoia that haunted his waking life. He had been repeatedly traumatized leaving layers of scars over his soul and it was time to deal with his damage and make himself a better person. He wanted to do it for him and for their relationship, but the only problem was he didn't know how to start. Laying in bed and looking up at his darkened ceiling, he decided to do the only thing he could, fake it till he made it. It was his will alone that had forged him into the man he wanted to be and his decision felt great.

Morning came and after his daily routine, Kole went shopping for new clothes. He didn't want to start his new relationship with Enora in his grubby hand-me-down coveralls, they both deserved better. He took a cab to the garment district, a tall building dedicated to fashion at the heart of the city. Fashion and clothing styles trickled out from there, rippling into the lower ends of town. To Kole it was another form of separation where a person's clothing dictated what district they came from. He didn't like the idea that a person can be classed before they open their mouth, but all sides were to blame. The under privileged, with their pride of being the hard-working salt of the earth and the well off who liked to have their stature recognized. And if a person crossed those class lines they became too posh to go back and not well off enough to go forward. And no matter what class a person belonged to, they all wanted to see their life as special. Kole had never been part of that and was an outcast to all. And living where he currently did, there was only one uniform he could wear.

Kole knew he was going to a ritzy building when the cab descended to street level to enter the underground parking garage instead of landing on the roof. In the older and run down districts the landing platforms sat on top of the buildings, limiting the view. The newer buildings were designed with air traffic in mind, designating different blocks for descending and ascending traffic, keeping accidents to a minimum. The city even made profit by selling air rights around buildings to redirect the traffic, or to rent out traffic ways to the building owners of lesser stature to boost their sales.

The cab entered the parking garage and followed the flashing markers to the entrance where a traditionally dressed doorman opened his door. Kole stepped out and the doorman gave him a funny look. Remembering that he wore coveralls, he showed him his cash card and was escorted to the unusually large glass doors with the building's company logo etched into it. The doorman opened the door for him and he stepped into the lobby's marble floor.

He didn't know where to go and was annoyed at the selection of floors. He was used to walking across the open market up to a cart and picking the clothes that'd fit. Now he had to know what he was looking for and where he was going. He stepped into an elevator and asked its attendant where he should go. The man cheerfully helped him then selected an upper floor. Kole stepped out of the elevator onto an open light green carpeted floor with tan trim. He expected the clothes to be on racks, or folded on tables, or carts but the sample clothes laid under glass in stained wooden display cases. But before Kole could look around, a man in a plain grey suit approached him. The man directed him to a small room where he was measured. Kole wasn't sure if it was procedure or if he was being molested by the store's employee. With his measurements recorded, Kole was free to shop. The store wasn't crowded and had mature and wealthy looking patrons. Kole wandered through the rows of displays with the man following him. He was told to pretend that the man wasn't there and when Kole wanted to see something, the man accessed his data pad and told him if they had his size of article in stock. And if Kole really wanted something that they didn't have, a custom order could be made at no extra expense.

Kole talked with the man to get to get advice then decided on several sets of clothes. He didn't see a price tag and asked before he tried anything on. The man then discreetly pointed to the lower corner of the display case where a little manila card sat with a number hand written on it. He almost gagged when he saw the cost then was encouraged to try his clothes on. At first Kole was hesitant, but the quality, comfort and look made the clothes worth the cost. After his shopping spree, he passed a lady in the lobby with three times the amount of bags, putting what he thought was a lot into perspective.

The cab took him to a gift store located in another building that housed many shops dedicated to rare and wonderful trinkets. After strolling through the different shops and finding artifacts dated back to before the Purge, he found a flower shop. He thought flowers being sold among artifacts was strange until he thought about how rare and resource consuming the flowers were. He thought about how long it took them to grow, what they needed and the attention spent on them to keep them alive. Out of all he'd seen and thought would be a great gift for Enora, he chose to buy a single red rose. For what it was, it cost a lot, but what he was truly buying was the look on Enora face when she sees it and that was priceless. He was surprise to even find them. He hadn't seen roses in a hundred years and thought they were extinct. There were so many other flowers out there that were alchemically made, making him wonder if they'd been choked out and driven into extinction.

After his last purchase, he expected to see his cash card burst into flames from all the cash he threw around and decided to call it quits. He went home and put away his clothes then dressed himself up, but hesitated to surprise Enora. She hadn't gone shopping and turning up without something for her to wear felt wrong. He went through her drawers looking for her size and found a nightgown where he was able to deduce her size from the tag, but after what he went through to get his clothes, he doubted knowing the size was enough. Everything fit differently depending on the manufacturer, so he had only one choice. He envisioned her, allowing his power to flow through him and visualized how the nightgown would fit on her. Seeing that it was slightly bigger and remembering that she liked to sleep in loose fitting clothes, he engaged with the Universe and was able to get her measurements. This was the future of peace, using his powerful reality altering abilities to get his wife's measurements.

He took a cab back to the clothing store and found a beautiful dress Enora could wear out for lunch. He wanted the dress to look good and feel great because he knew that some women suffered to look good and he didn't want have that for Enora. He wanted her to look and feel good in whatever she wore and spared no expense finding what he was looking for. He was pleased with himself and didn't pick the first thing he saw. He selected the nicest dresses then felt the material and for the first time noticed that women's clothing was very different than men's. He'd manifested women's clothing before, but his conscious mind didn't need to know the details and he didn't care. He made product that people were happy with and that's all he care about. There were so many things he had missed out on in his endeavor to transmute and make the best product in the area. He didn't think it was important to know why things were built the way they were, he just funneled his knowledge and did it.

After returning home to collect the rose he made his way to Enora's lab. He came up to her locked door and looked at the keypad. In one hand, he carried a box and in the other, the rose. The dress had been placed in the box in a certain way and he carried it so it wouldn't wrinkle making him not want to fumble with the box when he played with the keypad. Maneuvering the delicately wrapped rose was his only option. He carefully extended his finger and slowly punched in the code getting more aggravated with each crinkle he put into the wrapping. He knew that she wouldn't care about the crinkles, but he had a way of wrecking nice things over time, especially things that weren't his. She had told him a couple of times to respect her things like he did his own. She had seen how he treated his things and wanted the same for hers. He didn't want to let her down or hurt her feeling, but he knew he'd slip up, so he avoided touching her stuff all together. As for the flower, it was just wrapping, but he wanted to keep it in the best condition to show her how special he thought she was.

With the last beep, the door slid open. Enora was so wrapped up in what she was doing that she didn't acknowledge him. Though her hands moved and her body was in front of him, her awareness was high above them building satellites. He watched her work like he did the night before and realized that she hadn't moved. He then thought surprising her might not be the best idea. Bringing her back into a body that'd been standing still for twelve hours might suck, but that didn't apply to her. He body was a pure manifestation of self. He doubted she'd even be physically tired, but knew that she'd be mentally drained. He pictured going to lunch at a fancy restaurant with her in her new dress and having her fall asleep, slamming her face into her soup. He chuckled at the imagery then watched her hands slow.

"I'll be with you in a moment," she said without looking. "I have to finish this component."

"Sure," he said, telling her that he'd heard her. He watched her hands move and thought about how heavy the little dress in the box and the rose were becoming. He thought about using his shield to encase his body to do the heavy lifting, but that made him wonder what his power was going to be good for when there was no conflict left in the world.

He thought about the time before Alchemy and how spoiled the world had become. The bored masses looking for ways to entertain themselves, glommed onto Alchemists because they were the fad. Looking at what the people of Winter Haven had built and the future that Sarah promised made him realize that Alchemy was never needed. Everyone in the distant past had what they needed and threw it away, condemning their future, but they were never bored after that. Was Alchemy the manifestation of human consciousness? Was their cry of boredom answered?

Seeing the world in that light pushed Kole's mind and inch further to make him wonder if the other races including the Alchemists are destined to become extinct. Once peace returns and the human race flourishes, will there be a need for Alchemy? Will the world heal and return the human consciousness to the state it once was. The thought intrigued him, but he couldn't condone what James had done. James' planning to kill off, or shoot the other races into space was still wrong, but having the Universe lessen their birthrate was okay? At the scale he was thinking, morality didn't play a part because if he was right, the Universe introduced Alchemy to the human race to give them something to talk about. What is life to a Universe that with the wave of its hand, it can extinguish worlds? But with another wave, remake life. If the human race drove itself into extinction, in the right conditions something else would take its place, the Universe will continue.

"Are you okay?" asked Enora. "Your face is all scrunchy."

She came into focus and he met her concerned eyes. "I got these for you," he said then presented his gifts. Kole didn't want to think of the human races' extinction and focused on what was standing in front of him, his future.

Chapter

13

After sending her awareness into high orbit, Enora worked far from her body and lost track of time. She wanted to leave with Kole, but the work needed to be done and the faster she did it, the sooner the Trolls would be dead, but she lost herself in the details. She thought only minutes had passed and didn't realize she'd worked through the night, pouring her mental energy into the new satellites and remaking the old one. It was the sample Sarah had provided that inspired her, connecting her ideas, giving her what she was looking for, a way to kill off the Trolls and leave the mystery as to where they went. In time the Trolls will be forgotten. She slipped into a state of hyper awareness and was startled when she heard the first beep from the door's lock. At first she ignored it, but the second beep rippled into her awareness, hurting her skin and drawing her attention back to her body. She didn't want to lose focus, but the beeps were slow, making her think that someone she didn't know was messing with the door. She didn't want to stop, but she also wanted to know who was trying to break in and this disturbance divided her attention, slowing her down, but when she felt for the person, she sensed Kole. Annoyed, she wondered why he was taking so long to open the door. It was like waiting a couple of minutes between each beep and when they finally came, the beep noise hurt her.

She didn't mean to get upset and stuffed her feelings into a box. She wasn't being rational and all Kole did was punch in a door code and enter her workshop. She knew she was under a great deal of strain and having Kole there waiting was like having someone tap the back of her head with their finger, sparked another wave of negative emotion. Kole entered and finally ended the beeping. She knew he was being polite and waiting for her to finish, but she could feel his body heat on her back. She struggled to concentrate getting lost in the rhythm of his breathing, but she had to finish the satellite she was working on before she stopped.

She finished the satellite she was working on, but didn't want to come back to her body and Kole right away. She needed to vent the layers of stress resting on her, or she'd take it out on Kole who didn't deserve it. The emotional energy had to go somewhere and she couldn't swallow it. Her awareness drifted away from orbit and into the vastness of space. The clarity of the stars and the emptiness before her calmed her mind, humbling her. Looking into the Universe made her forget about all the meaningless crap in her life. All of the stress, arguments and heartache in her life diminished returning her to a state of peace. Floating there in space reminded her of being submerged in a jar with two electrodes stuffed into her brain that robbed her of her power, impeding her ability to free herself. She knew what had happened. James allowed her to keep her eyes. He even let her see her body before he discarded it. He held the jar up, bringing her to his eye level then smiled. While she was in the jar, she never saw him again.

She was placed on the pedestal then left alone, trapped and in her traumatized brain. Over time her trauma faded, but her boredom grew until she could no longer remember which was worse. All she had was the control room to look at with unblinking eyes. She used her imagination to keep her mind busy and memories alive, but over time the color in her dreams faded, replaced with blackness and her imagination dulled until all that was left was an emptiness she has to face. Only when she ran out of hate, anger, love and peace was she able to find the Universe within. And being tangled in this mess with the Trolls and James, she'd forgotten what she'd experienced. Then using her awareness, she looked into the Universe and remembered.

Her stress melted away leaving contentment and suddenly the satellites weren't that important because they'll get done on time. James wasn't important to her because he'll pay for everything he has done, if not in this life then perhaps the next. What James did irritated her, but with all her power, what did it mean to her? When Kole freed her, she reformed her body. What value does a body hold in the light of that power? All James did, was give her an unwanted haircut. He came up behind her and took a lock of hair. It was the violation of her ego that bothered her and cried out for revenge, or justice. She could do it, or have someone else do it for her, it didn't matter. But in the vastness of the Universe and the power of life flowing through it, one life ends then another begins. What is it that keeps us bound to pain?

She returned to her body feeling contentment for all that had happened in her life. She turned around to see Kole looking handsome and holding box in one hand and a rose in the other. She could see why it took him so long to get through the door and she almost ruined whatever he was planning with her foul mood. She could tell he wasn't there, staring into space with an intense look on his face. She was happy to get a chance to see him first and wondered what was going on in his head. By his expression, it wasn't contentment. She hoped that when he comes back that he'd leave whatever he was feeling behind. She spoke then watched him come back to her. The expression on Kole's face changed dramatically from sour to a boyish grin. He looked clean and groomed in his new clothes.

He presented his gifts and she took the beautiful velvety petal red rose first. It was a real rose from a seed which was rare in her time, replaced by artificial and Alchemical representations. "This is real," she said surprised then smelled its slight scent. She took the rose out of its wrapper then playfully brushed her cheek with its petals while maintaining eye contact. She gave a slight smile and he blushed. "Is that box for me as well?" she asked.

He offered the box, but she made him hold it while she put her rose down. She lowered her chin and flashed a shy smile before taking the gift. She then slowly spun on her heels and placed it on her table before opening it and couldn't help, but gasp. She'd never owned anything so stunning. She picked the shimmery yellow dress up by its shoulders, careful not to snag its material on the box and felt the smooth fabric. "Where are we going for dinner?" she asked, excited to hear what else he had in mind.

"No, not dinner, lunch," he said.

"Lunch?" she asked, thinking she misheard. The dress wasn't for lunch, it was a dinner dress.

"Yeah, it's the next day. You worked through the night," he answered, not understanding what she was asking.

His eyes were filled with excitement and she could tell that he'd put a lot of thought into his gifts, leaving one question. "Right now?" she asked, hoping she could wiggle out of his surprise and postpone their date so she could properly get ready.

"Yeah, go put it on."

If she could make satellites in high orbit that'll blow away every Troll on the planet, she could do this. "I'll be right out," she said then took her new dress into the washroom. She closed the door then looked around the cramped bathroom for a hanger, hook, or anything to hang the dress on, but there was nothing. She wanted to transmute a shelf to put her robe on and a hanger for her dress, but stopped. She didn't want to risk it, knowing that the city scanners might detect the transmuted materials. Instead she tucked the dress under her arm then grabbed the bathroom's paper towel. She wiped the top of the toilet tank before putting down more paper towel then folded the dress, careful not to let it touch any other surface. Taking off the layers of her robe, she placed them on the toilet seat. Standing in her underwear, she held the dress against her body seeing how it'd fit and noticed that he got her measurements right, but the dress would fit too tight, showing the lines of her underwear.

She closed her eyes and sighed, remembering that he put in an effort to surprise her. She visualized his sweet smile and how happy he was to give her his gifts, she couldn't disappoint him. The dress was beautiful, but she was in the wrong place to put it on. If she got one drop of water on it in this cramped bathroom, it'd dry funny and show up against her body and she didn't have the right makeup or accessories to pull the colors together. She's going to look like a giant over dressed dandelion. She looked at her underwear and imagined how stupid she'd look with the creases and lines showing then took her underwear off. She hadn't showered in over a day and wasn't feeling fresh and now she was going commando.

She took off her bra, but when she slipped her panties off she noticed her dirty toes. "He forgot the shoes," she whispered then checked the inside of the box on the off chance he'd stuffed them in there and she'd missed them, but didn't. She looked at the sandals she'd been wearing under her robes then back to her toes. "You're killing me Kole," she said to her reflection then lifted her foot to awkwardly wash it on the sink. She ran the cold water across the top of her foot then rubbed the dirt, smearing it. She hit the soap dispenser then worked to clean her foot. Once clean she grabbed more paper towel to dry her foot off then pulled her foot out of the sink. The only thing she was looking forward to with her other foot, was that the water was warm. She lifted her other foot and awkwardly put it in the sink, but before she started, her other foot slipped an inch on the flooring, almost toppling her. Her arm shot forward and her fingers slid across the top of the paper towel dispenser finding grip. Her knee twisted and for a second, her toe jammed into the faucet's nozzle, spraying warm water across her chest. She fought to keep balance and her foot out of the nozzle and in her struggle she ripped the paper towel dispenser off the wall.

She caught the dispenser, gently dropping it on the floor then fixed her balance. This was not how she wanted her date to go and this was the first time Kole thought to surprise her. She felt awful. Everything was going wrong and all she had to do was ask if they could do it later, but that would kill the date's momentum. The thought of disappointing Kole was worse, making her cry while she cleaned her other foot. After gathering the last of the paper towel, she dried herself off then slipped into her dress. The dress was beautiful, making her figure look great. A perfect fit. But the color washed out her face and put a yellow glow up her neck and under her chin.

She slipped her sandals on, feeling the grit on the padding against the souls of her feet then fixed her hair the best she could. She looked at her reflection at her puffy eyes and wished she had the correct makeup and nail polish to go with the dress, but she was going to make it happen. She survived the ordeal and decided to own it. She had been through worse in her life, but not by much. Fighting with the bathroom and the whole ordeal around the dress made killing Trolls look easy. And she wasn't going to let any of her frustration seep into her date.

She felt heated and needed to cool down, fearing that any per-spiration would put stains and water marks on her dress. Feeling cooler, she came out of the bathroom and waited. Kole held the rose's stem, examining the petals while slowly spinning it in his fingers. "It's lovely," she said.

Their eyes met. Kole ran his eyes down her body then back up. "It's not as lovely as you. You make the dress look good."

All her frustration and insecurities melted away. That's all she needed. A warm smile, a bit of reassurance and she could face the world wearing a burlap sack. Kole put the rose down then took a step closer and offered his arm. She wished she had a shawl to hang off her shoulders and down her arms to tie their looks together. She slipped her arm in his and together they strolled to the cab waiting on a landing pad.

"Maybe later, when this Troll business is over, we'll buy our own hover-car to get around in," he said, hinting that they could stay among the Humans.

She didn't give too much thought to sticking around and didn't like the idea of anyone dictating how she should use her power. Kole had a nice dream, but he wanted to live in a gilded cage and she wasn't sure if she could. She saw it coming and while working on the satellites, she decided that the second target for her weapon would be the Rippers. She'd destroy them all, but had an inkling of doubt. Alchemists were still being born and the temptation to be a jerk is strong when no one can do anything about it. The question that made her rethink her decision was, if she removed the Rippers, who would police the new Alchemists? The next step in her thinking brought her to a place she didn't like. What if her weapon could remove Alchemy itself? But because the other races had Alchemy woven into their cells, it would kill them and she couldn't live with that. Even if someone got hold of her weapon and used to against the Alchemists, it would neutralize everyone equal to, or weaker than her, leaving only those stronger than her, and James. The thought of rebalancing the world appealed to her, but James would have to go. All the roads of her thinking went to reasons for James' destruction. It wasn't personal. She just needed to give him a permanent hair cut at the shoulders.

Kole cuddled with her during the cab ride, holding her hand and whispering more of his dreams into her ear. James did tell the truth. Alchemists were unable to procreate, limiting their influence on the world, but if Enora used her weapon to remove Alchemy, there was a chance her and Kole would be able to have children. In exchange for that, they'd lose their power then grow old and move on. She held her thoughts back, listening to him talk about hope and the future. She loved his dream.

The cab went to the newer part of town and descended into a parking garage. She hadn't seen much of the city preferring to work in her lab and was pleasantly surprised at the architecture and cleanliness of the buildings. The building looked strong, built to channel force through its structure to survive whatever the future will throw at it.

The cab stopped. Kole got out then held his hand out to help her. She graciously took it then together they walked into the building and along a path that wound its way through exotic plant life. Along the walls, seamless projectors showed faraway landscapes and low sounding animal noises played over the P.A. It was a lovely, setting the mood for when they walked into the restaurant. Enora enjoyed the new Human take on beauty and what was special compared to her life before the Purge. In the past, she'd never gone to such a nice place, even after she became an Alchemist. She could've easily afforded it, but it was unimportant to her. She had better things to do then to enjoy the moment. But that was the difference between youth and wisdom. Now she could stretch the seconds in this beautiful moment, enjoying every part of it.

When they were shown their table, Kole held her seat and his gentlemanly kindness touched her. He'd treated her better that any other man had, making her fight back her tears. If he saw her tears, the flow of the day would change and she'd have to put it back on track explaining away her useless history. For all his niceties her mind kept slipping into negative thinking. She kept her thoughts about the Trolls, James and the future of Alchemy to herself, hoping that Kole's dreaming and sweet words would inspire her. She had spent too long thinking dark thoughts and wanted to build pathways in her brain to snap out of it. And if she didn't change, those dark pathways would deepen and that'll be all she'll see.

They ordered water and after the waitress went away, Kole leaned closer, stretching out his hands to hold hers. His warm touch made her smile. "I'm a lucky man," he said. "You are more than beautiful, smart and strong. Each of your wonderful qualities adds a flower to the bouquet that is you."

"Thank you," she said and blushed. "When we first met, I could see the light in you and knew that we were meant to be together. I loved you from the moment I saw you."

He chuckled then said, "You made quite the entrance. It was hard not to notice you."

They looked into each other's eyes and she realized that she didn't know what the restaurant looked like. She'd been staring at him the whole time. In the lull of conversation she normally would've gone to touch up her makeup, but since she didn't have any, she took in her surroundings. The restaurant was open with an abundance of space between tables. Artificial light shone down from fake skylights making it look like morning and the screens on all of the walls showed the view from the top floor. She knew that they didn't go to the top floor and could feel the duracrete encasing them, but found that she enjoyed the illusion. She tapped her sandal on the floor that looked like stonework, but wasn't. She assumed it was a cheaper and more durable material. And at the back, behind Kole was the discrete bar that had a modest collection of expensive alcohol. She was pleased with Kole's choices and tried to hear the people next to them, noticing that the restaurant used noise cancelling technology, giving each table the sense that they were the only ones there.

Their meal came and they took their time dining. It wasn't about the food. It was the experience that connected them on a deeper level. Over their meal they talked about pleasant things, deliberately steering clear of all the bad things they've done. Kole brought up the Slaver party, mentioning the floats and costumes the Slavers made for their celebration. It was a crazy party that he hadn't enjoyed because they were on a mission. He had been in a hurry his whole life and wanted to slow down and savor the moments. She agreed, stopping his reminiscence before he got to the end where she killed all everyone there. And as funny as it was to find Nick sunburned and duck taped to a chair, it was still hurtful.

"Do we have any humor that isn't hurtful to someone?" she asked.

Kole looked up at the ceiling accessing his memories then said, "I can't think of any. People haven't done much since the Purge.

I've seen stage plays and old vids that claimed to be comedies, but someone got hurt for the laugh. What is funny without someone else's pain?"

She thought about it then answered, "Puns."

"Puns, like what?"

"I don't know I'm not that punny."

He groaned. "That wasn't funny."

"What do you expect? You gave me nothing to work with. Who can come up with a pun on the spot?"

"Well, in that case, you didn't do too badly. You gave me a slight tickle, but I can see what you're saying. I was thinking along the same lines. Since we've met, we don't have many happy memories that aren't tainted with something sour. I want to start something new and build happy thoughts and experiences that we can revisit to put a smile on our faces."

"That sounds fantastic. I'd really like that."

"Who knows, maybe Eric will join us, but he likes to push my buttons. It might take awhile to change."

She couldn't see Eric coming along on their quest for happiness. "You can't wait for him, Kole. He'll either join us in our positive thinking, or find his own way. That's how it works when people change. They grow together, or drift apart."

"I know. I always thought he would be like me, but now I can see that he's trying hard to be his own person. I thought his behavior was his way of proving to himself that he's not like me, but what scares me is the thought that his true self has come out and it has nothing to do with me."

She tried to remember when she was young, but the logic that drove her then was long gone. "Don't worry," she said. "Eventually he'll come full circle and return to what he knows. If you think about it, all we are is a collection of tools that we learned to use when we were children. Our body grew and our logic changed, but the tools to manipulate our environment are still the same."

"I guess you're right. At his core he is a good kid. It was my meddling that messed him up. Of course you have to raise the child, keeping them safe, but it was always a fine balance. You never know what will set them off and scar them for life. I might have accidentally stepped on his favorite toy and now somewhere in his mind he won't let it go. You never know. He'll have to figure that out."

"Good. Now let's talk about something else. Tell me something nice."

They sipped their after lunch drinks while Kole told her nice things, flattering her, but she could tell he was struggling. He wasn't the most romantic man, but his trying made everything he said special. After drinks they walked arm in arm down the flower garden path to the main entrance. She didn't want their lunch date to end and thought about continuing it at home then remembered what she promised Sarah. Once the sensors on her satellites were properly calibrated, she was supposed to search for a Troll army that might be near the city. The Trolls hadn't moved and probably wouldn't for the next little while, but the thought crossed her mind. In the past she'd learned to listen to the whispers, subtle hints like checking something for no reason to learn that it needed to be fixed. She suspected that the hints came from her subconscious and didn't want to listen. But she heard them and would kick herself for not listening if things went bad. Besides, it was a little detour.

They walked into the parking garage and waited for a cab. "I want to continue this at home," she said while giving him the look. "But I have to return to the lab."

"What for?" he asked.

"I promised to do something for Sarah, but I forgot until now."

"How can I say no to the look you just gave me, but don't take too long. I might get bored and wander off."

She laughed. "I don't think so."

They arrived at her lab and after Enora punched in the door's code, she walked strait to her work table thinking that the sooner she fulfilled her promise, the sooner she could return to her lunch date. She accessed her table, bringing up its holographic matrix. A light blue light shimmered in front of her, responding to her touch. Her fingertip moved, accessing the communications and connected to the closest Satellite above Winter Haven. Kole walked around to the other side of the table, casually watching with blue light on his face. Enora didn't expect to find much. A couple of Troll spies with a communication system, or a small team waiting to take advantage of the city's misfortune, but when an area several kilometers away lit up bright red, her jaw dropped.

"What is that?" asked Kole.

She didn't know and planned to ignore his question until she knew something. She magnified the area seeing an active Troll presence. There were more than ten Battle Barges, Flyers and Fighter surrounding several structures with weapon systems.

Kole leaned on the table. "Those look like missile silos."

Enora magnified and scanned. Small windows popped up identifying the warheads. She swiped and read more of the windows then released a string of profanity that made Kole laugh.

"Nicely put," he commented then said, "I guess the Trolls don't need us for food anymore."

"Is their end game? They must know about my weapon."

"It looks that way. They probably sent a team to the Battleships to investigate, but this couldn't have been built overnight."

"This was probably plan B," she said. The scanners picked up a power surge. "The weapons are powering up. They must have detected my scan."

Kole's optimistic and boyish look disappeared and was replaced with a darker scowl. "We can't let those missiles launch. The city won't be able to shoot them all down and we can't make them go away before the hit. If they see that, they'll know Alchemist among them and I'm sure they'll thank us for saving their lives before they lynch us."

"That's not funny."

"I'm not laughing. I like Winter Haven. I'm going to destroy their weapons where they are. I learned some things watching you work when I tried to help you. I can take care of them. What I need you to do is search for more Trolls in case they have a redundancy plan."

She nodded and went to work scanning the landscape, trusting that Kole would succeed. She took the statistics of the missiles and assumed that a second base would be within that range. She was right and found the second base. It was more of the same. Her fingers went through the satellites system, preparing to use her weapon, but stopped. She assumed that the Trolls knew about her weapon, but the bases have been there for some time. It was her scans that tipped the Trolls off alerting them that they've been found and if she used her weapon again, they might be able to defend against it. It needed to be a surprise, wiping out the Troll with the press of a button.

She powered down her satellite then looked through the holo-gram at Kole who stood with his eyes closed. His mind was far off, stopping the Trolls. She focused, sending her awareness to the other base. The landscape flashed before her mind's eye then dove into the earth and emerged in a silo at the base of a missile. The count-down had started and the missiles were preparing to leave. The thought of one missile escaping her reach and striking the city sick-ened her. She went further and entered the Troll's computer system. She overrode their security and re-anchored the missiles, but that wasn't enough. She closed the silo doors then linked the missiles to-gether before setting them off. She wasn't sure if the explosions would kill off the Trolls, but knew it'd slow them down. All she needed to do was finish building her satellite network then kill all the Trolls, ending the nightmare.

She opened her eyes to Kole smiling at her. "How did you do?" he asked.

Seeing his smiling face reassured her of his success and was about to tell him that she too succeeded when she heard a series of explosions through the duracrete walls, rattling her table and vibrat-ing the floor beneath her feet.

"I bet we'll be the first ones Sarah calls," Kole said with the hint of a joke in his voice.

She didn't doubt it. While she was destroying the missiles, she had instructed the satellite to continue its search finding a scattered Troll presence, but nothing that posed a threat. She didn't like how close the city came to destruction and programmed the satellite to continue its search and alert her if it scans even the smallest group. If five Trolls got together to share a smoke, she'd know about it. And the thought of setting up guided missile platforms to trash those smaller groups made her smile. She didn't want to give them the opportunity to rebuild only to threaten the city later.

"Well, shall we go my lady," Kole said then wiggled his eyebrows, hinting to their playful business.

She smiled. He walked around the table then offered his arm, but before she took it, the com chimed.

"Ignore it," he suggested. "We know who it is, she can wait."

"Speaking about waiting, we have to wait for a cab anyway," she said.

"That's a great idea. You talk to her and I'll fetch a cab," he said, rushing away then stood in the outside hall facing her saying, "But don't take too long, cabs are expensive."

The com chimed again. "Really, that's what you're worried about?"

"Are you going to get that? Tick, tock," he said then hit the door release.

Eric had come by his annoying demeanor honestly. Kole had a special way of pushing her buttons. He called it humor, or the cute factor, but she didn't think it was either of those things, but he did remind her not to take things so serious, or to get upset of the small things. And of course, she gave it right back, after she saved up. Releasing a torrent of verbal slaps when he least expected it.

She pressed the com and Sarah's face appeared over the table. "How can I be of service Mother Sarah?" asked Enora.

Sarah didn't respond. Silence passed between them making her think that her screen froze then Sarah's eye twitched. "Is that how you're going to play it, Enora?"

"Play what?" she asked, continuing her innocent routine.

"Whatever, so it was you. I take it that you found the Troll army outside the city. You could've warned me. I might have been able to prepare the people and curb the panic. Tell me what happened so I can get things under control."

She forgot how two massive explosions on the horizon would look to the city's citizens. She could only imagine the city wide panic, but wondered if it was as bad as Sarah said. As sad as it was, people have gotten used to living under the threat of destruction and she guessed that things were already back to normal. "I did what you asked and scanned for Trolls around the city. I found some, but my scans alerted them. Judging by all their missiles and lack of troops, I don't think they plan to take Winter Haven anymore. I think they were waiting until everyone was here to blow us all up."

"That's good news," Sarah cheerfully said.

Confused, she asked, "It is?"

"If I'm going to die, I'd rather be blown up than eaten. Knowing that the Trolls no longer want to eat us takes away so much fear. Now the Trolls are like every other person trying to kill us," she said making strange sense.

"I guess so, but no one should be trying to kill us."

She smiled softly. "You should know this by now, but people have been killing each other since the beginning of time and with our help, the human race will find true peace. Thank you for taking care of the Trolls. If Kole is there, thank him too."

"I will and you're welcome."

"Your news changes things. Our defenses are centered on direct contact. Now we're going to have to thicken our missile defense. I'm just glad the Trolls haven't gone back to nuclear or chemical warfare."

Sarah was also glad. She trusted her scan and didn't double check the type of warheads before setting them off. She won't make that mistake again. "I don't think the Trolls will go that far," she said. "They want to take the world, not destroy it and who knows what radiation does to their cells. They could be saving themselves from horrific mutations."

"That's true. When do you think you'll be done your project?"

"Soon, I'll get back to work after my lunch date."

"Aww, that's so cute. You've been working hard and I know how much pressure you're under. It's good that you're taking some you time," Sarah said.

"It was Kole's idea. He went shopping and bought me a dress."

"Just the dress?" she asked.

"He surprised me and I didn't get a chance to prepare."

"That's typical. Men don't think beyond the dress. It's our fault really."

"How so?" asked Enora, wondering if Sarah had ever battled a cramped bathroom.

"We make ourselves look good and they think we wake up that way."

Enora laughed. "That's it," she said.

"I know that time is of the essence with your project, but over-working yourself will make you careless and strip away the value of what you're going to accomplish. I want a one and done scenario. I want you to be good to yourself and let Kole worry about everything else."

"I'll make sure to tell him that. He's been under the gun for so long, I think he doesn't know what to do with himself," she said, playing with the idea that Sarah would have some work for him.

"Honestly, there isn't much for him to do, but sit it out like the rest of us. James is on his way with more survivors and we're all waiting on you. Remember, no pressure."

Enora wasn't sure, but had to ask, "Did you tell James about my project?"

"No," she said. "You and I talked about that and I haven't changed my mind. I'm on whoever's side that'll help me propel the human race into a brighter future." She became serious saying, "Your project needs to die with the Trolls and it'll take time for James to realize the Trolls are gone. He's not as observant as he thinks, but I can't lie to him forever. He will eventually look into it."

"I understand, but it sucks to have everything riding on my shoulders. What did I do in a past life to deserve this mess?" she asked and secretly wanted an answer. She would do what needed to be done, but would rather not.

"I don't think I have past lives, but life is life and when it's my time, I'll return to the energy that made me, hopefully somewhere nice."

"I hope so too, you deserve it, but I have to go. Kole warned me that if I take too long, he'd wander off, so I better go see if he's still here."

They said their goodbyes and Enora found Kole waiting for her in the back of a cab. He got out then helped her in. She slid over, allowing him beside her and they held hands on their ride home. Enora was happy to be with Kole. They worked together, anticipating each other's needs, all with the intent to build a stronger relationship. She couldn't wait to see what the future held for them.

Chapter

14

Jas sat on a park bench atop of one of the green buildings in Winter Haven. One of four buildings dedicated to the preservation of plant life. It was a pleasant walk from the lobby, up through the various ecosystems to the top floor. She stopped at various spots and sat on a park bench to admire the beauty of nature. She wanted to have a quiet moment to herself, contemplating her future, but people took it upon themselves to sit with her. She didn't invite them, expecting them to sit on the other benches, but she attracted them. It didn't matter who, men, women, young and old would sit next to her, sharing their life story. As far as she could tell, she did nothing to instigate the conversations and dropped social clues that she wasn't interested, but they kept talking. She said nothing and learned all kinds of personal information about people she had never met. She was polite and would smile and nod, but tune them out. Eventually they would part and she'd continue her way up. On occasion she'd stop to admire a plant she'd never seen then feel someone looking at her. Compelled to look, the person would smile at her then inviting her over, but she'd ignore them.

The green buildings were made to filter out the city's pollution.

Fans pulled in the outside air, ran it through filters designed to cap-
ture certain particles then circulate the air inside the building and
blow it out. The city planners had forethought and decided not to
poison their citizens while trying to save them. No one knew how
long they'd be in the city, or how big it was going to get. They
thought in terms of a metropolis that way their support system
would be in place if it came to that. It also looked good for them if
society spread out. They'd be able to become the capital city of a
new nation. It was a positive structure made to bring peace of mind
to those feeling trapped, needing some real space. Most apartments
are small and cramped with video mats attached to the duracrete
walls and ceiling. A person could get whatever view they wanted,
the channel was free. The city's mental health department was in
charge of diminishing the stress from people living on top of each
other.

Jas continued on passing the last of the people. Few went to the
top floor even thought the air felt cleaner and it was as nice as anywhere else in the building. But if she wanted to be left alone, she
had to climb to the top. Knowing what she knew, she didn't understand why people who lived in a cramped environment went to an
open space to sit next to a stranger. Not only did they invade her
space, they flung their verbal garbage at her. She originally went
there to clear her mind and decide on what she needed to do next,
but they wouldn't leave her alone. In the end, she guessed that the
people who bothered her were venting, shedding the crap in their
lives so they could return to their duracrete coffins. She thought
about making a sign, shirt, or armband with a symbol meaning, do
not disturb. But would a person be rude to wear it? She didn't like
the option. Being and be held hostage by social etiquette, making
them the bad guys and you the victim, or snub them making you the
bad guy and them the victims. Either way, feelings were going to be
hurt.

She was sick of being the victim, first to James then to random
strangers. She wasn't a dumping ground for emotional garbage, but

people don't think that way. It should be an occupation, paid by the city, perhaps a call center where people can call in to vent, or air their personal laundry. Her idea was just as bad as people going up to a stranger to bare their souls, or maybe she didn't get it. She thought in a formula. If she got into an argument and said some bad things, a question would be asked. Does she like the person? If yes, apologize and make things nice. If no, walk away. It was a simple if and then equation that left her with no friends, but she didn't mind. Eventually everyone got on her nerves like the old lady who has a dying pet. She never had a pet and didn't understand why people poured so much into a dumb animal when they could get a new one. She thought the same way about children, but she kept that to herself. Voicing such things made her different, so she pretended to care, saying the right thing at the right time to make her look normal, but she knew she wasn't.

She always knew that there had been something broken in her, maybe from a head injury early in life. She thought her childhood was normal, but would say and do things to her brother and sister that her parents didn't like. The confusion in her head made things worse, but through it, she'd hear her dad tell her that she wasn't right in the head. She didn't know what that meant and wasn't allowed to play with her siblings anymore. Then her parents treated her differently, making her feel wrong inside and that was when she learned how to pretend, more for survival than anything else. She didn't feel safe in her own home, worried that they'd take her away and leave her in the forest for the Werewolves to eat. Then she was touched my Alchemy, manifesting in her at puberty.

It wasn't an exact science. Some children showed signs at birth while others shortly after puberty when their hormones shifted. In a way she was lucky. She didn't know when her mind got bent, but if she had Alchemy earlier on, people that had teased and smacked her around would've died. But by learning how to pretend, she had tools in place to channel her negative thoughts and redirect her toxic energy. At the time, she thought she was doing a great job at appearing normal, but she didn't understand that everyone saw right threw her and still thought she was weird. And when her power kicked in, she could tell that the people around her were afraid. They wouldn't talk to her and their faces would change when they looked at her. That was where James found her and took her away, giving her life purpose.

James pitched a dream to her, filling her little mind with a future where Alchemist and Humans stood side by side. She had never met anyone from the other races, but took on his hate for them. He said nice things and treated her better than her parents ever had. James became her family and over the years he taught her how to use her power, but now she could see his manipulations. She willingly became his tool, she didn't know any better, but he kept her blind to that fact. From the start, he'd altered pieces of her. One good thing that he did was make it easy for her to fit into society, she liked that part, but now it's gone. All she remembered was behaving and understanding things differently. When that old lady was whining about her dying animal, she bit the inside of her mouth to stop herself from grabbing the old ladies hands and slapping her with them. It was painful to listen to everyone's problems, there was nothing she could do to help them and she didn't want to. She didn't understand the emotions behind anything they were telling her.

She thought about her virus and her dream of global domination, but didn't understand that either. When James' programming was removed, she lost everything. It didn't all leave her at once. It slowly trickled away. She hid her virus and planted a note in Kole's pocket for some reason. It was part of her plan. She knew James wouldn't let her walk away, but didn't know why. It was now a feeling that he'd be upset if she took off. But what good was taking off when she didn't understand anything about the world. She'd have to make mental programs that'd help her decide who to trust. Starting over was a lot of work when all she had to do was take the virus to James, apologize and ask him to fix what's broken in her. He did it before, he'll do it again. And once she was fixed, she'd understand why strangers talk to her. She might even enjoy talking back, and that was the correct response.

She knew what she had to do. She needed to get her virus then take if to James. She walked down the trail, stepping close enough to allow the plants to brush her arms. Plants were good. Most of them didn't hurt people, so she felt safe touching them. It was people she worried about. She never knew who was going to hurt her, or why. If she hadn't been broken, she might have been able to tell if she was safe and feel things for others, but she'll understand when James fixes her. She passed by people casually enjoying the scenery and ignored their greetings and smiles. They were not her friends and she didn't what them to be. She was in a hurry and needed to get to her virus before Kole does.

She passed through the lobby and into the parking garage. She didn't have time to wait for a cab and went to the closest hover-car. She broke in and stole it. She was doing something important, she was going to get her mind fixed and was sure the owner wouldn't mind, but the only reason she justified her action was because her old programming told her that people didn't like having their things stolen. She left the parking garage and followed the rules to get to the landing pad she'd use before going to her lab. She felt safe leaving her new car there, few people knew about the pad. She opened her door and once her foot hit the ground, she remembered that the cars had anti-theft systems and locators. She abandoned her idea of returning to her car then entered the tunnels. The lighting was dim and it stank, but no one was there that'd hurt her. She initiated her shield incase the police decided to follow whomever stole the car, but doubted it. She'd be long gone by then.

She ran passing intersections that all looked the same until she had the feeling that she was lost. She was sure that she knew the tunnels, but part of her memory wasn't right. She knew where her lab used to be then walked through her memories. She backtracked and found the right side tunnel, but when she got there, her virus was gone. The only thing left to do is to confront Kole and get the virus back, but what if she didn't. James might be upset that she made the virus in the first place and he doesn't like Kole, or he shouldn't. She didn't need to confront Kole, she could frame him. James would believe her over Kole, she was sure of it. She'd lie and blame Kole then James would fix her so she could function in society. It was a good plan.

She let the weirdness of the day go and was happy with her decision, choosing a path to the nearest exit. The word around town was that James would be back tomorrow morning and she was excited to see him. She knew his morning would be busy and the best time to ask for what she wanted was before lunch. People are a bit cranky in the morning and hungry before lunch, but will grant you want you want to get rid of you faster. After lunch they're winding down the rest of the day and are more relaxed to give out lesser favors, or so she thought. Now all she needed to do was stay out of trouble.

Once on the street she found a place to spend the night then secured a room. It was what she should've done instead of walking through the green building. She grabbed the rooms remote and turned the walls and ceiling onto the nature channel then lay in bed watching the birds and wildlife move through the jungle. It was like being there. The scenery soothed her mind allowing her violent thoughts to diminish. James had always been good to her and he'll be good again. She remembered his promise to include her in his vision of the future and she couldn't wait for the morning to come.

Jas woke to the gentle alarm of the sunrise and the soft sound of birds chirping. Before she went to bed, she selected one of the preset alarm options for a slow wakeup and found it very pleasant. In the past when she had things to do, she'd set the alarm to shocking. Bright light and a pulsating noise startled her awake, pumping adrenaline into her sleepy mind. She didn't think it was healthy to wake that way, but it got her going. The rush would last for about seven minutes then she'd start coming down in time to collect her preset coffee.

This morning felt different. The alarm didn't make her feel rushed. She grabbed her mug and watched the scenery change to a tropical afternoon beach. She sipped her coffee listening to the rolling waves climb her virtual beach and relaxed into the moment. If you went with the illusion it was quite relaxing, but some people refused, calling it a sinister lie to get the population used to smaller levels of confinement. When the scenery was first implemented, the city allowed ads to play in a floating window, but people quickly tuned out. The ads broke the illusion making people feel suckered into believing a lie. They did want it and demanded the city to take out the ads, but the city was stuck in a contract. The whole project almost died before it started. Quick thinking and luck turned it around. The department of mental health was created, allowing people to be heard which lessened the tension and a new thin flat screen was developed, replacing the holographic projectors. It was a step backward technologically, but it completed the illusion. The screens were made and freely distributed at the city's expense.

Jas finished her coffee then set the machine again for when she got out of the washroom. After her morning routine she came out and grabbed her second cup. She was almost fully awake and ready to take on the day. The scenery on the walls changed to bright green grasslands and the ceiling turned into a dark blue sky.

Her mind went back to when she was with James in the Dark Elf Capital.

They were talking about Winter Haven when James scoffed then said, "There are many ways to kill a people, but the best is to kill their spirit with kindness. People won't know what's happening and will even thank you for it and later be too complacent to fight back."

She had no idea what he was talking about and didn't care. She responded the correct way, lying to him and telling him that she thought he was wise. But what he was talking about had nothing to do with her and it was up to the people in Winter Haven to reject the gifts from him if they didn't want them. There was something wrong in her head and she wasn't remembering the conversation right. There was more said, and she might have understood, but she lost it when Enora yanked James' programming out of her. The logic she used then wasn't helping her now. Everything in her mind was wrong, reminding her why she needed to get James to fix her.

She wore the same clothes as the day before, they still looked clean and didn't smell that bad but before she checked out, she mentally prepared herself. She remembered being with James on his Cruiser and what happened to her. Even though she was fixed at the time, her base personality was still there. She always had a problem being around people and being fixed just took longer for her crazy to bubble through the cracks. In the end all the qualities that James fixed merely suppressed her true self making her reactions worse. She figured that James used patches on her, but in the right place and time, those patches made things worse. She wasn't able to release the building emotional pressure because James' power hid it from her. It was only a matter of time before her emotional stress would've broken her mind. She might have ended up like Byron, The King, or worse. And if her mind broke under the stress of lies, the changes James made would've been tilled into her new personality.

 She patched into the news feed hearing that James had returned a couple of hours ago with more refugees. That was all she needed to know then turned off the feed in the middle of the announcer's blathering about how great James was. She ordered a cab and on her way to meet James, the only question rattling in her mind was, why didn't James tell her that some of her emotional problems were the result what he did? He didn't tell Byron or The King either and knowing that, those two might've worked through their growing madness. She didn't understand why he wouldn't have told them and assumed that he didn't know. She'll tell him. James had always been good to her and he'll fix her.

The cab went as far as it could and parked outside the military base. Jas paid the fair then ignored the cab, looking up at James' Cruiser. It hovered docked to one of the lower towers and from what Jas could see James had run into trouble. The Cruiser's hull was peppered with burns and had a gruesome scar across its underside. With all the damage, she figured the crew had fun. In moments like those everyone had purpose and people liked that, or so she thought.

She presented her pass, entered the base and instructing the guards to tell James' staff that she was on the way. James needed to know she was coming, or might not be there when she arrives. It didn't take her long to get to the elevator. She strolled passed the stream of refugees being directed by military personal on their way to the medical center then walked through a hatch into the Cruiser. The inside looked as bad as the exterior. She passed by blown conduits, ruptured coolant lines and severed wires on her way to the bridge, but was stopped outside its door. James' new assistant directed her to the dining room where she had eaten her meal with James. He was expecting her and she entered without knocking. The room looked like a dining room. All the monitors had been taken down opening up the room and the holographic table was gone, replaced with a chrome and glass one. The walls and ceiling were creamy white and the floor was light brown.

She looked around the room then met James' gaze. "I don't like it," she said. James didn't get up or respond. He sat there dressed in his white uniform with his hair slicked back. Several high backed chromed framed chairs sat around his table and when she went to sit, she noticed the magnetic locks on the chair's legs.

"These are fancy chairs. Where did you get them?" she asked, but James continued to look at her saying nothing. His expression wasn't what she had expected. His teeth weren't showing meaning he wasn't happy and the light in his eyes wasn't there. Something was wrong, but she didn't know what.

She implemented her plan to frame Kole, by laying down a series of lies that she can use to sell Kole out and get what she wants by guessing, "You're upset. I know I seem a little off, but that's Kole's fault. Do you remember those things you did to me when I was younger to fix my mind? He removed them and I need you to put them back."

James leaned forward, resting his elbows on the table. His hands came together in front of his face giving her a better view of his eyes. "Kole, you say?" he asked then went on saying, "I spoke to Sarah after you attacked her and she said that it was one of Kole's friends that had stepped in to save her."

"Well yeah, under his orders," she lied. "Don't listen to Sarah, she doesn't know anything, not like you and I. We've gone places and been in the world, she hasn't. I need you to fix what Kole did."

"So we're back to that are we? And I'm not talking about your persistent request to be fixed. I'm talking about the compulsive lying little girl I found all those years ago. I know that you don't mean to lie. Your mind gets confused and you remember things wrong. Why did you attack Sarah?"

Jas thought about it and saw a way to apply leverage saying, "I don't remember. Maybe if you fix me, I'll be able to tell you." His eyebrows came together and his expression darkened, telling her that he was maybe thinking about it.

His hands lowered, resting on the table and his face went back to normal, meaning that he was calm. "Shall we drop the charade? I'm not going to fix you, you're no longer useful and I know that you had Byron killed. My detective found Monique then questioned her and in exchange for her freedom, she gave you up."

Jas didn't know how to respond. His face hadn't changed and she couldn't deduce what he was feeling. "It wasn't my fault. I gave her the weapon, but she did it, besides Byron deserved it. How does this make you not want to fix me? You've always been nice to me."

He hissed a heavy sigh then enunciated saying, "You are a tool. I was nice to you because I was manipulating you. You have no idea what I'm saying because I'm deliberately keeping my voice and face neutral. I remember you as a child and how your mind works. It's nice to see that you know you're broken, before you didn't and that's real progress. You thought you had the world fooled, ignorant child."

She fought through her cloudy mind. Things weren't going well, or he would've fixed her by now. Confused, she asked, "So what you're saying is that you're not going to fix me?"

"Listen to my words and try to hear what I'm saying. I used you, Byron and The King to get what I want. I was happy when you killed them and yes I know you killed The King as well. I was monitoring his life signs via satellite when you arrived to save him. It's so close to the end now and everything is in motion. I no longer need you, in fact, I don't need any Alchemists. Things are looking up."

She decided that she was being threatened, but he hadn't attacked her, meaning that it's all talk until something physical happens and if nothing happens, he changed his mind. She wanted to use the virus as a bargaining chip, but it wasn't the time. She needed to turn the talk around. "I'm sorry, James. Everything got out of hand and I really believe in your vision of the future. We can still do this together," she said, firmly believing that a person's not caught, until they're caught. Without proof, there's nothing.

James laughed then said, "I lied and you lapped it up. All I had to do is play on your parental issues and you'd do anything for me. Let me tell you about my true vision of the future. I am the one and only true Alchemist and people like you were an accident, coming from a mutation. Let me widen your scope because you look lost. In the entire history of the human race, I was the first Alchemist. Through my intellect, I alone uncovered the key to the Universe. Do you know what that means? I'm pure and you are garbage. When I'm done with you I'm going to kill the surviving Alchemists then cure the world of the Alchemist virus, ending the plague, you manifesting monkey. I'll be the only one with power, the way it was meant to be. It was by accident that those stupid chimps denied me of my godhood and it's taken this long to recover. I've been systematically eradicating all Alchemical life across the planet without anyone figuring it out. Not even you, but you were always crazy. I'm going to say this again because I don't think you get it, you were easy to manipulate."

His face and tone weren't happy. She'd seen this look before when he was about to do something bad. It was too late for her to bargain the virus. She could throw it out there to see if he'd change his mind, but before she said anything, he continued.

"I hate you," he seethed. "I hate all of you false Alchemists. You're monkey crap that's been flung into the world."

She understood hate and realized that she was slated for death the moment they met. Hearing the word hate and seeing his unhappy face made something in her mind finally align, a moment of clarity through the fog, allowing her to know whose fault it really was for every bad thing in her life. James never planned to share power, making her feel good about making the virus and wanting to kill him. She was right and must have known on some level that he was using her. Everything she did for him was his fault. He didn't fix her mind. He twisted her thoughts, making her kill Byron and The King. He said so himself, she was sure of it. It was all James' fault and she was innocent. He wanted them dead and she must have picked up on that. She thought she was very intuitive, feeling things out, but now it was time for revenge. She might not be the one who kills him, but in keeping the virus a secret, she'll have a hand in his death. The thought pleased her, but since James hadn't killed her yet, she still has a chance to survive.

Jas' mind felt muddled. She was angry, or thought she should be angry that James had victimized her. She was innocent after all, but did enjoyed hurting people for him because he said they deserved it. She had good memories with him, but strange emotions ran thought her. Her guts twisted then she realized that she was panicking on the inside. She had felt fear before, but that was after James fixed her. It was a curious feeling, strange and unconnected like a train that never pulled up to a station, forever a ghost lingering in the back of her mind.

"I can see it in your eyes," James said. "You're finally putting it together. I didn't want to kill you until you understood how stupid you are." He frowned and wiggled his shoulders then said, "Killing you before that wouldn't have felt right. It's like beating on a helpless person. I could never stomach doing that, it's beneath me. That's what you and the other two idiots were for."

She had no idea what he was talking about. She hadn't put anything together, all she knew was that James lied to her and made her do bad things. That was normal stuff in her life, it wasn't a big deal. She was alive and capable of moving beyond that, so it didn't matter. She was looking for something more than hate. Something spectacular that'd blow her mind, but couldn't see it. But James was becoming more animated telling her that he was getting off on gloating over nothing. She couldn't deny that she was frightened and understood that she was fired, but didn't care about the rest. But James did and if she could get the right pattern of words, he'd let her go.

"It must be tough being you," she said sounding sympathetic and doing her best to give James what she thought he wanted to hear. "All these years of being alone with no one to match your intellect, I can't fathom that. I know how strong you are and you probably didn't need anyone, but for me I wouldn't be able to do it alone. I know how you see me, but I'm glad to be sitting here in this moment of honesty. Doesn't it feel good to be open and honest with someone? You've shown me the true you and I accept you." All she needed now was a chance to run and he'd never see her again. He was still listening and it was time for her to lay down some solid lies. She was going to bury him in lies until he could no longer see. In his confession and truth, the only thing she picked up on was his need to be seen as smart, so she planned to make him choke on it. "I still want to be part of your godhood. Sure, you'll have millions of people groveling at your feet, but will you be able to show them the real you?"

He raised his hand stopping her. "Yes, I'm going to stuff my feet inside them and wear them as slippers so my feet never touch the ground. I own the world and they're here to amuse me. Why would I need to hide? No one can touch me."

"I can't hurt you, so why are you going to kill me?"

"You're not listening. I told you like three times. I'm not killing you Jas. I'm killing the Alchemy in you. You're just its home. But now you're annoying me, so I think I'll be killing both of you."

"I'm confused."

"Shocker, let me explain again," he said. "Picture yourself as a house with someone living in it and there's me firing a rocket at the house to kill the guy inside. That's you. Try not to take it personally."

Jas finally understood what was talking about, but didn't know how she'd get out of his scenario alive. She was beginning to think that James was crazy and worse, in denial. "I totally get it," she lied. She could feel her fear deep inside her, a real feeling, but her attention span was waning. James was officially crazy. There was nothing special about him and she was losing interest. But she needed to keep it together. "You plan to eliminate Alchemy in everyone, but yourself, that's commendable," she said. "I'm totally onboard. You'll save the world and will earn the right to rule it. Even if you cull the weak and stupid, there'll be plenty of people to go around. You'll be able to perfect humanity. That's what gods do." James leaned back into his chair, studying her. She liked his long pause, it was a good sign telling her that he was thinking about letting her live, or not. She honestly couldn't tell, but it felt good.

"I like what you're saying and your honesty," He said, but it sounded like he was mocking her. "If I let you live, eventually I'll take away your Alchemy and I'm not sure what you think about that. But I do need people around me who understand the bigger picture."

She nodded then humbly said, "My Alchemy is nothing compared to your future. I'd gladly sacrifice the man in my house to better your human race."

She could see her way out. All she needed to do was get though this meeting then she can tell Kole everything and he can risk his skin to kill James. Her day was brightening. Kole kills James and she keeps her power, double win, but she's not free until she was free. She has him thinking and now has to nudge the conversation in a different direction to make him think that keeping her alive was his idea.

She remembered James being upset over Byron and The Kings deaths or pretending to be upset, she didn't truly care. She didn't understand why he pretended then, but it gave her fuel now. "I understand that I overstepped when I killed Byron and The King, but they were damaging your plan and I did it to protect what you were building," she lied and smiled on the inside. Their deaths made her great and placed her into an excellent position to survive now. "I should've talked to you first. We are your tools and I now can see how wrong I was. All I can do is make it up to you. I am still willing to be your right hand and help protect your future endeavors."

"Jas, to be honest, you are my favorite tool. I've had many servants over the years, but none were as devious as you."

"Thank you," she said then lowered her chin to bat her eyes at him.

"I didn't fix you. Sure I rewired portions of your mind to make you controllable and gave you power. When Sarah told me that you were going to kill her, I thought you were making your move to seize power. Then you got neutered robbing me of my victory. I wanted to do that. I was going let you attack me then strip you of my power making you understand how feeble you are before I killed you. I had everything planned out and I was looking forward to it. What a thrill. Of all my tools, you were my best, but you've forgotten who taught you how to manipulate. All you've done was regurgitate everything I taught you. I look at you and I have no idea what you are. Sociopath, schizophrenic, I'm not sure, but what I do know is that you're dangerous. And as annoying as you are for arguing with me, I do have a soft spot for you."

"Wait," she said interrupting him. "I thought you decided to let me live."

"No, the truth is, I was stalling because I was having a hard time letting you go. You'll never give up until someone puts a bullet into your heart and you'll always be looking for a way to end me. I'm proud of you."

That was all she ever wanted to hear and it satisfied her, but before she could respond, the floor opened up beneath her. She slipped off her chair and fell. Her instinct took over trying to remake her shield, but failed. She didn't know when her shield had come down, but was sure that she'd raised before she got there. It doesn't matter, she was falling. She pushed out the useless arguments in her cluttered mind and tried to reach out, grabbing for a passing deck, or someone she could grapple with, but couldn't reach. She fell too quickly and saw no one. She was alone, plummeting toward the ground.

Her mind slowed then her life flashed before her eyes. All her memories and experiences were centered on James and in her moment of helplessness she found that she actually loved him. In her mind she always thought and told herself that, but feeling it was different. The mind could lie and tell you many things, but when the heart speaks it makes things real.

Warmth pulsated in her chest, a comforting hug that soothed the terror and loneliness within her. He had become her father and it became clear to her that even if she'd been normal, she'd still be right where she was, falling to her death. Would he care? Would he miss her? She was sure he would, because with all her heart, she missed him. She felt the connection between them then sent her forgiveness through it.

All she had ever wanted was his love and as she sped toward the duracrete, she could see all the lies her mind had told her. By joining him, there was only one path for her and that was to end in a bright red flash then darkness.

Chapter

15

Eric hid the virus near the highest concentration of Ripper am-munition in the armory, gambling that someone more powerful than him wouldn't find it. He had his identification ready when he walked onto the base, but no one stopped him. He looked at the guards at the gate and they nodded back, irritating him. He wanted to be stopped and subjected to their procedure, but assumed Sarah was behind his all access pass in case something bad happens and he doesn't have time to be stopped. That type of special treatment drew attention to him when he was trying to blend in and he didn't like it. The base, like the city was clean, but had a layer of discipline. All the grass had been cut to the same length, the perfect Human flag flew high on the gleaming flag pole and the duracrete walkways were free of bird crap. Kole had said many things throughout his child-hood, going on and on about stuff he tried to tune out, but was right when he said that the cleanliness of a place sets a certain mindset in those living in it. All Kole needed to say was that a person's envi-ronment contributes to their mental state. Eric understood it back then, it was obvious, but this time it was the first time he saw it. It was having someone tell you that the sky is blue, you know it, but it takes on a different meaning when you look up and see it for yourself.

He'd pass military personal along the walkway drawing their attention and receiving nods. He'd nod back and by the time he reached the armory he realized that wearing street clothes and having piercings wasn't the best way to blend in either. He assumed people would ignore him, like everyone else in his life, but he was the intruder, disrupting the balance of their environment. He was no longer mad at the guards for letting him in. He should've conformed to their uniform to blend in. It was his arrogance that assumed people wouldn't notice. It was their job as protectors to notice what didn't belong.

In the armory, he found the thickest overlapping layers of void and stashed the virus there. The virus knew he was going to leave it there and reached out, touching his mind, asking when it'd be able to find its home. Eric felt its energy ripple across his skin and pretended to examine the Ripper Round surplus when soothing it. He assured the virus that he'd take it to James and convinced it to hide by shrinking its unique void, making it harder to be detected. He was sad to leave the virus and missed it when he left its influence. The other voids tried to consume him, tugging at his energy, but the virus felt more symbiotic, but he wasn't James. Eric suspected James wouldn't be thinking fuzzy thoughts when he and the virus get together, but that wasn't Eric's problem. He was just the package boy.

He left the base then spent the day shopping for clothes. He didn't like the fashion from just one district and decided to roam between them all. He searched for the unique items that'd best display his personality and was surprised. Out of curiosity, the people who he talked to asked him where he lived. When he told them they were shocked. They asked because they couldn't figure out which district he belonged to with his mismatched clothing. He didn't think shopping all of the stores would matter, but he drew more attention to himself. It seemed that they didn't like his originality, but called him eccentric when they found out where he lived.

He didn't know that most people in the city didn't have windows. He didn't think it was that important, but it was to those who didn't have them. He learned that since the buildings were close together, the city decided that widows weren't needed. And because he had a view, the city didn't install the thin video mats in his apartment. The mats were for mental health and if he wanted them, he'd have to pay which he thought about. On his shopping trip, he found games and movies that could be played on the walls or ceiling and with powerful surround sound a person could feel like they were the movie, but he wanted to sleep on his decision.

The next day, Eric sprang out of bed in his underwear then flung open his drapes to greet the afternoon sun. Looking across the city between the lines of traffic, he could see James' Carrier. He thought about retrieving the virus and going to see him, but didn't feel that it was the right time. He doubted he'd get very far and James would see him coming. It needed to be a surprise, or James wouldn't co-operate and die. Besides, if he told the virus, it'd shoot a beam of energy into his forehead, a constant begging for Eric to do its bidding. It didn't sound fun. He also knew Kole and Enora, thinking that the perfect time to introduce the virus into the mix was when Kole and Enora face off with him. Right now everyone was playing nice, but when the pressure of the Trolls is gone, old hatreds will re-emerge. It's only a matter of time.

He turned around and was tempted to close his drapes. The sun-light coming in showed the dust floating in the air and revealed all the garbage he had scattered around. Takeout boxes, wrappers, dirty laundry and random bits of garbage were strewn across the floor. Eric cringed. After all the things he'd heard about how others lived, he was wealthy, but lived in squalor. They didn't have to room to be slobs and here he was rubbing his filth in their faces. To make him-self feel better, he opened a window to air out his stink then cleaned up after himself. He did it for himself. He was lucky to have the apartment and treating it badly, jinxed any further gifts. It didn't take him long to gather all the garbage, but noticed the dust on the coun-

ters and toilet. He hadn't been there that long, but somehow had
made a huge mess and decided that his first major purchase would
be robotic cleaners. That way he'd always have someone cleaning
up after him. He truly felt privileged.

Using his data pad, he searched through the city's shopping network and discovered that there were different layers of robotic cleaners depending on the task at hand and he chose the brand that would
match his decor. Their store was on the other side of the city and
having nothing better to do, he decided to walk there then take a cab
back. But before he left, he wanted to listen to the latest foot traffic
report to avoid the crowds. He turned on his wall mounted com
and tuned into a news report. In a red banner at the bottom of the
screen, the topic read, "A city in morning." The announcer reported
that a woman committed suicide by jumping off James' Cruiser. He
watched the footage. The camera panned across James' Cruiser then
zoomed in on a person falling underneath. He was glad that the person disappeared behind a building because it wasn't hard to imagine
what happened next. It made him sad to watch.

Eric remembered the woman who snuck into his hospital room
and slipped a note into Kole's pocket. He stepped closer to his com
and when they played the footage again, he zoomed in the best he
could, seeing the smear of color that was the same as the woman
clothes. He remembered what her note said and knew that she had
confronted James and lost. The news announcer went on to saying
that the department of mental health has offered grief counselors
for all those affected by the city's loss. He changed the channel and
listened to the foot traffic report then took a shower. Cleaning his
apartment in his underwear made him aware of how he smelled and
also made him feel dirty. He showered then dressed in his new de-
signer t-shirt with ripped grubby pants then threw on a thin dress
jacket, sneakers and a wide brim sun hat. He enjoyed what he
bought, picking the best from each district and mixing them all together. The last thing he grabbed before he left was his lucky rock
that was perfectly round and almost flat. It was special because he

had found the other day in the middle of the city where it shouldn't have been.

Eric felt bad for the woman on the news who had fallen to her death and was glad that he stole her note. Kole would've been enraged and gone on the offensive to bring James to justice, but it wasn't time for that. He entered the crowd on the street and avoided people handing out black armbands to those who wanted to show how much they were affected by the woman's suicide. He knew the truth and didn't want to wear the armband, but most of all he didn't want people thinking he was a callous dick. No one knew her name or why she did what she did, but her death made people look at how they treated others and didn't want anyone to feel invisible, or unheard.

He did his best to follow the traffic report, avoiding the milling crowds, but with overlapping start times, certain buildings in the business district were hotspots to be avoided. Some larger businesses took up an entire building, offering their employees housing. Later those businesses got together with other businesses to provide everything their employees would need and those employees rarely left their block. The woman's suicide made people reach out and connect with their neighbors, filling the walkways, altering Eric's path. He didn't think what they were doing was bad. It bothered him because he knew the truth and wanted the city to know that a wolf lived among them, but he couldn't prove anything.

The energy of the city plummeted and a day of mourning was declared in the hope that people would reach out to each other for support. The department of mental health assured the masses that new programs are in the works to help those contemplating suicide. The streets filled and Eric had to go the long way around to avoid the major walkways. All he needed to do was get into the newer districts and jump on the moving walkways because people couldn't gather on them.

He came to the corner of the next street and looked down the street to see if there were any crowds and spotted Monique across the walkway. His face flushed and heart pounded in his chest. He planned to call her later after he cleaned up after himself. He watched her, she was hard to miss with her long strait hair pulled into a ponytail over her tall black jacket and over the noise of the wide walkway Eric could hear boots clicking on the duracrete. He didn't know why some women wore noisy footwear, he assumed it was to get attention, but Monique didn't look like she wanted company. Eric stepped close to the opposite building then leaned against its wall.

She walked slightly slouched with her head down and shoulders up. Her hands were crossed at her stomach as if she was holding her jacket closed. She didn't look hurt, or in danger, but he debated on letting her pass or joining her. He wanted to be with her, but was that because she was attractive? If she was ugly, would he care? But the answer was that he'd met her for a reason and in a way knew her. If he didn't know her, they would've passed each other then after he purchased his cleaning robots, he would've went home and had a cold shower.

He remembered her cookies and decided that if she could make something that tasted so good, she couldn't be that bad of a person. He timed her pace and walked, intercepting her. At first she didn't see him. Her eyes didn't come off the ground until he stepped in front of her. She stopped, startled. Surprise crossed her face. She grabbed his arm, squeezing hard. Eric could feel her nails through his dress jacket when she dragged him off to the side.

He noticed how worried she was. Her sad eyes spoke volumes, making him wish he could hear her story. She thrust her hands into her jacket then pulled out a holo-com, holding it on her palm. She initiated the device and a screen appeared between them. Eric had seen the commercials for the holo-com. She held the latest advancement in holographic technology. Smaller and faster than the wall mounted com, it was a database in the palm of your hand. You could tie in all the electronics in your home as well as your robots. You didn't even have to get out of bed. Your robots would clean and go shopping if you fridge and cupboards needed it. All Human technology was merging, allowing one tool to access it all. He wanted to snatch it out of her hand and play with it.

Her fingers moved in the air typing on her holographic keyboard saying, "I need to talk to you."

"If you want I can hold that," he said, more to feel the holo-com's weight than to help her type her message. "You can increase the keyboards size and use both hands."

She passed it to him then used her fingers to adjust the keyboards size. "I know the woman who died," she typed.

Eric didn't read her message at first. The holo-con felt lighter than he thought. The commercial said that the battery would last all day and had an electromagnetic charger. He wanted to flip the device over and see if he could get into it. The little pings of her typing had stopped, interrupting Eric's speculation on how the device worked. He looked up and met her weary gaze. "Sorry about that," he said then read her message. "She worked for James."

Her fingers went to work and this time he paid attention to her. She went on to say, "It's my fault she's dead. She helped me once and to thank her, I gave her up to the authorities."

He could see the fear and regret on her face, but had no idea what she was talking about. "I don't think it was your fault," he said, remembering the woman's note, but didn't want to go anywhere near his secret. He looked into her sad eyes and wanted to help saying, "Start from the beginning."

Her fingers went to work on her holographic keyboard typing, "When I lived in the Dark Elf Capital, I was in a bad place. A man that worked for James killed my family and I sacrificed everything to get close to him. I tried to kill him, but failed. He owned me after that until the woman who supposedly committed suicide freed me. I escaped the Capital, but the people I paid to get me to safety betrayed me, collecting the reward. James sent an Investigator after me and for my freedom all I had to do was betray that woman. I thought getting revenge for my family would make things better, but it didn't. When I stabbed him, his chest exploded and what was left of that little girl in me, died."

Eric was confused. He remembered hearing about the destruction of the Dark Elf Capital ages ago. "When did this happen?" he asked, hoping to clarify her story.

She deleted the text on her screen then typed, "To a Human these events appear unrelated, but Dark Elves hold on to evidence for hundreds of years, waiting for the right time to what they've collected to destroy their enemies. I proved to James that she was guilty of murder and he tucked it away until he was ready. By our law, you're not allowed to kill someone outright. There has to be a trail of failure, or betrayal before you're allowed to kill them. If you haven't collected enough proof against your enemy, the victim's family can seek retribution."

After hearing how messed up the Dark Elf legal system was, Eric was glad Kole never took him there. But something bothered him about her story and he didn't want clarification, but was compelled to ask, "You said that you failed to kill the man who killed your family and he ended up owning you. What did you mean?"

She frowned and her hands furiously typed, "Without my family, I became property. I had the right to kill him and because I failed, he had the right to own me. We were a small family with little influence and I was the only survivor. I didn't know who Byron was and when I was found, I'd been struck mute. No one wanted me and was sold into slavery. After I killed Byron, I was an escaping slave. I traded my freedom for hers, or my contract would've gone to James and he would've owned me. It's all about who's protecting who and who has the power. I knew Byron was protected and didn't care. The proper procedure was to go to James and ask him if I could kill Byron. I'd present my evidence and if Byron was out of favor with his protector and the evidence was moving enough, Byron's protection would be revoked. Of course there are always bribes, but where's a slave going to get that kind of money. And I didn't want James telling Byron that I was going to kill him. So I broke the law."

"What about your previous owner? What happened with them?"

"As punishment for not controlling me, or looking into my life to see what evidence I had, they lost my contract and it went to the offended."

"That's so messed up," he said, feeling bad for Monique.

While she typing her story, Eric read along, but he mostly looked through the words at her. He watched her stand tall. He couldn't see the years of slavery and abuse on her determined face. He almost didn't believe her. He compared the harsh world she grew up in to his, making his life look like he'd been frolicking with Unicorns. She was the toughest chick he'd even met and suddenly all his tattoos and piercing felt funny. He didn't know what to say to her and felt his face grow hot. "Um," he said, stalling. A bunch of things to say flashed in his mind, but they were all stupid. He liked and respected her. Between the two of them, he was the idiot whining about his past. He felt her pain and the guilt she was going through. He also could understand why she turned on the woman who helped her get revenge. He didn't know how long she'd been a slave and understood how desperate she would've been when James dangled her freedom in front of her face. "What I mean is that I think James killed her, but it's not your fault. I know how it looks. James might have used what you did to justify her murder, but he still chose to do it. He could've forgiven her."

Her gaze returned to the walkway and her shoulders relaxed. She typed, "I guess so. I feel bad that I had played a part in it. By Dark Elf law, James had the right to kill her, but I don't have to like it."

Eric deleted the screen. He didn't want anyone passing by to read it. "It sucks, but James will get his. I'm sure of it," he said then reached into his pocket then pulled out his new lucky rock and showed it to her. It was light and fit perfectly in his palm. Like her, it was a rare find. "I want you to have it."

She looked puzzled, but took the rock. Eric had seen rejection on many women's faces, but Monique looked curious. Eric turned off her holo-com then handed to her. "If I buy the ingredients for your get well cookies, will you make me some?"

She smiled slightly then nodded. Eric was warming up to her little smile and smiled back. He took a step then spun around to stand beside her, placing his hand in hers. In one motion his intent was made clear. He wanted to be with her and if she pulled away, he'd understand, but the way she looked at him told him that she'd take a chance on him.

To his relief, she didn't pull away. Eric became so nervous that his words stumbled out when he asked where the nearest food store was. She pointed the direction and he matched her pace. He didn't mind the silence between, it allowed him to calm down and get a hold on his tongue. It also allowed the heaviness of the previous conversation to dissipate.

In the store shopping for her cookie ingredients, he'd glance at her every couple of minutes. It was more than admiring her beauty. He wanted to learn to read her body to see if she was comfortable, or looking for the door. As he watched her, he found that every movement she made had purpose. She didn't waste her energy touching things more than once. And when she wanted his attention, she'd gently touch his arm, communicate with her eyes then point to what she wanted. At first it was a guessing game and Eric wanted to put in the effort to learn everything about her. When she touched him, he focused all his attention, deepening his connection with her. She was patient, deliberate and had many layers of expression. He loved every second of it and didn't want to see her communicate through her holo-com until she was done making his cookies.

He bought all the ingredients and the tools she'd need then carried the awkward bag, but it was uncomfortable for him to carry it and hold her hand. The bag's weight threw off his step and he couldn't shift his body to compensate, but he didn't care. He was connecting with her and didn't want it to stop. He found himself talking softer and stepping closer to her and to his delight, she leaned her shoulder against his.

They reached his apartment. Monique hung up her jacket then unpacked the supplies. Eric did a discrete looked around, checking for any garbage he might have missed, but saw none. He had no idea that his day was going to go this way and was glad he did all the surface cleaning. He only hoped that she didn't see any dust. Monique wore a delicate long sleeve tan colored blouse with embroidered flowers. She rolled up her sleeves and went to work making the dough. Eric watched, keeping her company and when she looked up she'd smile at him, Eric felt a surge of joy within and smiled back as if she told a joke. She'd then go back to mixing. Her joy was infectious and Eric couldn't take his eyes off of her, he didn't want to miss anything. She put the cookies in his oven and together they waited, looking at each other. It became a game of noticing and responding to expressions. It was a language that Eric was new to, but was happy to learn.

When he got distracted and wasn't watching her, she'd touch him. He liked her attention and almost wanted to pretend to ignore her so she'd to touch him again. He thought about it. She could make a noise to get his attention, but she chose touch. He compared it to two people trying to talk to each other in different rooms. They could yell at each other or get off their butts to find the other person. Not only did he like her touch, it showed him respect and how classy she was.

The cookies came out and she placed them on the stove's burners to cool. She took off her oven mitts then turned around to face him. He waited to see what she was thinking and the look she gave him made his face flush. She stepped closer to him and his body got jittery. He was so nervous he forgot how to line himself up with her. Her gentle smile took some of the tension away, but when she tapped his forehead with her finger, it knocked him out of his nervous frame of mind.

He relaxed and she moved in, pressing her body against his. Her soft lips touched his and he let her show him what she wanted. Between the kisses, she grabbed his hands and placed them on her body. She was intoxicating. Eric started slow, feeling her body respond to his touch. He could feel a pressure between them building. She stepped away, took his hand then guided him to his bed. Eric forgot all about his get well cookies.

Chapter

16

Sarah let her servants go early to mourn the passing of a woman who no one knew. The footage and surveillance records the media had didn't show much. The camera was focused on something else then caught her falling in the background. But people were wondering how a woman managed to sneak into the base and get onto the Cruiser without anyone noticing. Sarah knew who the woman was and also knew that she must have presented her id when she passed through the gate. It was James who was keeping her name from the public, but she didn't know why. The situation made the military look dumb and with their no comment response, it only aggravated the people. The people wanted to know why she did it and how no one was able to stop her. They wanted to find a note, or video to make sense of the tragedy. Sarah did what she could, giving people the basic explanation, the day off work and encouragement to connect with the person beside them. Jas died alone, but Sarah was going to use her sacrifice to bring people together.

She walked into her kitchen, placed her tray on the counter then collected the tea set James had given her. The black teapot felt light and deceptively fragile in her hands. It was beautiful. She had heard about how the Dark Elves made their art using heat and wondered what her warm teapot looked like to their eyes. She thought about making tea, turning off the lights and wearing goggles to watch the art in her pot come to life. The pot was priceless, an artifact from a people who have been scattered across the land. She didn't know if there were any survivors and didn't truly care, but she appreciated their art.

She made her tea and placed the tea tray on her coffee table then sat on her couch. With her remote she adjusted the view screen of her video com to focus on her then placed a call. The com chimed and no one answered, but she let it go until it'd annoy the person on the other end. She knew he'd still be there even though everyone else in the city had the day off.

The close up of a bald man's chubby face appeared on her screen. "What!" the man demanded. His eyebrows raised and his nostrils flared. Sarah almost laughed at how huge the man's eyes looked in his glasses.

"Sorry to bother you doctor," Sarah said.

His face backed away. "Ah Mother Sarah, I didn't know it was you. If I did I would've answered before the twentieth chime."

"I know. How is our patient?"

"He's demented," he said.

"He's awake?" she asked surprised. She specifically remembered telling them not to wake him up. She was a little bit more than annoyed. She felt that people were no longer listening to her. First she was left as Troll bait and now this guy disobeyed her. She quickly reined in her anger, knowing that the good doctor doesn't respond well to confrontation.

"I did," he said then quickly added, "I read through his files and it was suggested that he was responding well to his incarceration, well that was before he was experimented on. All his work in therapy was thrown out under the pain of his transformation. His tormentors didn't treat him well and I thought I could reach him. What he did to himself is beyond my knowledge and I thought that he could explain what he was doing to defeat the Troll's regeneration."

She couldn't change the fact that the doctor disobeyed her and woke the first Troll, but there was something about the way he talked that raised her suspicion. "Are you talking to him now?"

The doctor awkwardly chuckled deepening her disappointment. "He'd not that bad of a guy. He had a horrible upbringing and was coming around before he was experimented on. I need his help because I don't want to hurt him and you can't make me, or I'll leak his whereabouts to the Department of Mental Health."

Sarah was done. The way he was talking and what he said saddened her. She knew crazy when she saw it. Her doctor had been emotionally compromised and she was surprised that she was more sad than upset. "I understand," she said, stalling. "I've seen what you're going through before." She used her remote and shrunk down his face on video com then accessed her secret files. "Help ease my mind. Did you follow procedure with your support staff?"

"Oh yes. I'm the only one that has engaged with him. I didn't tell my staff anything."

She used her remote to pan through her files and open the floor plans to the lab. She wove her power into her words then asked, "Tell me the truth. You wish to save him?"

He became still and his eyes glazed over. "I do," he said. "I think he has much to offer the human race. He believes we can use his modified version of the Troll's regeneration to cure diseases."

"That sounds really good," she said while bringing up the lab's destruct code. "What does your staff know about this?"

He relaxed until his shoulders slumped and his head arched back, giving her the view of his tonsils. "I lied," he confessed. "They know everything. Only one of my people was doing what you wanted. We saw the future in his work. With his help we could develop vaccines and become masters of our evolution, but don't worry, all of our research is still here."

Sarah was so angry she couldn't speak. She saw the end of the human race. Her thumb hovered over the button that would incinerate the lab making the good doctor die screaming. She wanted him to feel pain for his stupidity. The Trolls nearly ended the world and he trusted the man who'd finish the job. She wanted to tell him that he was being manipulated. That those vaccines would infect the population with the Troll regeneration, allowing Mini Trolls to spring from people's chests.

She was livid. She placed her thumb on the button and wanted to looked into the man's vacant eyes, but couldn't. All she saw were his teeth. Enora had the weapon that'd end the world's pain and she no longer need the doctor's research anymore, but she doubted that he would comply with destroying his work. He'd never let it go and the human race needed to be protected from it.

"Look at me!" she commanded.

The doctor's head jerked and eyes flickered. She knew her effect was wearing off and quickly opened the file to the research team's implants. A list appeared and she selected all. She didn't want to take any chances that the Trolls would ever come back and did something evil for the greater good.

While the scientists were tucked away in their beds, she had a team break into their apartments, sedate them then implant a small device containing a neurotoxin at the base of their skulls. She was assured that their deaths would be painless, the implant would dissolve and that they would die in a way that looked natural. But if a person looked closely at their murders, there'd be too many questions. Having a small group of people across the city die at the same time for the same reason would set it all off. An investigation would take them to a burned out lab and she was careful not to have anything leading back to her.

She took Kole's advice and told no one, but he was right. All Troll knowledge needed to end. She tapped the button on her remote and watched the doctors face go slack, eyes roll up and jaw drop before he disappeared off her screen. She heard him hit the floor then maneuvered through her filing system, hitting the button again to incinerate everything in the lab. She heard a hissing noise as the lab filled with gas then on the little screen she watched jets of flame shoot out of the ceiling, filling the room with an intense flame before static filled her screen.

She felt dirty and tossed her remote onto the floor then grabbed her tea cup. She drank the tea down barely tasting it then it hit her, a painful tinge in her heart. She felt a deep pit open up within her then curled up, hugging knees and wept for the team she had murdered.

She didn't know how long she wept for, but the hurt in her heart didn't go away. She had done bad things in the past, but not to her people. This time was different, or she was the one that had changed. She knew her power wasn't effecting her people as well as it used to, meaning that they were outgrowing her, or she was losing her power. She wasn't sure what was happening to her and was afraid to ask James incase she was weakening. She didn't want to see him then become the city's next suicide. Of course he'd kill her in secret then replace her with a fresh clone and she didn't want that. She wanted to live and not waste all she'd learned. She'd grown with and cared for her people.

She was miserable and didn't want to clean herself up. She dried her face on her sleeve then downed another cup of tea, but no matter what she did, or thought, her pain didn't diminish. Her heart felt bruised and she didn't think it'd ever heal.

She retrieved her remote then sat down again. She centered her image on her screen then looked at herself. She tried to smile and appear like there was nothing wrong, but her sad puffy eyes gave her away. She wiped her face and thought of nice things then when she felt better she placed another call.

Kole answered wearing a plush dark blue, almost purple housecoat. He was close to his screen and off center showing his apartment in the background. Sarah didn't like looking into people's lives, seeing pieces of how they lived. "What's up?" he asked.

"Do you know that you can put a mark on the floor and program your video com so all you have to do is stand there, hit a button and have a perfect image?"

He looked at the floor then back to her then asked, "You called to tell me that?"

"No..."

"Hold on," he said interrupting her. He walked off screen then returned with his remote. "I'm still getting used to this thing."

She watched his face change while he read and fidgeted with the remote. He looked ridiculous and she'd laugh, but she wasn't in the mood. "Are you done?"

He took a step then backed up centering himself. "There, is that better?"

She held it together for as long as she could then before she could stop them, hot tears ran down her cheeks. Her hands came up covering her eyes then she collapsing, resting her elbow on her knees. Her body shuddered and her heart hurt so bad she thought she was going to die. He asked her what was wrong, but she couldn't answer. He waited and when she was able, she lifted her head then said, "I destroyed the Troll research."

Kole face contorted looking a cross between worried and confused. "Okay," he said. She wanted to say more, but was afraid the lump in her throat would choke her. "Oh, you mean the first Troll?"

She nodded.

"Yeah, I figured that was going to happen. The first Troll had to go, or somewhere down the line someone else would try again."

He didn't know how right he was. She dragged her sleeve across her face then said, "I don't care about that. There was nothing we could do about him. His body was living knowledge on how to remake the Trolls."

His face softened. He asking, "What are all the tears for? You make me want to come over there and give you a hug."

She chuckled. "You hug me? Enora has changed you."

He scoffed then said, "That hurts, I wasn't always a jerk."

She felt better and thought about telling him the rest of her story. That she'd murdered the scientists who were supposed to be working on creating something that'd stop the Troll's regeneration, but were compromised. That they were tricked into believing that they could use the regeneration to create cures for diseases, but fell quiet. She didn't want to him to ease her burden. She never wanted to forget what she'd done. "I wanted you to know that you were right. We should've terminated the first Troll when we found him."

"Thanks, but I understand why you didn't. Enora has a good plan and everything will work out," he said. She knew he was trying to make her feel better and that was sweet, but her heart was too heavy.

She smiled. "I just wanted you to know. I have to go. You and Enora have a good day."

"You too," he said then disconnected the call.

She centered herself then savored her next cup of tea. She wanted to fall back into routine before she made her next call. She didn't want to rush and get into another conversation while pushing her emotions out of the way. She wanted to honor what she felt and not have her emotions used against her. James had killed Jas and made her murder into a spectacle, telling her that he stopped caring about discretion.

There are different kinds of people in the world. Some keep it together until they cross the finish line while others lose it once they see the line and she figured that James is overworked. He's been hiding in the shadows for so long he might not be able to stand in the light. Or, the stress of keeping his plan going for so long has made him impatient. He could also be tying up loose ends. Regardless of his reasons, he could've taken care of Jas quietly. Whatever his reasons were, she didn't like it.

Her call went through and James answered saying, "Sarah, I was expecting to hear from you sooner." He looked comfortable, leaned back in his black high backed chair that looked like a throne.

"Were you? My hands were full redirecting the mess you made."

"I mean before that. Last time you contact me to find out how many people I've rescue before I got here. Has something changed?"

She didn't want him to look into her and confirm her fears. "No, nothing's changed," she partly lied. "I've been preoccupied. The city is getting close to bursting and people are stressing that there's not enough room."

He didn't answer. He stared at her with his dark eyes then said, "Something's changed in you and your power has diminished, everything happens for a reason and it might be a good thing. Sometimes it's hard to see truth when things look bad."

She released a sigh of relief.

He laughed then said, "You knew that your power was waning and were worried that I'd replace you?"

"What did you expect? I've been watching Jas'..." she said then made quotation marks with her fingers, "suicide on the news all morning. And you've been quiet. You didn't call when you got in."

"Do you know how much paperwork I have to do? When I took on this job, doing paperwork was the furthest thing in my mind. Remember when you pitched this idea? You made it sound fun, but this is an actual job. I expected to walk in, snap my finger and everything done for me. Now I'm responsible for all sorts of crap. I didn't call you because I was busy delegating," he said sounding overwhelmed. "I don't know, maybe I'm doing it wrong."

This was a new side to James. She'd never seen him look vulnerable before and wasn't sure how to react. She treated him like anyone else and said, "I get it, it's a big job and I'm glad you're doing it."

His face brightened. "I have the support of good people," he said then smiled. "I have a surprise for you."

She read his face and his expression said he was genuine, but there was a flicker of darkness hidden in his eyes. She had manipulated many people to get humanity to where it was and could tell that his sudden mood change was bunk. "A surprise?" she asked feigning curiosity.

"After we fought our way in and rescued the people, I went to the lower decks to assure the refugees that they were safe. While I was down there, an old lady gave me a gift and it's perfect for you.

It's a re-gift, but I'd rather be honest and tell you where it came from."

She looked at her teapot then took a sip of tea. "Is it tea?" she asked.

He looked shocked. "How did you know?"

The more she watched him the more weird he acted. His facial expressions and mannerisms were off. She didn't want his gift, fearing poison and in her mind she saw herself falling like Jas to her death. She wished James had acted normal and been the same inconsiderate jerk she'd always known, but it was too late for that. She'll accept his gift, keep it around until he forgotten about it than disposed of it. If he asks for some later, she'll lie and say she drank it all. "What kind of tea is it, the old ladies horde the best."

He grinned. "They do indeed. She was the local tea maker. That was her job. She gave me her best blend from her garden. I don't know if it's any good, but it smells nice."

Despite knowing that James was trying to manipulate her, she dropped her guard and gasped then said, "An actual tea maker. Her knowledge is more valuable than the teas themselves. She'll need a shop with students." Her mind filled with possibilities and she could smell the flavors of the teas she no longer had. "Teas and coffees are getting harder to find. There're a couple of stores in town, but eventually they'll run out of the good stuff."

"I knew you'd feel this way. I've already set her and her family up. In exchange for housing they've agreed to be suppliers. It's going to be a family business that'll supply teas to the shops to keep the economy going. They could do it all themselves, but we need to spread the jobs around."

"That's wonderful," she said, thinking about meeting with the old woman.

James licked his lips then said, "I'm sorry about Jas. I didn't mean to cause so many problems for you."

"It's done and I used it to bring people together," she said, disliking his sickly sweet tone.

"When she came to see me I could tell something was wrong with her. I tried to get her to focus, but she lost it. She became irate and I was forced to open the floor beneath her. It was the only thing I could think of. I couldn't have her attack me there. She would've burned everything we've worked for."

She was stuck, he was clearly lying, but she had to play along, saying, "I wasn't expecting her to turn on us, but she wasn't happy when we sided with Kole. It must be the hardest on you."

"What do you mean?"

"Weren't you and Jas close?"

"We were and it did hurt to put her down, but I'm glad it's over. I do have to say that you've handled yourself well. Jas, Byron and The King weren't the best people to work with."

"They were volatile," she said agreeing. She went to refill her cup, but the pot was empty.

"It seems that my gift of tea came at the right time."

She chuckled. "It would seem so. When you come by, I can make us some."

"I'd like that. Do you think Kole would like to join us?"

She thought about Kole and Enora's plan to rid the world of the Trolls then kill James. The only thing they disagreed on was what they should do with the other races. "I think Kole has his hands full at the moment. He's settling in, but his apprentice is occupying his time."

They were quiet for a moment then James said, "It's funny. I get back to town and hear all kinds of funny things. Did you know we have a Dark Elf living here? The King brought her and somehow she was accepted. Your teaching must've changed the public's mind."

"I haven't heard that."

"I asked and found out she's a baker. She makes cookies at a tea shop and with your love for tea I figured you would've met her."

She shook her head then said, "I don't have time to shop. My servants go for me."

"She's hard to miss and a young man has been seen with her. I believe it's Eric, Kole's assistant."

Sarah knew there was something he wanted to say to, but his meandering way of getting to the point annoyed her. "Do you want her thrown out of the city?"

"No. I heard they were making googly eyes at each other." He paused tapping her last nerve. She had no idea what he was looking for then he said, "Its Monique, the hooker Byron was obsessed about."

Confused, she asked, "The woman who killed Byron? Seriously, what are the chances?"

"Tell me about it."

"What are you going to do?"

"Nothing, I brought it up because after Byron's death, I hired and investigator to track down Byron's murderer and he found Monique. I made a deal, her freedom for the truth."

This new information brought her back memories of Byron. Mostly of his volatile behavior and muddy boots that the kicked up on her coffee table. "And what was the truth?"

"Jas gave her the weapon and used her to kill Byron. When I found out, I was floored. I thought we were all family, but I guess not. Jas killed him to get closer to me. It was my fault really. I knew she was having problems and I didn't reach out to her. I tried to look past Byron's murder and needed time to process her betrayal. When she came to attack me I confronted her and you know the rest."

"Why didn't you lead with that?" asked Sara, feeling more confused. "It would've helped me understand,"

"To tell you the truth, I didn't know where you stand. Cid, the Trolls, the Orks and Jas, people are betraying me and I was worried that you've been turned. And if you doubt me, ask Monique."

Her secret slapped her. By not telling James that Kole and Enora plan to kill him, she too is betraying him. "I don't need to talk to Monique. The survival and future of humanity is my only concern," she said, reminding him. "You made this way."

He smiled then said, "I'm glad. When I'm done sorting everything out I'll swing by and we can have tea."

"I'd be delighted," she lied then he disconnected the call.

She sank into her seat feeling like she'd been punched in the gut. There was no doubt in her mind that James was going to kill her. She went over what he said, thinking that he had wrapped everything up in a nice package and put a big red bow on it. His story was too convenient making her wonder if James had planned this all along, maneuvering Monique into Winter Haven to justify Jas' death.

Sarah didn't like her next thought, that he ordered Monique to find Eric, but dismissed it. It was too fortuitous. All James needed to do is have her in town to point to when things didn't go his way. But he can't spoon feed Kole the answers without making Kole suspicious, meaning that Eric and Monique found each other by chance.

Sarah found it amusing that one event could change so much. She saw Monique as a beam of light that'll pierce the darkness toppling all the lies. If Kole goes up against James and mentions Jas, for whatever reason James could've pointed to Monique, who would've verify his story and stall Kole. But now, because Monique and Eric have met, she'll look planted and convenient. Kole won't care what she says, thinking James is behind it all. Regardless, Monique is innocent. Sarah smiled, deciding not to say anything, hoping Monique will be good for Eric.

Chapter

17

Kole left Enora's lab and stood outside the outer hatch waiting on the landing pad. The delivery truck was late. He looked up at the landing pad above calculating the clearance, guessing the truck could fit then wanted to know why the truck was delayed. He cleared the delivery with security, gave the store the correct address and clearance codes, but forgot to tell them of the pads clearance. Enora's lab was one of many, piled atop one another and separated by a meter of duracrete. The landing pads were made for smaller vehicles to limit traffic and cover from the buildings guns, in case someone tried to invade a lab. Kole also lied about the delivery, telling security that it special scientific equipment. If they knew what it was, they would've denied him and forced him to waste time going through the proper channels.

He wanted to be with Enora, but had nothing to do while he waited and apparently his waiting bothered her. With him standing there, rubbing his arms against the wall pretending to make angles in the duracrete wall, she felt pressured to hurry. He assured her that it wasn't the case. That she could take her time and he wasn't pressuring her to finish, but when he started making mouth noises, she lost it, almost throwing him out of the lab. She came unhinged and he almost got caught up in her explosion of frustration, adding his defensive anger to the mix, but he was able to see her frustration and backed off, defusing the argument. He decided to give her space to cool off and went shopping. He gave her a couple of hours then returned with some fun food and drink, but didn't want to go in until his other purchases showed up.

He looked out over the gleaming city. The afternoon sunlight reflected off windows and building art making the city sparkle. Most of the shorter buildings were solid duracrete, allowing the architects to be creative. Colored plastics, metal and glass art created massive displays for the company logos. It was much better than looking at the bare duracrete that gradually darkened over time. The art also hid the buildings' ugly air recycling, purification and cooling systems. People working in the lower portions didn't seem to mind. Thanks to the thin video matting, every office was a corner office that had the best view in the city, but those in the taller buildings who had the real thing were still envied.

Kole looked across town at one of the taller buildings that was supposed to have windows. Construction platforms hovered near the building allowing work crews to put up scaffolding. He squinted and watched the workers install rolls of flat video matting, slowly descending to cover the side of the building. Kole thought he had status symbols figured out then imagined what could be done with the matting. The building could use its exterior, selling space on its matting for ads. And as far as Kole knew, there weren't any regulations regarding that type of light pollution, restricting who could do it and where. Kole smirked, thinking that the person who thought of turning the side of a building into a wall of ads probably presented the limiting regulations once they were allowed to do what they wanted. But if not, he hoped someone would quickly button it up, or the city will become a garbled mess of ads that could be seen from space.

Kole got tired of watching the construction and was about to call the delivery company when he spotted a truck coming his way. He looked at the truck, guessing its height and hated being right. The truck won't fit and will probably turn around, making him wait forever. The truck had a fat base with a two man cab and a rectangular cargo hold. The truck slowed slowly spun around, lowering a cargo ramp onto the landing pad making Kole wrong. They never planned to land. The two young workers dressed in gray work clothes walked around the sides of the truck to the back then opened the cargo hold. Kole didn't see the walkway from the cab, around the hold to the back of the truck, but it made sense. The men carried a big black plastic bag down the ramp and placed it at his feet.

"Here you go," the larger worker said then produced a data pad. The taller and thinner worker went back up the ramp to close the hold.

"You're going to leave it here?" asked Kole.

"We're not allowed in this building. You're going to have to carry it from here, sorry," he said then walked away.

Kole frowned and watched the two men disappear around the cargo bays corners. The ramp went up then truck left. The bag wasn't heavy, but it was awkward, getting through the hatches alone. He had no other choice. He pulled the back off the landing pad, dragging it to the hatch then went in to get Enora. He walked into the lab and Enora stopped. She had her schematics open on her holo-table, but Kole knew she wasn't using them. It was a diversion for anyone who'd walk in on her while her awareness was off making things.

Enora turned to him saying, "I'm sorry for being grouchy at you. I'm under a lot of pressure to get this done and I didn't mean to take it out on you."

Kole walked up and gave her a hug. "I know. I like keeping you company and I got something that'll satisfy both of us," he said then clasped her arms, pulling her out of the lab.

She looked annoyed, but reined it in asking, "Where are we going?"

"To the landing pad," he said then led the way.

Outside she stood beside him and together they looked at the large black bag. "What is that?" she asked.

"It's a surprise."

"It's a chair," she corrected him.

Kole signed then said, "The point of it being a surprise is that you don't look into the bag."

"I don't have time for this, Kole."

He held her hand. "Help me bring it in. I can't do it alone."

"That's a big chair. I don't have that much room in there."

"It's not just a chair," he said trying to entice her. "It's the Uber Relaxation 2000 Reclining Chair. It has heating and sonic massage."

She cocked her head looking skeptical then said, "Wait, you didn't buy this for me. You bought it for yourself."

"No," he said trying to sound hurt, but she wasn't going for it. "Fine, I honestly bought it for both of us, but mostly for me."

She sighed letting her fatigue show. Her eyes looked heavy and slightly bloodshot, worrying Kole. But she yielded, saying, "Let's get this over with."

"I'll go in first. You grab the other side."

She walked around and picked up her end. "You know I have lots to do?"

"Yes, but you're allowed to take a break and you never know, you might like this Uber Chair."

She frowned and her eyes brows furrowed telling Kole that it was time to stop talking. They maneuvered the chair into the lab where Kole cut the bag open then positioned the chair. Enora went back to work then shuddered when he grabbed the plastic bag and rolled it up. He tossed the bag into the incinerator then fetched the food. He held the bag of fun food and looked for a place to put it. Then with a long slow screech, he dragged Enora's little table over and placed it within arm reach of the chair then put the bag down.

"Are you sure you don't want to take first turn on the chair?" he asked.

"Enjoy," she said smiling, but her salty tone said, "Do not enjoy." He placed his hands on the arm rests then slowly lowered his rear onto the plush leather seat. When he bought the chair, Kole didn't think of the acoustics of the small lab with duracrete walls. The slightly squeak and pop of the leather reverberated through the lab sounding extra loud in his ears, making him cringed. He then slowly slid to the back, trying to make less noise until Enora hissed a venomous sigh, telling him to hurry up.

Kole threw himself into the chair then became still. It took a moment for Enora to return to work, but she did and he relaxed, slowly sinking into the shuddering leather cushions. But it didn't feel right. His feet couldn't touch the ground and the chair bothered the backs of his knees. He leaned over sending the squeaking sound of leather across the room then grabbed the chair's side lever and pulled, bringing up the footrest with a series of clangs and springs.

Enora slammed her hands down onto her table. Breathing heavy, she leaned with her eyes closed then whispered, "Do you mind?"

And even though she whispered, Kole could hear her loud and clear. "No, I'm good, thank you," he said, thinking that it was a good thing to say to avoid a fight. He was distracted. The chair was bigger than he thought and he was having trouble getting comfortable. He wiggled in feeling entombed by the chair's comfort and was finally able to relax.

Enora turned to him with her arms crossed and her hip leaning on the table. "Are you comfy?" she asked.

Kole could almost see flames flickering in her eyes. Her gaze unnerved him and he almost regretted his previous want to get to know her on a deeper level. "Yes, thank you," he nervously replied.

"That's good because you don't seem to understand the pressure I'm under. I'm the only one on the planet that can end the Trolls and save the world. I almost want to ask James for help because I'm taking too long. In every passing second, I imagine little children being trapped, hiding from the Trolls that have devoured their parents. Can you imagine what that feel like for me? Wondering if children are dying while you're being distracted by a leather chair?"

Kole didn't know what to say and watched her return to her work.

He didn't move and watched his lovely Enora. He thought about what she had said and saw how much her heart hurt. He worried that the weight of the world would crush her before she finished, but whatever she needed to heal, he'd give it to her.

His mind drifted. He sat there trying to amuse himself by designing a new Transport in his head and felt a bit peckish. He reached over and slapped the top of the bag open, reached in and grabbed a plastic bottle of carbonated water. He half smiled and anticipated the water quenching his thirst then twisted the cap. The bottle hissed, but before he drank, Enora was beside him holding a manifested silver knife. She was a blur, moving from the table to his side faster than he could recognize her. He gasped in surprise, but before he could react, she thrust her knife through the water bottle exploding water over him and his new chair.

Shocked, he cried, "You crazy bit…" but her glare silenced him. He sat there and let the water spill on him. She then flicked her wrist, flinging the water bottle away then raised an eyebrow silently asking him if he wanted to finish that sentence. Kole said nothing and didn't move. The silence between them felt heavy, but it wasn't his turn to speak.

The knife in her hand vanished then her hand dropped to her side. She spoke with tender caring and warmth saying, "I know waiting is hard for you Kole. Your entire life you acted on one level or another and now it's you that needs to rest. Enjoy this moment of inaction because it may not ever come again. And look at it from the Universe's point of view. It has given you the gift of time and you're squandering it. By not resting, all that you're telling the Universe is that you crave conflict and hearing your wish, it will gladly give you what you want. Now think about what you're bringing into the world. All small actions matter."

Her words cut through the noise in his mind giving him permission to be calm and still. Kole didn't know what to say. He could feel the conflict within, begging for him to take up a cause and fight for anything, but all he did was tap dance on her nerves to pick a fight and he got it. He treated her bad and she didn't deserve to have him poking at her, but he didn't know he was doing it until she pointed it out.

The water soaked through his clothes and stuck them to his skin. "I'm sorry for treating you badly," he said then slipped out of the seat. He stood in front of her and looked into her sad eyes. "I love you and you're right. I've been running my whole life and I'm having a hard time sitting still, but I want to sit still with you." He stepped in and held her tight against his body.

"I can see that you're trying," she said, her voice muffled against his chest. "I guess I can let you sit still beside me."

They laughed together. "I don't know how you do it, even when I'm angry, you can always make me laugh," he said. "But, in a good way."

She looked at his chair. "You couldn't have picked a worse chair?"

"What do you mean? I got wicked deal."

"There's a reason why you got the deal. No one else wanted it. Look, it even has cup holders."

Kole looked for the cup holders, but couldn't see them then asked, "Where?"

She pushed herself away and gave him her "seriously?" look then leaned forward touching the side of the chair. A small panel slid open, allowing a thick tray with three holes to extend. Kole searched the other side and found another panel. Now the chair looked tacky, a gimmick for a home entertainment system that those in small apartments couldn't have. He saw her point, but didn't want to admit it. He had spent good money on that chair no one else wanted. "I was wondering why they had a lot of them," he finally said, admitting his defeat.

"I'm sorry. I thought you bought it to mess with me. I was mad before we brought it in. This isn't a big lab and your chair eats up a lot of space. And it takes most of my concentration to make the satellites. Squeaky leather is a bad choice. Then there's the cup holders, I know it's a little thing, but it beneath you. You could have a classier chair with a small table, but you shouldn't be eating or drinking in that position anyway. There's a risk of making a mess of your nice clothes. You should take better care of yourself."

"All sales were final. I can't return it. Now I understand the funny look the salesman gave me after I bought it, the bastard."

"Were stuck with it, but it stays here. I'm not filling up our nice home with duck phones, singing fish and leg lamps."

He had no idea what she was talking about, but her tone told him that she was teasing him. "I don't want any of those things, but if I did, I'd have them," he said teasing her back.

"I'm open, but if you cross that line, accidents happen. Oops."

He became serious. "Do I own anything that you don't like?"

"No, you don't own anything. But, now that were not using Alchemy, you're a bit messy. You do your best to clean up after yourself, but you never had to learn how to be clean. It's always the little things that get you. I can tell that you've stopped using Alchemy to look into things. The moment I saw the chair, I sent my awareness into it. It's cheap junk."

He shrugged, thinking that it wasn't important. "I've stopped looking because I don't want to be killed in my sleep by our neighbors. Collecting garbage is good camouflage." He thought back to his time pretending to be a wasteland scavenger, slapping rusted chunks of metal onto his Transport and wearing clothes made of scraps. "I guess it's an old habit."

"After all of this is over, where do you want to be? You're not going to be able to hide here forever because people are going to notice that you don't age."

She made him think. He had adapted to being normal and forgot about that and knew she was right then felt weight of being an Alchemist return. "I suppose not."

"We are what we are. We have a once in a lifetime opportunity to shape the future. After we're done with the Trolls and James, we should disappear into the waste to live our lives. We can be alone and study Alchemy and the Universe, but before we go, I think we should use my weapon to dissolve the casing holding the Ripper Gel. We can set it all off and be free from it."

"What about the Alchemists who come after us? They'll be nothing keeping them at bay if they choose to go bad," he said, liking where the Humans were going and didn't want to see everything they've built blown apart.

"That's not our problem. Be realistic, there's only so much we can do and we can't be everywhere. Children are going to fall through the cracks and grow up to be Alchemists. It's outside of your control. Besides without James, the world will run out of Ripper Gel. It's only a matter of time." She met his gaze then smiled warmly before saying, "I know that you don't want to hear it, but we have to talk about this because I'm almost done building the satellite network. Decide on how you're going to handle this. Are you going to transverse the world collecting alchemically touched children to teach them, or not risk that they'll go bad and put them down? Because in the end, one of your children might go bad, manifesting your fears."

"Speaking about children, I did hear you earlier. I'm sorry for distracting you. I had no idea that you were thinking that children were dying with each passing second. No wonder you blew up."

"It's okay," she said then closed her eyes. Her tension faded and she relaxed, but looked sad. "It was all in my head. I'm sorry about the water."

He felt bad for adding to her stress and tried to make her laugh saying, "Who cares about the water, you scared me so bad I almost filled my pants."

She laughed and he thought about what she had said. He didn't want people murdering helpless children because they were different, but also didn't want the children to grow up and maybe destroy the world. But she was right, it was better to clean slate the world. "No matter what we do, it won't be good, but you never know. People might learn to live together and not all Alchemists will be bad. As for us, we'll do what you said and destroy the Ripper Gel then run off together."

She nodded then returned to her table, but before she went back to work, Kole asked, "What about the other races? We can use your advanced sensors to find them."

"We can," she said. "But we need to deal with James and I'm not sure that we'll win. There're three outcomes. We win, he wins, or no one wins. I didn't want to add the other races profiles to my system in case we lose. James will figure it out and kill everyone anyway, so he has to go, but if we all die, I don't want someone else finishing what James started. Nothing is ever truly deleted and I don't feel safe leaving the information on my system." She turned to him and asked, "Every time I finished a satellite, I thought about this. What if we find them and see that they're in trouble and we're not ready? Do we fire early to save the other races and tip our hand, giving the Trolls time to figure out a defense, or do we let them die? In the end, it's better not to know. That's why I'm in such a hurry to finish. Every second I'm idle, I imagine people dying."

"What if they're doing fine? Wouldn't you like to know? The main thing we can do right now is kill off the Trolls. That's more important than James. Kill the Trolls then destroy the Rippers. You can program instructions into your network then once they're done your satellites can self destruct. And you're right, once James realized that the Trolls are gone, he'll figure out what happened to them, but it'll take him time to rebuild your network."

"It's not just about James. I'm worried," she said.

"About what?" he asked.

"What if we're the only ones left? What if Kyra, Reece and Nick are gone? There's a strange comfort in not knowing when there's nothing you can do about it. All you can do is hope they're living well and happy."

"You've been putting way too much pressure on yourself," he said finally getting to what's been bothering her. "You're rushing because you feel that you'll be too late to save our friends? And when you finish, you'd rather blow up your network than find out that you were too late."

Tears welled in her eyes. She rushed forward then wrapped her arms around him. "The Trolls have taken so much from me," she said sobbing. "They ruined my life and I can't stand the thought that they killed my friends. What if my weapon doesn't work, or some escape? More will die and it'll be my fault."

He held her tight. "I hear you," he said.

"I can't search for the other races because if I find out that their gone, it'll destroy me. Let me finish and we'll end it, saving as many as we can. Maybe later we'll find our fiends and make new memories."

Kole rubbed her back then kissed her forehead before letting her go. She stepped away and wiped her checks then went back to work. He watched her wanting to say more and tell her that it was going to be all right, but he needed to trust her. Trust that she knows what she's doing and that she'll have to courage to face her pain.

Kole stood there for a couple more minutes watching her. Her awareness was off doing what she needed to do and her body stood relaxed. He looked at his chair and focused then with the wave of his hand the water on his seat evaporated. The tension in the lab had diminished and he felt better knowing that she wasn't really upset over the chair, but she was right about it being crappy. The energy from their fight soiled it, making him decided to leave it there when they abandon the lab. There was no room for it in their lives. He slid onto the warm chair, making as little noise as he could then relaxed and made himself comfortable.

A couple of minutes past and he couldn't help but ask, "When you're done, do you want to get something to eat?"

Her head dropped and she let out a low sigh. "Sure. Sure we can. Let me finish and we'll go and get something to eat."

Kole smiled, remembering how much fun they had. "Do you want to go back to the restaurant where we had our lunch date?"

She laughed then said, "No." She leaned on her table and massaged her temple. "We can go somewhere else where they won't remember us."

She wasn't making sense. He didn't remember them being out of place at the restaurant and wanted to ask her to explain, but his interruption had upset her. "I'll think of something," he said cheerfully, trying to pick up her mood again. "I'm going to be quiet now. You do your thing."

"Are you sure?" she asked letting the strain in her voice show again.

Kole shut his mouth and looked at the stab wound in the plastic bottle on the floor. She waited for a minute as the tension in the lab subsided then went back to work and he didn't dare interrupt her again. She was right, he had a problem being quiet in his own head and it was time to change. He wanted to be a better person, not only for himself, but for her. He sat dreaming of strengthening their relationship and walking beside her forever. All he had to do was find the silence within.

Chapter
18

Enora closed her eyes and leaned heavily on her table. Her trembling arms threatened to buckle, making the surface of the table look comfortable. She slowed her breathing, drawing in and exhaling long breaths, watching the dim holographic light dance in the inside of her eyelids. She wanted to sleep, but had a little ways to go yet. She had finished the last satellite and double checked its systems to make sure that it'd fire when she needed it to. The thought of having any of her satellites misfire or delay firing, frightened her. She didn't want to give the Trolls a chance to react. If there was a mistake in her calculations allowing a Troll to survive, any deaths after would be her fault.

She pushed off the table to energize her body and looked over at Kole who slept in his new chair, gently snoring. He looked snug, sunken into the chair's cushions, but she knew how stiff he was going to be when he woke up. She thought about waking him to share in her moment of victory, but it was a personal moment, a bag of mixed feelings. Before the first Troll became a Troll, he was her stalker who destroyed her way of life, forcing her to become the person she was today. She found it strange that she was the one who was going to end him and without his evil, she wouldn't be there in the first place. She thought back to the person she was when she went to the coffee shop and compared herself to the woman she chose to be after. Things could've gone differently. Without her stalker she would've kept her friends and might not have moved when her Alchemy manifested. And if things would've progressed the way it did, she might not have had the willpower to survive being placed in the jar. On the other hand, she had no idea how she influenced his life, or if she even did. She was his unfortunate fixation, the character in his story that could've been played by anyone.

She tapped the keys on the hologram and accessed her system then tested her relays, connecting the satellites. When each satellite lit up green, she brought up an image of the globe then searched for Trolls, finding fewer than she anticipated. In her nightmares when she'd search for the Trolls and the entire world glow red, overrun with Trolls hiding in every crevice, but to her relief, there were only small pockets of little red dots scattered across the land. She was happy to see that the Trolls around Winter Haven hadn't come back to rebuild their missile silos and went to work targeting the dots on the surface. Her system beeped alerting her to several larger dots underground, in the oceans and upper atmosphere. She widened her attack to include the new targets then her sensors told her that the Trolls in the oceans and air were engaged in search patterns.

She rechecked her findings. The Trolls were indeed searching, telling her that there were survivors. A wave of joy rushed through her. The other races were still alive. If the Humans were the only ones left, all the Trolls across the planet would be heading their way.

Excitement flushed through her like a shot of cold water. She picked up speed, programming her targeting system then searched for all the Ripper Gel, finding more bullets than the combine population of the world. Judging by the reserves, Humans would be able to cull any Alchemists they find for centuries to come. James wasn't messing around, making her doubt that he was going to let the other races go and send them into space. She targeted the Ripper

Gel and hoped the explosions wouldn't kill too many people in Winter Haven. There was no way she'd be able to get everyone away from the gel and trying would only tip off James to her plan.

She looked at the red dots on her global map remembering that all the races had Ripper Gel then had an idea. She turned the dots representing the Ripper gel yellow then overlapped the red Troll signatures finding the other races. The other races were alive, split up into small groups being pursued by the Trolls. She wasn't too late, but destroying the Ripper Gel might make things worse, but there'd still be survivors to continue on. And if James had his way, everyone but the Humans would die.

Kole choked making her look and felt relieved when his snoring continued. She watched him sleep, thinking how handsome he looked even when he was drooling. She didn't want him to wake. She couldn't look him in the eye and press the button, killing so many innocent. She knew that he loved her and would support her decision, but it didn't make her feel any better.

She finished targeting the Gel then set the instruction to self destruct. She double checked her instruction to make sure she'll get what she wanted then brought up the satellite's commands. It was her humor the make the proverbial big red button that floated in front of her face. The button didn't look like it had a chance of ending the world, but she didn't expect to fire into the oceans and deep underground. She had to trust her work. Trust that the satellites will pass through the water and earth to find their target without creating earthquakes and tsunamis.

She raised her hand then hesitated, looking at the button that represented large scale death. She had killed before. She didn't blink when she destroyed the Slavers. There were plenty of innocent people there that she'd justified away, but somehow this felt different, making her humanity feel cheap. Something inside her hardened, removing her hesitance, too many lives were on the line. She pressed the button then waited. Her system came to life and she watched her holographic satellites fire. The red dots across the globe flashed then blinked out of existence and when they were gone the yellow dots appeared.

Enora clutched her chest waiting for her network to acquire their targets then fire. She spun the map around to find Winter Haven then heard muffled explosions outside. She waited to feel a rumble or something through the duracrete while watching the yellow dots disappear, but was too far from the armory and feel anything. Another series of explosions surprised her. She had under a minute before her network would self destructed and zoomed in on the city trying to remember what she had missed. No one told her that James had returned. She watched the image of James' Cruiser fall into the city, collapsing buildings as it fell. Enora's jaw dropped. She imagined all the chaos and death she'd caused.

Her building shook, rattling her furniture and she watched in horror as the ground open up above the underground hangers then her system went dead. She was cut out, unable to see what she had done. She trembled, barely able to breathe. She couldn't move, or speak. She only thought of the armory and forgot about the city's defenses.

Her com chimed startling her. She jumped, breaking her paralysis then the com chimed again. She knew who it was before she looked. She didn't want to talk to Sarah, but she had to make sure that Sarah knew it was an accident.

Sarah's angry face appeared on her screen. "What have you done?" she demanded.

"It was an accident."

Her angry eyes widened and she became quiet saying, "Oh, that makes it much better. This city has survived so much only to be taken down by you. Tell me that the Trolls are dead so my people can put out the fires, collect the dead and grieve in peace without the threat of an impending Troll invasion hanging over them."

Her words were nails driven into her heart. "The Trolls are dead," she said then realized that Sarah wouldn't know that she had targeted the Ripper Gel and caused all the destruction.

"What happened?"

Sarah's eyes plead for the truth, but Enora couldn't stand other people knowing her shame. "Somehow my weapon reacted with the Ripper Gel when I made adjustments to kill the Trolls hiding deep underground," she lied, not wanting Sarah to know that she deliberately targeted the Ripper Gel to save the future generations of Alchemists. "But the Trolls are gone."

Enora watched the anger in Sarah's eyes fade. "What's done is done and even if you did it on purpose there's nothing I can do about it. You're a powerful Alchemist," Sarah said.

"I said that it was an accident and I meant it."

"I know," she said. She blinked and tears ran down her cheeks. "A lot of my people died for nothing and I have to spin this tragedy so my people can blame the Trolls. Grief is a funny thing, my people can't know that there was an Alchemist behind these deaths, or nothing will change. For humanity's sake, we have to put away our hatred so we can build a future together."

But before Enora could respond, Sarah disconnected her call. Enora turned off her table, mourning the city's losses, staring at the duracrete wall across from her.

"I'm sorry Enora," Kole said startling her. His sleepy voice sounded loud in her ears.

"For what?" she asked. "You didn't do anything."

He sat up and put away the footrest then moved to hug her. He held her tight comforting her and said, "When we talked about destroying the Ripper Gel I didn't think about where the Gel was, or what would happen. I knew it would explode, but I guess I saw what I wanted to see."

She leaned into him, feeling his warmth and Alchemical shield. "How long were you awake?"

"Sarah woke me. When you were talking, I sent my awareness over the city. There's nothing we can do here. Sarah's right, the city can't know there are Alchemists here, or they will blame us forever."

"We can help dig people out from under the rubble," she said thinking of several other things they can do, but she wanted to tell him some good news. "I found them. The other races are still alive, well those that I didn't kill."

"Well that's great," he said, sounding chipper then became serious. "I'm sure there're survivors, but now it's time to end James. If he gets away from us, he'll make more Gel then he's back to business. This has to end today."

She knew he was right. She'd been waiting so long to extract her revenge against James, but all she could think was that there were worse things than death. She liked her life with Kole and felt lucky to have found him, but Kole was right. "Are we going to get Eric?" she asked knowing the answer.

Kole placed his hands on her shoulders then stepped back to look at her. "No," he said then smiled. "I think we can handle James without him. I want him to have a life and if things go bad, I know he'll be out there working against James to save the world later. That's what we do."

"If we can't let people see that we're Alchemists, I guess we should call a cab," she joked, thinking that it was funny to ride a cab into battle. "Do you think he's still in his Cruiser?"

"I don't know, but I can find out," he said then accessed her com.

Sarah's face appeared again looking stressed and upset and by the way the background moved, Enora could tell that she was using a data pad. "Kole, I hope this is good news," she said.

"Where's James?" asked Kole. "It's time."

Sarah stopped and closed her eyes. She sighed heavy then said, "You guys suck so bad. You're going to do this now?"

"We have to. We can't let James get away."

"Kole, he's not going anywhere. We just finished talking and he knows that you two were behind this. He wanted me to tell you that he's waiting for you in his Cruiser. He sent out his crew to help the city and is there alone. I honestly hope you kill each other because I don't think the world can take your kind of damage anymore." She sighed again letting the anger in her face fade. "I'm leaving. James wants me dead and the city doesn't need me anymore. I'm off to help those in need elsewhere and if you live, I'm sure we'll meet again, good luck," she said then disconnected the call.

Chapter

19

Eric woke from his nap happy to find Monique next to him with her head resting on his chest. He didn't expect things to move so fast and fall in love with her so quickly, it was wonderful. After they had played and had their messy fun, she draped her leg over his and snuggled, running her hand across his chest. He held her in his arms feeling cozy, warm and loved then drifted off not knowing where his body ended and hers began. Coming to, he thought he had dreamt what they had done and for a second didn't want to wake in case he was right, but there she was beside him. Excitement swelled within him. He finally understood the advice his friends had given him and wanted this moment to last forever. He caressed her shoulder giving her a gentle hug then ran his hand down her smooth naked back. She tilted her head looking up at him then he leaned closer and together they kissed. His body became hot and he guided her, pushing her onto her back. She smiled and her eyes encouraged him, but before they could play, multiple explosions erupted across the city.

Surprised, Eric's head shot up. His apartment windows flexed inward then bounced back shaking, threatening to burst, but held together while a loud rumble vibrated through his building. He didn't know what was going on, or how to protect Monique from it. He sprang out of bed and rushed to the closest window. He thought the Trolls were attacking and was shocked to see that half of the armory was gone. He could see clear blast pattern of debris that had shot out and peppered nearby building, starting fires. Smoke bellowed from the destroyed pillboxes on the outer walls and the artillery emplacements in the older part of town. He looked across town at James' Cruiser as it tilted, breaking free of its dock and fell, collapsing several buildings.

Eric ran to another window looking for attackers and felt his building shudder. He grabbed the windowsill for support as a black rolling cloud of smoke rose between the buildings over the underground hangers. A hole appeared in the ground, quickly opening, raining broken chunks of duracrete below and Eric watched in horror as his neighboring building collapsed then slid into the hanger. He waited for his building to list then collapse into the growing hole then spun around meeting Monique's fearful eyes. She stood near the window wrapped in their bed sheet. Even terrified, she was beautiful.

If they fell, he planned to rush to her side and encase them in his shield, but they were lucky, the hole stopped growing. Her eyes asked for an explanation, but he didn't have one. She rushed to his side and he held her. He could hear the alarms and sirens far below and didn't know what to do. He just found Monique and didn't want to lose her, rushing out to help others only to have a building fall on her. People were hurt and dying and all he could think of was her. He felt selfish and petty then remembered the virus, the only thing that might be able to kill James. He leaned back then shifted his head around Monique's to look at the armory. He didn't want to leave, but he needed to know if the virus was still intact. He grabbed Monique's shoulders and gently pushed, but she held him tight, refusing to let go.

"I have to do something out there," he said and tried to get her to let go.

She held fast and looked up at him pleading for him to stay.

He saw everything in her face, love, despair, pain, loss, hope and his future. He didn't want to go. The thought of being away from her hurt, but he couldn't let the world burn. There was no future for them as long as James existed. No matter how far they ran, eventually he would find them. But if it came down to it, he'd gladly get shot into space to face the unknown as long as he was with her.

He held her tight, resting his forehead against hers. He kissed her deeply then stepped away. "I won't be gone long," he said then found his clothes. He enjoyed their messy fun, but felt sticky, itchy and pleasantly dirty. He focused then brought forth his Alchemy to clean himself before dressing. He looked back at Monique. She stood watching him silently weeping, wrapped in the bed sheet. He felt everything he could for her and let her see it in his eyes then left.

In the elevator, on his way to the lobby, he raised his shield then stretched his awareness to access the building's computer network. He attached Monique to all of his accounts in case something happened to him in the armory. He imagined a minefield of exposed Ripper Gel and really didn't want to go. Things were finally going his way and for the first time, he couldn't wait for tomorrow.

He flung open the front door of his building and ran out onto the front steps then stopped. The sirens from the hovering emergency vehicles fighting fires hurt his ears and the destruction looked worse on the street. Crowds of people had gathered to help the injured, carrying them out of the hole. People in the area who had vehicles dropped down to load up the injured and ferry them to the hospitals and rescue those trapped on burning buildings. It was clear to Eric that he needed to find another way.

He turned around and ran back into his building, taking the stairs to the parking garage and after finding a vehicle to steal, was on his way. He quickly gained altitude, carefully avoiding those in a hurry to save others. He took the long way around and didn't have a problem landing in the base. He expected to be questioned, or shot down, but the base personal were too busy saving people to notice him.

His heart sunk when he saw the gutted armory. Large chunks of duracrete with broken mesh lay strewn over the ground. The armory looked like it was peeled open, spitting its exterior. He expected to feel the exposed Ripper Gel's void reaching for him, threatening to consume him, but there was nothing. The air felt funny, reminding him of the Ork city that he destroyed. He made his way over the debris and into the armory. His eyes told him that he was in a building, but he felt like he was walking in death. He didn't want to be there and thought of Monique. He felt her beside him and all the weirdness of the place melted away, comforting him.

He moved on finding familiarity. He retraced his steps and found where he had hidden the virus, but the case was gone. His heart dropped. He panicked, thinking that the virus was gone and James would live and destroy his future. He closed his eyes regretting his idea to put the virus in the armory. It was good at the time, but felt something different. He stretched out his awareness and following the feeling. He rummaged through a pile of debris and found the broken vial. He backed away, worried that the virus was airborne and that it would kill him, but was still alive.

He calmed down so he'd be able to think clearly then reached out to the virus. It was dying. There was very little left of it and he didn't know what to do to save, or recreate it. He wished the woman who made it in the first place hadn't died. She'd know what to do. The virus touched his mind back and he felt its desire to live and find its proper home. Eric then knew that the virus wouldn't kill him right away. It only wanted to consume James, its home. He thought of Monique and felt connected to her on a level that he'd never felt before. He loved Kole and Enora, but Monique made him feel something along those lines, but something deeper. He relaxed and let everything in his life go, but her. He knew that if James lives, he'll take her away from him and he'd die inside.

He wanted to see the truth within himself and doubted that Kole and Enora could defeat James. They would try and might even come close to winning, but there was something in the virus that told him they'd lose. He shook his head and tried to disengage from the virus. He didn't like what the virus was telling him, thinking that it was lies to manipulate him and get him to take him to James, but the virus, even in its weakened state caught Eric's awareness, locking him in place. Eric wanted the truth and the virus gave it to him. The virus ushered his awareness away, and in his mind's eye he saw James' power.

Normally an Alchemist could only see the work of those less than or equal to them, but James wasn't an Alchemist. He acted, sounded and looked like an Alchemist, but his power came from a different place. Eric could see it, but his mind couldn't handle it. He tried to stop, but the virus held him, forcing him to look into James' power. Eric's body trembled and his mind weakened. He wanted to fall asleep and escape the wicked yellowish orange maelstrom of power, but the virus pushed him deeper into James until Eric was outside of the reach of James' power.

Moving past James, Eric was filled with calm and felt the purest of energy. There was nothing in his life to compare the raw energy that passed through his body. In his mind's eye, he floated in infinite energy and found the virus looking back at him. He then understood that the virus was James' balance created by life itself, made manifested in the right time and place to correct the ripples James had made. The clock ticks, the Universe turns. Before that, the right conditions were met for humanity to experience Alchemy, but there is always room for surprise and disappointment.

In James case, he horded the Universe's gift, creating the first imbalance, but life found another way. Eric knew the story. Kole had bored him on countless time repeating it, but now Eric could see its value. The Alchemy he knew wasn't the real thing. It was a side effect from James' greed to keep him from utterly destroying all life on the planet. If he was the only one who had Alchemy, his ego would've crushed humanity. The gift wasn't meant for one person, it was meant for all and only when everyone had the gift, would the world be safe.

Eric's awareness floated in the power of the Universe and in his greatest moment, all he could think of was Monique. After seeing James' power, Eric knew that Kole and Enora didn't have a chance against him, but he was in the right place and time to shape the future for all of humanity. He knew what he had to do, but didn't want to do it. He wanted to see Monique again and fall asleep in her arms, but if he did nothing, James will kill everyone. It was only a matter of time before James' massive ego would poison the world.

Eric opened his eyes. He was back, standing on the rubble in the armory. He took a step then knelt. He pictured Monique's face and the way she looked at him then reached for the virus. He took the vial and dumped the blackened mess of its contents on his palm taking the virus into himself. He became the virus' incubator. Its power coursed through him, merging with him, consuming one cell at a time. Eric knew he didn't have long and reached out, feeling for James. He felt him right away and knew that the virus had always known where James was. The virus told him that he needed to be close to James and that it would consume them both, but in doing so, Eric would be able to wrestle the Universe's gift from James and be able to give it to its rightful owners.

Chapter

20

Kole called a cab company, but was unable to secure a ride due to state of emergency. All air traffic was suspended until further notice, forcing them to steal a vehicle. On their way to James' Cruiser, Kole wasn't sure if he should say anything. The city's destruction was worse than he thought. He had heard some explosions and felt rumbling, but was shocked to see the damage. Fire tore through the old district, but slowed when it hit the duracrete. None of it was good and Enora looked miserable. She leaned on her armrest looking at the street below.

"Try not to think about it," he said, knowing it was a terrible thing to say, but he needed her to focus and put her guilt away, or she'll make a mistake against James.

She shifted in her seat to stare at him. He felt her eyes burning into the side of his head and glanced over to see the murderous look in her eyes. "I need you to focus," he said.

"I am focused," she said in a calm that scared him.

Her tone shut him up. He wanted to tell her that he loved her and was happy that they met, but didn't want to shift her gears. If she needed to become death itself to finish off James, he welcomed it. He knew she was going to do all the heavy lifting, but he planned to be there to cheer her on. But what worried him the most was that her satellites weren't powerful enough to attack the Ripper Gel directly. She had to destroy the casing and expose the Gel to her Alchemy to set it off. He knew he was driving them to their deaths, but there was always a chance that James would succumb to his narcissism and allow Enora to kick him in the batteries. All it'd take was one good hit and he'll be there to stab James in the back. He wasn't proud of his strategy, but what can he do at the feet of giants?

Kole slowed and planned to land in one of the hangers, but they were all blown out. Black holes of twisted and burned metal were all that remained. Smoke wafted from several holes on the outer deck. The Cruiser had battle scars, but the huge rupture in the engine room was what killed the gutted ship.

Enora's sad eyes, showing her doubt, but they were there instead of doing what he truly wanted, running for it. He turned to get a better look at the Cruiser and stopped. It took him a moment for his mind to sort out the wreckage and find and open escape hatched that James' crew had used.

"Can you feel him?" asked Enora.

He slowly lowered the vehicle toward the hatch and opened himself to his power. He searched, feeling for James, but couldn't feel him. "No, I can't," he said.

"It reminds me of the time when my friends and I went to face him. It wasn't much of a fight, but I not the same person."

Kole remembered finding her friends and releasing them from their jars. He tried to understand what she had gone through, but he'd never know, unless they lose and James does the same thing to him. He shuddered at the thought. "Let's get this done," he said then warned, "Try not to play with your food. If he remembers you, he'll push that button."

"This is too serious to mess up. I'm beyond listening to him."

"Good," he said, remembering the first time he'd met James and got caught up in the man's crazy.

Kole pulled up beside the hatch and opened his door. "We ready?" he asked. She nodded and together they entered the ship. Kole offered her his hand and helped her in then played with the hatch's door controls checking for power, but ship's systems were powered down. In the dark hallway, Enora pointed the way. Kole knew she could feel him and adjusted his eyes to see in the dark then they passed by burned out corridors, stepping over roasted corpses. The eerie silence unnerved him and all that was missing was the spooky sound of scraping metal.

They went down a set of stairs to a lower deck to a T-intersection. Enora stopped. "He made this level," she whispered.

Kole could tell that it was getting darker and wanted to put up his shield, but later would lose the ability to see in the dark if he wanted to attack. Kole couldn't see James' work, but the grate walkway had changed to a smooth metallic floor and after being around natural things, Kole could see the difference in its perfection. "No wonder people hated us," he said.

"What do you mean?"

"Look how perfect his work is, it's like he's rubbing our faces in it."

"That's exactly what he's doing," she said.

Kole frowned. He realized that James was demonstrating his superiority and telling them that they weren't a threat. "Cocky bastard," he said then asked, "Was it like this when you first faced him?"

"Yes," she said sounding a bit happier.

Her tone confused him. "What do you see," he asked, hoping she'd have a plan to beat him.

"His work hasn't changed a bit. It's been a thousand years and he hasn't evolved as a person."

What she said didn't make him feel any better and wanted her to explain. "What does that mean?"

"He a dork," she flatly said.

Kole laughed, but he already knew it. "That was funny. Thank you, I needed that."

"I wasn't being funny. Life happens and people grow, but this guy hasn't changed since the first time I met him."

"Are you sure? Maybe you're not strong enough to sense his change."

"You can perceive what I do to a point and you'll always be able to know my work because of my Alchemical finger print on it, but the nuances of what I do will change over time. Our work is a manifestation of who we are, so it changes as we grow, but his didn't."

Kole grasped what she was saying. "He believes he's done learning and has closed himself off from the world," Kole said, thinking about how he Enora and Eric have influenced each other. An isolated person only has one mind to reflect off of, their own, which limits their growth.

"Yeah, I'm disappointed. I was hoping to see something new to show me that the gift he'd been given wasn't mistreated, but this shows me that James is a waste."

"I thought him being a narcissistic racists, made him a waste."

"That too," she said then smiled at him.

He was happy to make her smile and felt less stressed about being there. Seeing how much James had changed his Cruiser showed him that James didn't care about hiding anymore. There was nothing that James' people could do or say about his remodeling, except for encouraging words from his future slaves and Kole didn't want the human race to live under tyranny.

He followed Enora along the seamless hall to a large circular arena in the belly of the Cruiser. James stood in the center of the arena waiting for them and when they entered the walls sealed up behind them. Kole stopped and watched their escape vanish then sensed the air change. He reached out with his senses and realized how much trouble they were in. All the materials around them were manufactured by James, making everything useless to him. There was only one thing he could use to transmute and that was his body.

He then understood how Enora remade herself after being freed from her jar. That was something he'd have to quickly learn before he consumed himself. He didn't like walking into James' trap and wanted to say something funny, but understanding the level of Alchemy he was about to be part of, silenced him.

Enora encouraged him to continue on. There was nowhere else they could go. With Kole's altered vision, James' white uniform looked bright against the dull black huge of the distant metal walls. He had a feeling that James saw him as the speed bump of the party and had made all of this for Enora.

James let them get close before speaking to Enora saying, "I thought all of the Alchemists from my time were dead. You can't imagine what I thought when I felt your presence. I thought I was being nostalgic and dreamt you up." He then looked at Kole saying, "Don't think I didn't notice you too, but I'd expect as much from the student of Carl the Mad."

"What do you know about my teacher?" asked Kole, hoping to stall James and give Enora time.

"I guess I can tell you. We're not going anywhere," he said then smiled. "Carl used to work for me, but when things got too dark for him he quit."

"No," Kole said, stepping away from Enora. "I could tell what kind of person you are by looking at you. My teacher would've never worked for you."

James turned to him laughing. "Why would I lie to you? I can stop if you can't handle what I have to say."

Kole had buried his teacher a long time ago and had dealt with his feelings, but used it on the chance that he'd lure James into a false sense of security saying, "Fine, no more lies. Tell me your side."

"You're a funny guy," James said. "The only truth is that there is no truth, only shades of perception, but we'll never get around to talking about that. Now where was I?" he asked then said, "Oh yes, I didn't care that he quit until he started spilling my secrets, but he had no proof. He went around warning the world about me, but the louder he yelled, the crazier he looked until he earned his nickname." He clapped his hands twice then laughed. "I didn't have to do anything. Nobody listened to him. To me he was like a layer of camouflage making me invisible. And when anyone thought to ask me about whatever I was doing, I'd accuse them of being like Carl the Mad and they'd shut up. Once Carl realized what was going on, he disappeared and that's when I took notice."

Kole was relieved when James stopped talking and it pained him to play along, asking, "What was my teacher up to?" Kole tried to expand his awareness beyond his body, but whatever James did to the air trapped his awareness inside his body. He glanced at Enora and as poised and polite as she looked, he could tell that the fight had already begun.

"This is my favorite story. Before you were born Carl knew that no one could beat me so he turned to the Universe and ask for a student that'd be able to defeat me. On faith alone he wondered the world waiting for someone to give him a student. He couldn't go shopping, he had to wait, or it wouldn't be a gift. Time passed and when he was forgotten, you appeared. But I kept my eye on things because I was fascinated by the idea that one day our destinies would cross. Of course, Carl couldn't say anything about me or he'd taint his manifestation."

"And here we are today," Kole said. What James said made everything in his past fit, explaining why his teacher shot weakened Rippers at him, took him to the most horrific battles and held impending doom over his head. But it was no way for a child to grow up, but he teacher believed that he was given the key to James' defeat and maybe James believes it as well.

"When Carl went to one of my Ripper Factories and took a look around, he got my attention. He popped in, set off my alarms then wondered off. That's when I decided that I'd had enough of him. I added a new man to my team and as a loyalty test, I had him Kill Carl. The test was to see how creative he could be and the only rule was that Carl's death wouldn't come back to him. He used Pixies and that set off the chain of events that led you here, as I said, fascinating."

Kole put it together. If Carl hadn't annoyed James, James would-
n't have killed him. Carl needed to die that way. That event ce-
mented Kole's path and he didn't like feeling that for his entire life
he'd been in one way or another, manipulated.

James smirked then said, "I can see the sparks going off behind
your eyes, but I don't see anything special about you except that you
have a hot girlfriend. I was expecting…" he made a circular motion
with his hands as he searched for the correct words, saying, "the Universe to show up and imbue you with the power to at least defend
yourself. But here you are. What it really shows me is that my way
is the right way." He turned his attention to Enora asking, "What's
your story?"

In a swift motion, she sprang forward. Kole matched her speed,
circling to James' back and watched her hand transmute into a blade.
Kole couldn't imagine what that felt like and didn't have time to think
about it. James didn't move as Enora rushed in, thrusting. With
both hands, Kole touched James' side and felt his uniform. He
planned to use his arms to block James' shoulders, opening him up
for Enora's attack, but changed his mind. He expected to feel his
shield against James' and maybe help out, but instead he felt cloth.

He knew his shield would be useless and dropped it. This was a
battle of the mind and instead of going up, he went down. This was
his last dance and he had to give his all. He had to match Enora's
strength and ferocity to create a chance for them to survive. Kole
opened himself up, delving deep into his power and mimicked
Enora, turning his hands into blades. He slid down James' legs and
drove his blades into the tops of James' feet.

James arched back and cried out in pain as Enora's blade met his
chest. Her blades sunk deep into him, but with a loud snap, her
blade shattered leaving chunks metal in his chest. Kole didn't like
that noise and worried that Enora was hurt then listened to her
bloody stump slap against his uniform.

Enora didn't miss a beat. She made more weapons out of her
body and slammed them against James. Shattered metal rained

against the floor and through James, Kole felt Enora's flurry of attacks, knocking James back against him.

Kole followed her example, stabbing his way up James' legs, but in the back of his mind, he wondered why his blades hadn't broken. But as he stabbed he looking around James, watching the love of his life dwindle, sacrificing her body to kill James.

James side stepped then yelled, "Enough!" He then slapped Enora knocking her back.

That was when Kole saw what she did to herself. She wasn't as tall and was very thin. Her bloody clothes hung off her bony shoulders. She remade smaller hands, but the look on her face told him that she saved enough for one more farewell gift.

Kole didn't want her to become a bomb, knowing that it might be the last resort. He didn't know if it would even work. James might let them die then defuse her energy. But now it was his turn. Whatever happens, he needed to buy Enora time.

But before he could so anything, James spun around and Kole had never seen such rage in a person's eyes. Enora painted James' white uniform with steaks, splatters and deep red bloody splotches. But before Kole could react, he was sailing through the air. He didn't see James move or know how he got there. He hit the ceiling and his face slid against the metal. It was cold and burned at the same time. Kole landed on his shoulder and with a blinding flash of white light, he slammed his head against the floor then slid to a stop.

James glared at Kole and said in a scary calm voice, "For a second there I thought I was in trouble."

Kole sprang to his feet then charged. James hunched, bearing his teeth then opened his arms to take Kole's assault. They collided. Kole sunk in with all his weight then lined his blades up to dive into James' rib cage to puncture his lungs and heart, but his blades snapped. Unbelievable pain shot through his arms numbing his chest. He fell to his knees then Enora sprang into action.

James looked down at him then smiled and with a clawed hand he reached out, exploding Enora's knees. But before she fell, James opened the floor a short distance away. His claw turned into a fist and Enora flung into the air. She cart wheeled through the air spraying blood on the ceiling and floor.

She was hurt and dying. Kole couldn't let her go. He forgot about James and his bloody stumps. The pain no longer mattered. He chased after her, channeling his power to create new hands. She hit the floor and he dove, catching her frail hand in his. He slammed onto the deck and together they slid.

Kole tensed, dragging himself trying to stop them, but Enora fell into the hole. She almost pulled him in. The edge of the hole came and Kole arms slipped in but he managed to slap his hands together grabbing hers before he stopped them. He tore away from her terrorized gaze and looked past her to see the thin layer of Ripper Gel coating the bottom of the pit.

Chapter

21

Eric ran through the Cruiser's corridors. He knew Kole and Enora were ahead of him and could feel James' power saturating the walls and decking. The virus pulsed, filling his mind with knowledge. He suddenly had insights to the different layers of reality and knew that Kole and Enora were in trouble. He wanted to warn them, telling them to run away, but caught up to them after they had entered James' arena. He wanted to call out to them before they met James, but the wall closed up behind them. The air shifted becoming James', encasing Kole and Enora within their bodies. But when the air shifted, Eric stood within James' power seeing two of him. The first James stood in the center of the arena and the other off to the side near the wall.

Eric was confused and felt a growing pressure within him. He looked at his hands, seeing the blue glowing energy of the virus coursing through his veins. The insecure part of him blabbered on about running out of time, but time was all he had. His power grew. He could feel the edge of James' power and Eric knew that he wouldn't be perceived by anyone there. He was a ghost and was now the strongest Alchemist on the planet, but in his greatest moment, all he wanted was to hold Monique one more time.

He drew closer watching Enora's power bubble against James' while Kole attacked in his opposite side. He watched Enora burn up her body in a fierce attack on the fake James, spilling her blood against its uniform. Kole continued as well, but it was like watching two people attack a tree. From across the room the real James approached, circling to get a better view, watching with mild interest. James' double shouted, "Enough!"

The real James waved his hand, blowing Enora's knees apart then shot her away. With a gesture from his other hand, James opened up a pit in the floor and created a thin layer of Ripper Gel at its bottom.

Eric saw their horrific end and wanted to move and help them, but calm filled him. He knew the timing of it all and watched Kole saved her at the last moment, partly sliding into the hole. Eric could've cheered, but also knew that his time was close. The virus swelled within him aching to be released.

While James' double walked up to watch Enora, the real James walked over to Kole, placing his foot on Kole's back then leaned in, making it harder for Kole to pull Enora to safety. Watching James savor Kole's pain and distress fascinated Eric. Because Kole couldn't perceive James, Kole's mind would make up a reason why he was having problems. Eventually Enora will fall and he would willing join her.

"That was it?" asked James' double. "I've waited all this time to see the end result of Carl the Mad's manifestation and this is all you could do? I feel ripped off."

Eric walked around to see the horror etched on Kole's face. Kole didn't answer. He struggled and jerked, trying to get a better grip, but his fingers slipped. Enora's cried out and it was the most painful sound Eric had ever heard.

James' double squatted beside Kole and watched him. "I can see that you're busy, but you have to see the scope of it. You see, manifestation is a group effort where everyone gets what they want.

And if two people are in conflict, the Universe sorts it out and the more you trust the Universe, the more you'll step out of its way. Can you tell that this is a big deal for me?"

Kole grunted, tears flowing from his eyes. He jerked forward, slipping further into the hole. His legs went stiff and Eric could tell that he was losing her and wanted to help, but the virus flooded through his muscles paralyzing him. All he could do was watch while the virus merged with his consciousness.

"Do you know what this means. I've been right this whole time. The Universe chose me and when I'm done with you two, I'll kill off the other races and remove all forms of the false Alchemy. I'm going to rule the world and why shouldn't I? It was the Universe that gave me this planet."

James watched Kole's grip slip. Kole screamed and Enora fell, but in that moment, Eric gave himself to the Universe, allowing its power to flow through him. With a thought, the Ripper Gel at the bottom of the pit became inert and Eric gave Kole a gentle shove, pushing him in. The real James' eyes went wide, expecting to see them explode, but it was his turn to feel pain, fear, loss and hopelessness. It was a prism of emotional reflection within James himself.

Eric took a step, thrusting his glowing hand out. He felt nothing for James. He expected to feel hate, revulsion and even pity, but his emotion was clean, peaceful. A massive beam of blue energy shot out of his hand into James' back. Eric knew the truth. James was right, everyone gets what want. James got to see the full manifestation of Carl the Mad, but it wasn't Kole he should've been looking at, it was Eric, the grandson of Carl the Mad that had always been his end.

The fake James vanished and the real James cried out and in that moment, James became the victim, but his scream of pain was hollow compared to the love that echoed between Kole and Enora. Power tore through Eric. He could feel the molecules in his arm come apart as his hand then arm dissolved. It was a contradiction of extremes. He experience pain, but it didn't hurt. It was an intriguing feeling, but he didn't want to waste a second in his confusion.

He blocked the pain in his body and focused on James. It was time for him to take back the gift meant for humanity. He could see it within James, a darkish golden spark sitting within his consciousness, the essence of Alchemy. He reached out with his other arm and ripped it from James' body. Eric watched James go through an array of hateful emotions mostly because he didn't know who was attacking him. All James knew for certain was that he was dying. Eric could see it all and held him while the life in his body drained away and once James was dead, Eric vaporized James' body.

The golden gem, the essence of Alchemy hung in the air before Eric, but it wasn't meant for him. His other arm dissolved and he stepped past the gem. He walked to the edge of the pit to see Kole and Enora, beaten up, but alive. He shifted his reality allowing them to see him. He smiled and through Kole's eyes he saw himself as a pillar of liquid blue flame. Kole didn't understand what he was looking at and Eric wanted him to understand. Eric didn't have much time, the virus was chewing through him, consuming him, but he had enough energy to allow his Human form to appear. He was once again, Eric son of Kole. Worry, fear, hope and happiness washed through Kole. He reached up to Eric, pleased to see the boy he knew, but also felt that there was something wrong.

There was so much Eric wanted to say, but only one thought found his lips. "I love you guys. Take care of Monique for me."

"I will," Kole said with tears of pride flowing down his face, knowing he'd never see his son again then asked, "Who's Monique?"

Eric could only smile at them before growing too weak. He faded from their sight and stood beside the essence of Alchemy. It was now his decision. He could fade away along with the Universes gift, or he could use the last of his life to give the Universe's gift to the world.

He felt content knowing that Kole and Enora were safe then stepped into the essence of Alchemy. Its golden light flashed merging with the virus and his life force. He stoked the light, feeding it the last of what he was then focused on his love for Kole, Enora, Monique and then the world. He then exploded in a massive blast of energy that touched the hearts of the surviving races. Out of love and his final spark of life, he birthed a new reality for all those on Earth giving everyone the Universe's gift of Alchemy. Now all would be equal and no longer separated by their abilities. His spirit hung in the air for a heartbeat, a million shimmering stars before he returned to the welcoming arms of the Universe.

Chapter

22

Several centuries later on a warm summer's day a young and beautiful Elven maiden strolled along an old path deep at the heart of a lush forest. She merged her consciousness with the forest, feeling the many forms of life within and walked barefoot on a wide path of millions of ornate stones made by the people from all the different races. The stones were special symbolizing the people who have come before, an alchemical gift of gratitude, a fingerprint, signature and picture that she could feel. Days before she wanted to know where she came from and desired to connect with the past.

She decided to go on a spiritual journey and saw the stones, recognizing the Alchemy of the different races then took off her embroidered slippers to feel a stronger connection to the past. She undid her ponytail to let her long blonde hair flow over her pointed ears and down her back then looked into the cloudless blue sky, feeling the sun's warmth through her long elegant dress.

She felt pulled and with each step she was drawn down the path until she came to the foot of a large statue. The statue was of a person, but moss covered its base and leafy vines had climbed up its legs and over its body. She reached out her hand and with her power, she gently dislodged the vines, laying them on the ground then cleared away the moss.

She connected with the statue and could feel the essence of three people who had made it, a male and female Human and a female Dark Elf. Together they combined their energies to create a statue that would last forever. Although she didn't know their names, their love for the person that the statue portrayed, was immense.

Their love vibrated through the statue washing over her. The intense emotion touched her heart and with tearful eyes she looked up at the statue. A young Human male stood tall and proud and dressed in humble garments. He looked strong and handsome. She held her breath as she read the words carved into the statue's base.

Eric the Lightbringer
Who freely gave his life
so that all could share in the
Universe's gift of Alchemy

Eric's get well Cookies

Into a bowl:

1 Cup – Grapeseed Oil
1 Cup – Raw Brown Sugar
1 tbsp – Baking Powder
1 tbsp – Alcohol free Vanilla
3 – Eggs

Mix then add:

4 ½ Cups – Flour
1 tsp – Cloves
1 tbsp – Ginger
2 tbsp – Cinnamon
100 grams – Raisins

Bake at 350 degrees.

Shape into balls and freeze what you don't need on a cookie sheets then place the frozen cookie balls in then a baggie to enjoy when desired.

Thank you for reading the Alchemist Series

Look me up on www.goodreads.com

CPSIA information can be obtained
at www.ICGtesting.com
Printed in the USA
LVHW020727170619
621444LV00002B/322